THE GIDDY DEATH OF

THE GAYS

& THE STRANGE DEMISE OF
STRAIGHTS

REDFERN JON BARRETT

AMBLE
PRESS
ANN ARBOR

2024

Amble Press

Copyright © 2015 Redfern Jon Barrett

Print ISBN: 978-1-61294-293-3

Amble Press First Edition: May 2024

The Giddy Death of the Gays & the Strange Demise of Straights
was originally published in 2015 by Lethe Press,
Maple Shade, New Jersey

Printed in the United States of America on acid-free paper.

Cover designer:
TreeHouse Studio

Amble Press
PO Box 3671
Ann Arbor MI 48106-3671

www.amblepressbooks.com

FOREWORD

I don't know where to begin. Since this novel was first released in 2015, it has been studied on university campuses, discussed at conferences, and been the subject of doctoral dissertations. Despite being a true labour of (unconventional) love that took many years to write, I never expected the book would make such an impact, and I've been continually delighted to see it reach so many people. Someone even fashioned an adorable fridge magnet featuring the novel's front cover—not an easy task considering the title!

What touched me the most, however, were emails and messages from readers who formed a real connection with the story and its characters. There's still not a lot of sympathetic literature out there featuring polyamorous and genderqueer people, especially those living in everyday towns, and these are tales that need telling. Not many would consider Swansea to be a hotbed of radical living, but scratch the surface and there's a thriving underground of people doing just that. I spent eight years living in south Wales, and I still marvel out how many unique and unorthodox experiences play out in otherwise conservative places. As the story's drag queen, High Hopes, points out:

"Your friends there, they have a fucking polyamorous trio thing going on, right in chapel country. Do you know where the largest Faerie sanctuary in the world is? Tennessee. Tennessee of all places. You don't need to move a thousand miles to fit in. Make the place fit you."

Yet many of those living in reactionary places are isolated.

In such locations, living your life outside accepted norms can be truly dangerous: I was attacked multiple times while living in Swansea. It was the early 21st century, but you simply didn't leave the gay nightclub at the marina alone—drunk straight men would often swing by the city's LGBTQ+ spaces looking for a fight, and for safety you would wait until someone else could go with you. A former lover of mine made the mistake of braving the narrow, cobbled alleyways by himself, and wound up in the hospital. The violence in this story is also, sadly, inspired by real-life events.

Yet there's an even deeper, more insidious form of violence we must deal with. It's hard to convey how damaging it can be to your sense of self when everyone you see is straight, cis, binary, and monogamous—it's like you don't exist, or, worse, like you don't *deserve* to exist. Without positive representation it's easy to feel like a freak. Alison Bechdel once remarked on the importance of seeing yourself reflected in the cultural mirror, and for queer people of all kinds, that reflection is the surest antidote to shame and humiliation.

You are not a freak. There are many more of us out there, just like you.

Since the novel first released, I began using gender-neutral pronouns, before finally coming out as nonbinary in 2020. Reading over the story for this new edition, it's actually astonishing that it took me so long. I mean, I wrote a book about being genderqueer! But it's also clear that writing this allowed to to explore my sense of self, scratching beyond the surface to discover what lay beneath. As we see through the stories of Rutti, Richard, Caroline, and Dom, our identities are vast, complex, and ever-changing. The worst thing we can do is make assumptions about ourselves.

On the subject of nonbinary pronouns, readers familiar with the first version of this book may notice there's been a change for this re-edition. Even just a decade ago, there was no agreed-upon pronoun for gender-nonconforming people. The original text's 'sie' and 'hir' were among the more common ones in use before society settled on 'they/them'—the pronouns I feel most comfortable with. As most people outside the gender binary now use singular 'they', it makes sense that this is reflected here. I hope it's a change which allows more people access to that cultural mirror.

This re-edition would not exist without the support of Salem West, publisher of Bywater Books and its imprint Amble Press, and I'm extremely thankful—in the years since the book has been out of print, I've received many emails asking where copies can be found, and I'm delighted to now inform them of this new edition. My sincere gratitude also goes to the author and scholar Meg-John Barker, for both their warm friendship and the wonderful afterword featured at the end of this book.

I'll be forever honoured that this novel has meant so much to people. Of all the messages I've received since it first came out, the one that touched me the most was from someone who said it made them feel less alone. Reading that brought me to tears. Literature allows for deep and intimate connections with total strangers, and I swear it's a very real form of magic.

If nothing else, I hope this story makes you feel less alone.

–Redfern Jon Barrett
Berlin, Germany
December 2023

PROLOGUE

SWANSEA

CAROLINE

There was a problem. I mean, there's always a problem when you're a bartender in south Wales, but there was a *larger than usual* problem. The problem was Debbie.

"I'll bisect yer fuckin' cock wi' my teeth, yuh fuckin' arse'ole."

Or, possibly, the problem was her husband.

"Yuh mad fuckin' bitch, I'll cut yuh tongue out an' ram it so far up yuh fuckin' arse it'll come out your mouth covered in shit."

The two were perfectly nice when they were apart—in fact, Debbie was one of my favourite regulars. It was when they were together that they were a larger than usual problem. The cook had hidden himself away in the kitchen, whilst the other regulars watched them from a semicircle. It was up to me to sort it out, but I didn't even get a chance to speak before Debbie pointed her thumb at me.

"Ask Caroline 'ere. Caroline, do you—"

"No," the husband interrupted, "You jus' said I should ask, so I'm fuckin' askin'. Sharline," he gestured at me with the point of his finger, "Is it *reasonable* to go out to dinner wi' a friend of yours? A woman friend? Debbie, she's got a temper, see, she's all jealous."

"You're not tellin' 'er the 'ole story, you lying arse'ole," she

1

flicked his shoulder with her fingers and turned to me. "Caroline. Not just dinner. Dinner *an' a film*. He took 'er to the cinema after. That's a date, that is."

"Nothin''appened, like. No hugs, no kisses, nothin'. It's not a date if yuh don't kiss," he appealed to me, his thick grey eyebrows raised. Debbie's black pencil-thin eyebrows lowered in response.

"'Cause she wouldn't let yuh. If you 'ad 'alf the chance—"

"I still wouldn't kiss 'er, like. Tell 'er Caroline, I love 'er, the daft cow."

"Yuh loves me when yuh not tryin' to kiss other women."

"I never want to kiss other women. Or blokes for that matter. I only want you."

Debbie didn't look at him. She kept her small eyes fixed on me. She would make him work for this one.

"Yuh—you're the one who's special, like. You're the one I wanna see ev'ry mornin'. It's you, Debbie. Debbie is the one I love."

"Really?" she asked, turning her head toward him a little.

"Really," he replied, kissing her on the cheek. One or two of the others cheered.

The problem was resolved.

The Tail and Tugboat called itself a bar, but it was more of a tatty old pub. It squatted at the edge of the marina and had its small share of regulars who were almost always found propped up by the counter. I mostly enjoyed working there—the torn cushions and peeling wallpaper made me feel at home—though I never had enough shifts: I only just had enough money to both eat and pay rent. Such is the life of a geography postgrad.

"You can come out now," I called to the cook. He was frightened of the locals.

My shift ended fifteen minutes later, which meant I actually finished thirty-five minutes later—that's how things usually go. I made my way through the darkening streets in a half-walk half-jog. In Swansea you always feel like you are being watched: rows of tiny, terraced houses staring down at you from the hills, their bright gaze eyeing you.

2

I checked my phone, working out how long it would take to get to the girls—they would kill me for being late.

"Fuck you, Caroline, I'm not talking to you if you're gonna show up this late. D'ya think we've got nothing better to do than wait for you to waddle in here, drunk already? Don't argue with me, I can smell the fumes, and I know they're not all from serving at that shitty place that calls itself a bar. Poor Christina has been waiting ages to tell you about her new job, and now you've let her down. *And what are you wearing?* Do you always go to work dressed as a homeless alcoholic from the seventies? I don't know why we spend time with you, I really don't."

Nomi pursed her thin lips and folded her arms across her chest. She was short, and her round face gave her a child-like appearance, an appearance which was not helped by her tantrums. She waited for three seconds after her tirade before she burst into laughter. Christina and I just looked at one another.

"Hi-i-i-i-i Caroline," Christina greeted, before reaching out an arm and pulling me into a hug. Christina was the opposite—she was in her mid-twenties, like the other two of us she lived with—but her long face and careful manner made her seem a good two decades older.

"It's at least good to see you, Christina," I said, glaring at Nomi.

"Oh, come off it, Caroline. You'd be totally fucking lost without me. Look at yourself, you can't even do your hair properly if I'm not there to help."

I looked around for a mirror.

"Your hair looks fine," Christina told me, "she's just making fun. Even though it's only fun to her."

Nomi burst into a throaty laugh once again.

This bar was one of the trendy recently-refurbished ones down on Wind Street, all bright colours and two-for-one offers that still wound up twice the price of the student's union. The place was absolutely heaving, and I made my way through the roar of the crowd toward the bar, doing my very best to avoid the more aggressive drunks. From the corner of my eye I could see a woman hitting her boyfriend in the arm with the long heel of her shoe.

I ordered a drink—my first of the evening, aside from *one* I'd snuck in earlier in my shift. It was hard work, after all, what else was I to do? I ordered one for Nomi as well. Christina was still nursing her beer—she never seemed to drink much, she said she'd drunk too much back in Barcelona. She'd come to Wales to study, and start over a 'fresh leaf', though why she'd chosen Swansea for that was a total mystery.

I returned to the table with the drinks. Christina told us about her first day working in the new call centre.

"That's it. Nothing special. I have people shout at me all day, either through the telephone or in person, and I imagine what it would be like to blow up the building. I'm telling myself it's temporary, even if I know it isn't. There is no other work. Nothing."

"There are at least three brothels within a five-minute walk from our house," Nomi reminded her. Christina didn't respond. She was better at ignoring Nomi than I was.

"Now going out with Zebedee is a full-time job," Nomi stated, oblivious to Christina's wince at the shift of conversation to men. "Caroline, can you get Dom to tell him to cut his nails, just once? I'm like a bloody zebra right now."

"Tell him yourself." Now that I was going out with her boyfriend's best friend she thought we were in some sort of secret club, one I suspected she enjoyed all the more for its implicit rejection of Christina.

"You're right, I've seen the state of Dom's nails. Ugh, hippies are so *grotesque*. And don't tell me 'he's not a hippy' just because he has short hair or studies maths or something. It's the fingernails, you can always tell by the fingernails."

"Come off it, Nomi," I said, getting annoyed in spite of myself. I'd only been seeing Dom a couple of months and she'd spent the whole time insulting something about him—his clothes, his politics, the way he drank tea. I didn't let it affect me—I loved Dom. He was even doing his masters in maths in the building opposite my postgrad office. It was working out well.

"He does have a nice arse though," Nomi announced, which was the same thing she always said after insulting him. Nomi was under the impression that if you gave a compliment after disparaging someone then it somehow balanced out.

Christina threw an ice cube at her. I could see the stiletto-heeled girlfriend being escorted from the premises by security. I craned my neck in the direction of the window to see her being dumped face-first into the street. I craned my neck in the other direction and peered through the bodies, managing to catch a glimpse of her boyfriend raising his plastic pint glass in celebration, along with two or three of his friends. I was going to tell the other two when my phone rang. Dom's face flashed over the screen. Nomi snatched it from my hands.

"Dom, you and Zebedee are to meet once a week to cut each other's nails. No it is not gay. No arguing, if I have to put up with—"

Christina grappled the phone from Nomi's hands and handed it back to me. I was about to apologise to him, but he spoke first.

"Caroline, you have got to get down to the Kingsway—you won't believe it."

It was Nomi who didn't believe it.

"There is no *way* Skyline is burning down," she stated as the three of us tramped arm-in-arm down the street. "Dom's delusional. He smokes too much weed, he's imagining it all. Zebedee's the same. He's on his way too, by the way."

I didn't ask why she'd invited her boyfriend if she didn't believe anything was going on.

5

And there it was: the burning club. It was a large building, a great concrete cube which squatted against the four-lane road in front, the once dull grey of the walls now scorched black. The bright uniforms of the firemen swarmed around. A few people were sitting around in blankets next to ambulances, whilst the majority of the crowd blocking the road gazed wide-eyed at the spectacle. A group of angry lads were screaming at one another. You could feel the heat of it even from the distance the police were guarding.

Dom and his new roommate found us right away. Nomi was holding onto Christina's arm, her eyes wide and mouth ajar.

There was a loud bang and a shower of sparks—the large neon 'S' of the 'Skyline' sign exploded, and the crowd shielded their eyes as the police forced them back, attempting to take control. One of the ambulances roared away as the flames soared higher into the sky. This was not good. I didn't know why but seeing the black smoke chilled my stomach. Dom put his arm around me but it didn't help. I could feel it—something was coming, something terrible, something we wouldn't be able to stop. The others looked pleased.

Why couldn't they see it?

RUTTI

Don't avoid the other children. Don't play with dolls. Don't be so sensitive. Don't be a wilting wallflower. Don't doodle. Don't dream. Don't wrestle other boys. Don't forget to shave. Don't kiss male friends. Men don't love men. You certainly can't love more than one at once. The rules-to-a-happy-life are the same in south Wales as anywhere else.

Happiness is boring. At least I think so. Contentment makes for the worst stories. Contented people live and die as though they never were—there is no imprint to be left by the contented. Now *discontent* is worth something. When we live among masses of those with whom we disagree—those we find abhorrent—that is when we fight to leave a mark, that is when we have something worth conveying. That was my life in south Wales. So I avoided who I wanted, I played with what I wished, I was as sensitive as I needed to be, I wilted and doodled and dreamed, I wrestled whomever I felt like, I didn't close-shave anywhere. But I hoped that people would kiss me and people would love me and that maybe there would be more than one at once. At some point.

I was twenty-five, and it was three nights after I had been evicted. I was standing outside a ratty café which was the meeting place of The Lesbians, watching passers-by trying not to slip or trip on the wet, cracked hazard of the pavement. I'd fallen over, myself—twice in the past month, in fact. And I was smoking. Smoking is as much a cliché as pointing out that something is a cliché, and I don't enjoy it. I smoke for something to do with my hands. It makes me feel terrible—the claggy sensation in my mouth, the fatigue from the nicotine. If I'm home I'll have some fruit after each cigarette just to feel a little better again. Lemons work the best. I am not good at smoking. I smoke as though I'm imitating someone smoking.

Waiting for The Lesbians was like that: something to do. Steph was the one I was waiting for. In a few minutes they would come out of the special summer solstice Women's Meeting, looking for all the world like a pixie; small and lithe with turquoise hair.

There was a shriek of laughter somewhere inside—the group would be finished soon.

The fag smoke choked my throat, the wet Welsh mist bouncing from my face. Now and again the cackle of laughter from the lesbians inside cut through the cold air, which was brightly lit by garish signs. I actually liked the tacky glow, it did a lot to hide the crumbling faces of the buildings. I slumped against the wall and waited for the meeting to finish. No men allowed, not even queer men.

Someone stumbled by, a person in their fifties, head down against the elements, a tattered carrier bag in their hand. They didn't see me.

Then someone else, thirty-four, hurried past me into the building. They saw me and smiled.

A young guy, eyes filled with tears, wiped the sleeve of their trendy jacket against the wince of their face, not noticing me. I asked them if they needed anything, but the roar of traffic and gush of wind drowned my voice.

A rough-looking hetero couple clamoured into me, cursing me then resuming the rage they shared toward each other, screamed as a public spectacle—both had hair that was plastered to their faces with rain, their inexplicably bare arms soaking wet. Be aware I might be paraphrasing a little.

"You make me feel inadequate in my masculinity and I find the thought of you finding other men sexually attractive threatening to an ego which was damaged by a hyper-masculine, overbearing father."

"I retreat into a shrill media-based portrayal of hysterical womanhood as the only response I know to dealing with your insecure aggression. I'll screech over and over that I didn't sleep with anyone, protesting my innocence so I can resume my campaign of passive aggression against you, which I learned both from school and from my parents."

"I monitor the direction in which you cast your eyes when we're in public together, watching for any sign that you find anyone else physically attractive. When I feel sufficiently justified in my fear-based rage, I shall shout at you and then attack the poor individual who played no part in the gradual and inevitable breakdown of our ridiculous relationship. I shall threaten to murder anyone who is foolhardy enough to endure orgasm with you, thus proving I am a man."

"I shall cite your lack of sexual potency as motivation for any possible infidelity."

"You're both a canine and a bovine, and finally you're an apparently offensive word for a female sexual organ which has its roots in old English."

"You're a fuckin' wanker and a fuckin' stupid prick an' all," the girlfriend squawked back. Then the two stumbled into the pub opposite. I could see only shadows inside.

I lit another cigarette. The glow of my phone and roar of traffic passed the minutes.

"Rutti, how long have you been waiting out here?" Steph. Small and lithe, though it was too dark to ascertain the current colour of their hair.

"Not long."

"Not long," Steph repeated, eyes narrowed. They snatched the cigarette from my hand and smiled.

"How was the girls-only club?"

"Women's Circle," Steph corrected. I grimaced at them.

"Homowomen's Institute. Sewing Circle. Lesbian Support Group."

"It's not a lesbian group."

"You're all lesbians though."

"Not all. Kitty's bi, you know that."

The Lesbians began to scuffle out to the pub opposite. One of them muttered to me as they passed by. "You coming, Rutti?"

"Am I allowed? I have a penis you know," I called after them (less aware back then that not all men had penises).

"Show me," they called back, breaking into a cackle.

"You're well aware you're allowed to the pub, Rutti," Stephanie sighed. "Stop making a fuss."

"I don't make fusses."

"And we're not all lesbians," Steph answered.

"We're not you know," Kitty stepped from the doorway to back Steph up.

"Token bi."

"I'm not going over this again," Steph's voice hardened a little. "You could form a men's group if you wanted."

"Jesus fucking Christ," I answered.

A small cluster of us waited in silence to cross the street. The pub was louder inside than I expected. Steph and I headed alone to the bar.

"So what's up, Rutti?"

"What's up?"

"You only criticise the women-only thing when you're in a bad mood."

"I've been kicked out."

It had only been a matter of time. Four years, in fact. I already missed the run-down, mouldy apartment with its ragged furniture and cupboard doors that wouldn't close, situated next to an old betting shop so that the street outside was always clogged with the chain-smoking desperation of middle-aged men. It had been home, but it had never really been my place—it had always been Richard's. Richard, the straightest of straight roommates.

"Richard kicked you out? Did he get sick of your heterophobia? What did you do to him?"

I was about to answer when Richard called. Speak of the uptight, heterosexual devil.

"What do you want?" I answered, not giving Richard chance to speak first, and trying to sound aloof.

"Rutti, there's something you should come see."

"*Something I should come see?* Are you fucking serious? *Something I should come see.* You evicted me all of three days ago."

"I was kind of hoping there'd be no hard feelings about that."

"I'm hanging up."

"No, Rutti, look—I just couldn't live with you any longer, that's all. I still want us to be friends. Really. It was just too much for me right now. And now this thing is happening and you're the first person I thought to call. And it's something you would really want to see. Are you listening to me?"

"I'm listening."

"Get to the Kingsway, I'll see you here."

"But I'm with Steph—"

"Bring her."

"Rutti, you do realise you're not honour-bound to do everything your weird ex-roommate says?" Steph asked, hurrying to keep up with me. The rain had subsided, but the pavement was bogged down with puddles which soaked our socks. An ambulance raced past us, splashing me and soaking Steph.

"Fuck—fuck your fucking ex-housemate, Rutti."

I took their hand and tugged them along, following the path the ambulance had taken. Somewhere in the distance we could hear a cacophony of sirens.

"That's got to be something good, right?" I asked. Steph seemed to cheer a little, prancing along the soaked concrete. We reached the Kingsway to find it clogged with drunks. One slumped a heavy hand onto my arm.

"Skyline's up in fuckin' smoke," they slurred. Over the crowd we could see flames licking upward, as a young man missing most of their shirt buttons almost urinated on Steph's already-soaked feet. Steph didn't seem to notice. The huge concrete box of a building was burning. A neon light burst, showering the firefighters with sparks.

"It's fucking beautiful," Steph sighed, their gaze fixed firmly on the fire, the sparks reflected in their eyes like fireworks.

It was. The concrete eyesore was being destroyed. More precisely—we discovered as we forced our way through—it had mostly burned already. The doorways and terrace to the side were blackened, chairs and posters of scantily clad girls equally charred. A giant baby and a chicken were fucking in a nearby shrub as the firefighters fought the last of the flames.

I turned to Steph.

"One down, fifty to go. Perhaps this city can be saved after all."

RICHARD

I like to think of myself as a tolerant person. No, scratch that, I don't even like that word, 'tolerance', like us straight or white or able-bodied people should have to grit our teeth and bear the presence of people different to us. I'm not tolerant, because I don't think these are even things that need tolerating. Individual people, on the other hand, that's different. You can be close to someone and still need to tolerate them. You can really like them, in fact. Even in these circumstances, though, there are limits to my tolerance.

I didn't expect to have to find a new roommate—I mean, things had been fine with Rutti, for the most part. I'd overlooked him pouring coloured dyes into my plants, or sticking black labels over groceries I'd bought (an 'act of protest', as he called it). Or his attempts to set up profiles for me on dating websites. I could cope with that. What I couldn't cope with was his bringing a girl home for me. That was too far.

So I like computer games. I like trying and comparing different open-source operating systems. I like reading tech news. That doesn't mean I'm somehow emotionally crippled— scratch that, I mean *awkward*. I don't usually use such ableist terms, they sometimes just slip out when I'm angry. My point is, being a geek doesn't mean that I can't take care of myself. That had always the problem between us, if you ask me. Rutti never understood that basic point.

He'd introduced the girl as I walked in through the front door of our admittedly grotty and damp apartment (I'd always meant to get it sorted with the landlord). As always he used his ridiculous *theys* and *theirs*. "This is Ichie," he told her, pointing to me ('Ichie'—taken from the central part of my name and pronounced 'itchy'—was one of Rutti's pet names for me, something else I'd learned to tolerate).

He was perched on an upturned bucket like an overgrown leprechaun, whilst the poor embarrassed-looking girl was given the armchair, which had long ago been clawed apart by some mystery cat.

The girl and I looked at one another, as awkward as could be imagined.

"Hello, Ichie," she said, looking at the floor.

"It's Richard. And hello," I'd answered, doing my best to

12

convey my absolute anger toward Rutti, who seemed totally oblivious.

"I'll leave you two alone," Rutti stated, walking into the hallway and hiding behind the door. Both she and I stared at him as he peered at us through the crack.

I offered her a hot drink, which she accepted, and for five stretched-out minutes neither of us said anything. The kettle clicked, I made the tea, and handed her the least-chipped mug. I looked over at the door. Rutti's eyes were still clearly visible through the gap.

She blew on her tea.

"I'm sorry about this," I offered, trying to untangle the situation my interfering roommate had created. She simply stared into her cup as through she were reading tea leaves. I tried again.

"How did he get you here?"

She looked up from her cup, first toward the door, then toward me. She flushed beetroot-red before stammering. Apparently just half an hour before, she had been browsing in the unbreathable perfume store where Rutti worked. He'd zoned in on her and suggested she meet his roommate. He had, apparently, insisted.

Rutti coughed.

We then spent sixteen more minutes attempting crooked conversation under Rutti's creepy gaze. We talked about work (she was unemployed, I worked in a call centre—nothing in common), about hobbies (she liked going dancing, I liked computer games—nothing in common) and, somehow, clocks (neither of us knew anything about clocks).

"What in the name of the gods is wrong with you two?" Rutti cried, bursting from his obvious hiding place. "Look, here's a discussion point."

He marched back into the hallway and returned with a carrier bag.

"This is Emily. Say hello to Emily."

He pulled the head of a sex doll from the bag, its mouth

agape in an obscene yawn. The girl's eyes widened.

"Put that away," I ordered.

"I found them in the dumpster behind the train station," Rutti continued, ignoring me. "I'm not sure why they don't have a body. Perhaps they're more portable this way, or maybe they were owned by a budding serial killer—that's something for you guys to talk about. Personally, I think it's a little grotesque—"

"Rutti," I barked at him.

The girl rose to leave, not taking her eyes from the severed head as she stumbled down the hallway. She didn't close the door behind her.

My blood absolutely fucking boiled. Why would he presume I couldn't get sex? I could talk to the opposite sex, I had women friends—they were just online. I could get sex, not that I'd have told him.

"Don't worry about it, Ichie, we can find someone else," he cooed, putting Emily back into the bag.

I wasn't going to let it get to me. I wasn't even going to get angry. I was going to stay calm. Nice and calm.

"I want you out, Rutti."

"I came out when I was twelve, Ichie."

"I want you out."

"No you don't." He went into the kitchen and returned munching on a carrot.

"Rutti, I want you gone by next week," I said, and my voice started trembling but I carried on talking anyway. "I don't want to live with you anymore. I don't want you here. I want you far away from me. I mean it." I'd started shouting but I couldn't stop myself. "Get out. Get the fuck out."

He'd gone by the end of the day. I placed an ad and found a new housemate by the end of the week. His name was Dom, and he seemed normal, even a little slovenly—he had yet to unpack anything other than a hoodie and a toothbrush—but by that point I'd have taken anything or anyone.

I was with Dom the night of the fire. To be honest I couldn't see what all the fuss was about. I mean, you've seen one fire

14

you've seen them all, and the whole thing had been ordered well. Judging by the clothing and banter of those stood outside, the place had been evacuated in good time, and those being led into ambulances were at least able to walk unaided. The building would be a ruin, but it hadn't spread to the neighbouring structures. So some stupid club was gone, there was no need for the huge audience—and I'd only called Rutti because he'd always hated the place. Plus, I didn't exactly want him to hate *me*. The burned club was a peace offering.

"Did you do this for me, Ichie?" Rutti was stood behind me.

"I'd do anything for you, Rutti," I told him without turning around. He walked in front of me, his too-long red hair loose over a tatty overcoat. He made the most over his height advantage, making sure to loom over me as he spoke.

"Except not throw me onto the street, of course."

Neither of us said anything to that.

DOM

Now this, this weird thing that happened, this was before we'd even seen the fire, and it was already a strange evening because there in front of us was a man with his head in a bucket. No, no, it wasn't so much a bucket as a bowl, a big bowl, one of those bowls that you wash dishes in—a big, pink, dish-washing bowl. He'd been sick into it. We saw him as we were heading home, and we stopped, not because seeing someone drunk and lying with their face in the dark road was unusual, but because of the other things: the man with his head in the dish-washing bowl was lying next to a small pile of rotting fish—three or four fish—and mumbling someone about Jesus.

Richard edged toward him as though he were going to the edge of a cliff, careful like, trying to get a closer look.

"She dumped me," the man cried, his voice echoing into the bowl.

"The fish," Richard said, "they're different kinds."

"What do you mean, 'they're different kinds'?" I asked him, holding onto my nose, trying to keep the stench out of my sinuses. Richard was more casual, he didn't seem to mind the smell at all. We'd found the man on the way home from the pub—we were heading back to watch a film—it was a getting-to-know-the-new-roommate deal for the both of us.

"The fish," Richard explained, leaning close towards them, "that one's a herring, that one's a kipper. Not sure about that one." I wouldn't have thought he'd recognise breeds of fish, he seemed much more the indoorsy-type—not so toned, a little pale—though to be honest that described most of us in Swansea.

"Do you think he brought the fish with him?" I asked, noticing at that moment that the drunk man had passed out, the bowl filling with a deep rumbling snore, loud as a cartoon.

"I don't reckon so," Richard reasoned, "I think he stumbled upon the fish and then the smell of them made him throw up. He looks like he was drunk enough already." He paused for a moment. "Do you think we should do something?"

So the two of us lifted him by the shoulders, bringing his face out the bowl, but he carried on sleeping, his beard full of sick down the one side of his face, then we half-dragged half-carried him to the bushes. Richard tipped the dishwashing bowl into the drain. The fish we left well alone.

"A good start to the evening," Richard said.

I'm used to better omens.

It was just as we were emptying the bowl into the drain that we heard the sirens—suddenly, all at once, a whole fuckload of them. I suggested we go check it out, and Richard replied sure, why not? We didn't have much better to do.

The sirens were further away than we thought, something like four or five streets away, and we could see the sky glaring orange before we even got there, the same sickly orange as the street lights, only brighter. There were crowds in skimpy night-out clothes: a stag party in nothing but oversized nappies giving drunken leers to a hen party in matching sexy chicken outfits, all under the blue lights of the emergency vehicles, fighting with the orange sky.

"Will you look at that," Richard exclaimed, and I did look. Skyline was burning. Skyline, the shitty nightclub with its tacky strip evenings and fourth-rate DJs, the chain with a hundred identical clubs in a hundred shitty cities. Burning. The squat box which housed it was billowing flames from all sides, as though the whole thing had combusted, spontaneously. It was like the city itself had finally had enough, that the match-book-like cube had been flared from below, the only mercy, the only concession to the blight being the escape of its occupants onto the now-warmed pavement and into emergency vehicles. Dark, murky water was oozing into the gutters, seeping from the shell of the old building. We wanted to get a closer look, but the rows of swaying skin-bared bodies blocked the way, so I chose to phone my girlfriend Caroline instead.

Now *this* was an omen.

CHAPTER ONE

THE MINIMUM WAGE MAGIC HOUR

RUTTI

I'd let my guard down. I couldn't help it, if I'm getting on with someone, I instinctively trust them, and with my words and my breath and my body I want to fondle them, caress them, feel them. Yet in that city there were two types of sexual connection: the cold, unfeeling robotic motion-going single-night encounters, which chilled me like metal, or an instant monogamous homo mock-marriages which may have been softer, but which smothered and blocked out the light. Neither would nurture an organic bond, one which grew where it grew and simply went how it went. Only idiots crave certainty.

I'd let my guard down. We'd met online—of course I'd have rather'd the gradual casual chat of knowing someone-through-someone, but with homos in Swansea it was generally the internet or the gay bars. That wasn't even a choice. This one had seemed different.

They had an obsessive interest in books filled with the past; they painted; they even hated the thunderous monotony of clubbing. And so we'd written one another, again and again, we'd flirted and joked and debated the fall of republics. And so it had begun to grow, organically, a tip of green sprouting from soft earth, nurtured by lingering glances and thoughtful smiles.

We'd swapped books and evangelised about them. Finally, we'd leaned toward one another, we'd kissed, we'd felt our bodies on one another, our legs and arms entwined, full of each other, of breath and flesh and hair, of sweat and cum. We'd collapsed into one another.

I'd let my guard down. We'd lain there together, a gentle finger circling skin.

I'd talked.

They didn't hear.

I'd smiled and they looked away.

I'd held them yet they remained rigid. Hard. Metallic. In one moment the green shoot withered and the seeds became bitter in hard soil. I knew even before they said that they weren't looking for anything serious—yet I told them I looked for nothing— that they needed to be by themself—but can't we just see what happens? Can't we just let something grow, and if it withers, if it dies, then that's fine, but can't it have a chance? No words were heard and as I lay in the dark, with the glimmer of rising light outside. My limbs grew ever heavier and more leaden, mercury coursing through veins and arteries, a heavy lump of loneliness made molten and slowly flowing through me. When the sun was higher this one would leave, a few words scattered for the sake of politeness before they went, taking a little of my hope with them.

When I awoke again, they were already gone. I was still staying on Steph's sofa bed, on the same rusty springs I had spent the previous four weeks. I quietly raised myself from the squeaky mattress and made my way into the kitchen. Steph had already left to work at the lesbian café—which they always swore was not a lesbian café—and the wall clock showed that I was late for work.

Each shift trundled by in the same way, the shwutz of the doors, the endless toxic artificial air and the patter-clack of heels on the polished plasticky floor. Mostly we just got frazzled spray-tanned young women and the odd anxious chubby-gutted heteroman looking for a gift for their girlfriend. I know Richard threw me out because I brought a girl home for them, but the girl had genuinely seemed nice, and to be honest the perfume store rarely housed nice people.

I rubbed my eyes with the balls of my hands. There was no sign of the piggish priggish manager, so I leaned against the countertop. I was wearing my regulation white shirt and navy trousers with a name tag bearing a name my friends never used. We weren't allowed to lean against anything at work—we were directed to remain bolt hand-up-your-arse upright at all times. I say 'we' as though there was some sort of united Worker Spirit in the perfume store, but there wasn't. Bored students, coerced teenagers, and those brainless, orange-skinned full-timers did not amount to anything like solidarity. I monitored the area with careful glances—I was on shift with one of the nameless full-timers and if they caught me slouching they'd tell the manager.

A customer in their fifties entered the store. The customer about half my height and gave me a pleasant smile. I stood straight and smiled in return as they nervously informed me:

"It's my grandson's birthday soon, a mere matter of days in fact, and I have absolutely no clue what to buy him, seeing as I have neither an original idea in my head nor any kind of functioning relationship with him. I want something perfect, something that will make him see me as an actual human being rather than some ageing obligation. Perfume seems as good a way as any to fritter away my money. What do you wear?"

I glanced behind me and told them I didn't wear perfume.

"How old is your grandkid?"

"Fourteen. He'll be fifteen years old on Tuesday."

I informed the customer that the grandkid would more probably prefer a book, something with zombies or some other horror, those were always beloved by bored teens. I wrote down a short list of which ones which might be appropriate and told them to keep the receipt in case the kid already had it. They thanked me and left.

The manager trotted toward me.

"What were you writin' down for 'er?" the manager spluttered through lurid pink lips. They looked up at me, their eyes crowned by tacky designer glasses and clumpen mascara.

I told them I was writing down a list of scents for the customer to consider.

You unavoidably learn things during the slow churn of years working retail jobs. For example, it is possible to tell in the first second of eye contact whether a customer is to be liked or despised: they will smile at you or they won't. It's that simple. In that first second, I then calculate how I shall respond to them in turn. If they smile at me then I shall do my best to serve them. The consequences of a scowl or sneer, however, varied according to the job. I had my first part-time retail job when I was fourteen and have had a succession of them since. Each one was spectacularly dreadful.

I actually once worked in a bookstore, which at first might seem like a dream job. It wasn't one of the hallowed and rare *real* bookstores, however—those basic retail jobs now required a master's degree in literature—it was a discount store which also stocked calendars, tacky paint sets, and faulty children's toys. There were no decent books sold aside from dusty, cheaply printed classics, but there were stacks and stacks of dreadful ones. I conducted daily acts of micro-sabotage, particularly against paperbacks by right-wing tabloid columnists: crumpling covers, tearing pages, anything to make a copy unsellable. I was caught defacing a racist homophobe's biography with green marker.

Of course, there was the obligatory fast-food chain. The stale stench of cheap meat would cling to clothes and hair and refused to wash out. It was hot and the old synthetic uniforms would soak up all your sweat. With the sweat and grease, you gained a grotesque sheen but after several days you simply stopped caring. Few customers were ever polite, even fewer would smile at you. You start to develop a dull loathing for them. I didn't receive any real training and had no idea what went in each burger—

each one I made was a random creation. Few customers noticed. I caused small fires. I spent a day cleaning all the tables with toxic chemicals and still don't know if it was deliberate or not. Eventually I stopped going in. It is not possible to be fired from fast food.

Then there was the maternity store. Despite the smug grins of expectant mams and dads it was actually the most bearable place I've ever worked. People purchasing miniature clothes, learning toys, and various nauseating baby accessories were generally pretty pleased with themselves, so you avoided the misery which customers usually inflicted on you in a shop job. I wound up finding myself helpful and polite the vast majority of the time, so the abrasive snarl of rude customers began to seem like a strange exception—though I actually resented the rude ones all the more for it and would reward their obnoxiousness by appearing as slow and dimwitted as I could realistically manage. Returned items were kept below the till and I would randomly swap their purchases whilst bagging them. Instead of a baby chair they'd get a pop-up animal set. Instead of a nappy storage unit they'd get a pop-up animal set. Multiple-sized bottle collection, pop-up animal set. The pop-up animal sets were unpopular. Eventually the entire chain collapsed under the weight of the recession. Swansea's pregnant now ordered online.

And so, I was in 'Per Fumes': pretension with a pun. The manager trotted to the back room—which they called their office—to rest their hooves. A pouting full-timer, the young unnaturally tanned girl sharing my shift, was maintaining perfect brain-dead silence, eyes as flat and lifeless as a mannequin.

I'd had enough of it all. I just had to save up enough and then I could leave—I'd go anywhere, it didn't matter, as long I was was somewhere else. I had to get out of the city.

RICHARD

The building I worked in was grey. In fact, most of the buildings in the city seem to be made of the same bare grey concrete—but the building I worked in had a more substantial effect. It was one of the largest in the city, both high (for Wales) and wide. My workstation was on the twelfth floor and faced out over the hills. Along the hills were rows of grey terraced houses. I had counted them. All four hundred and eighty-one of them. My flat was just in view if you craned your neck to the window properly, and at the moment it was empty—the new roommate Dom was staying at his girlfriend's place. So far, we'd been getting on all right, though in the month he'd been living there we'd not spoken all too much. He still hadn't unpacked, and I was starting to miss Rutti.

My phone started ringing. No rest for those working Customer Support. My station would ring constantly with irate customers having problems with their internet connections. Most of the time it was something the customers had done wrong themselves; very few of them knew how to operate a computer. When I was new at the job, I suggested to my supervisor that we provide a free half-hour of training to new customers—that way we could save on support costs. My supervisor had just laughed. He thought it was a joke.

The woman on the other end of the phone informed me that her dog had chewed through 'that cable that carries the internet'. I asked her if her dog was in the habit of chewing through cables. She said that both her dogs were, at least until one of them had been electrocuted. I told her we'd send an engineer round at the nearest possible opportunity and suggested in future she coat all her cables with nail varnish. If the cables tasted bad the remaining dog might survive. She sounded very grateful. Since I started my job, I had received eight personalised thank you letters and three gifts. I was doing a good job. It was important to do a good job.

My desk was one of the tidiest in my office. My co-workers had sweet wrappers and stacks of papers—even newspapers—or coins or paperclips or discarded elastic bands. My desk had been messy with all of those things too when I first arrived, but an

23

hour later it was pristine and had stayed that way ever since. The job had a 'high turnover', so I had been there longer than anyone (including the current supervisor). People tended to come to me if they needed help with anything.

My long-standing position also had the added benefit of small amounts of freedom: I had installed a second operating system on my terminal, which I could use as I wished, and which I tinkered with in between calls. This way messages I sent couldn't be monitored, though I doubted tech support had the competence to do so anyway. It also allowed for a certain amount of gaming, though I was careful not to push things too far.

This wasn't my only job, thought it was the only one that paid. I also had a job in the Shelter charity shop, sorting through bundles of clothes and worthless delicate knick-knacks hurriedly donated by bemused and grieving relatives. I'd started there even before the call centre job, when I'd left school and fallen straight into government assistance—I hadn't wanted to feel useless, and I hadn't wanted to stay indoors all day with my dad. Somehow, I'd stayed at the charity shop over the years, and to be honest it was because I enjoyed it. I didn't like telling people though— no one really likes earnest do-gooding beyond the earnest do-gooders themselves. Besides, I was only there for four hours a week.

It was during a lull in calls that I took another look at my apartment, straining my neck to the window, pressing my cheek to the glass—there was the roof of the building, a house sliced in two, roof ever-so-slightly buckled in the middle, the tiles a slimy green brown.

Shouldn't Dom have unpacked yet? Perhaps, I worried, he wasn't planning to stay. This sent me worrying further as I wanted him to—in truth it had been hard throwing Rutti out, and I wanted things to remain stable. At least for a little while. I had been lonely. Rutti may have been a pain in the arse, but he had also been omnipresent. I wasn't used to having the flat to myself so much of the time. I tried to strain my neck further, to see the full building. Five years I'd lived there—ever since I'd left home. Rutti had been there for four of them.

It was up to me to talk to Dom. If I wanted to have a housemate I actually spoke to then it stood to reason that I should actually say something. I peeled my face from the glass and stared at the spreadsheet on the flickering screen. I just had to message him. It was a simple enough thing to do. *Just send him a message.*

I got as far as opening my email account. I even got as far as writing his name before I closed it again. It was stupid. What would I even write? There was no way of wording it that wasn't totally insane, or weirdly desperate. Dom had already been there a month; it was too late.

Just as I closed my email my mobile buzzed against my leg. I wasn't supposed to have it on at work, but so many managers had come and gone I suspected the rule had been forgotten by everyone except myself. Besides, what if there was an emergency? An emergency was possible.

It was Dom.

"Richard, hey, I hope it's OK to phone you at work, I was just ringing to see if you fancied having a drink together, tonight? Only I've still to actually sort my room and my stuff out, and it's been long enough already, and the company would be good. Don't worry if you're busy or something, it's just a thought, no pressure."

"I'm not busy."

"Great, nice one, then I guess I'll see you at home then—though, could you grab a beer or two on the way back?"

"Sure."

CAROLINE

Fuck, what time was it? Nomi was hammering on my bedroom door, a heavy bog-standard fire door painted white like the rest of our cheap rented house. She was calling my name over and over. Where was Dom? The space in the bed next to me was

25

empty. What time was it?

"'Line," Nomi sang, and she dragged out my half my name like I was a dog. I was not in the mood.

"'Li-i-i-i-i-i-ne, it's me-e-e-e-e-e," she carried on. "Nomi." She pronounced her own name normally.

"I'm in be-e-e-e-e-d." I called back.

"It's three in the afterno-o-o-o-o-ne."

"Fuck o-o-o-o-o-ff."

"Let me in," she ordered.

"No."

"Fine."

I heard her footsteps go down the stairs and I drank some of the old warm water I'd left on my bedside table. Her footsteps returned and there was a scratching noise at my door.

"You've got the spare keys, haven't you?"

"Nope." There was scratching, a jangle of metal then more scratching.

"There's no point, I took my key off there."

"Off where?" Scratch-jangle-scratch. The door flew open and there was Nomi, in her pyjamas, the keys in one hand and a slice of toast in the other. "Look at that," she said, then she almost put the keys in her mouth before remembering the toast was in her other hand. Light flooded in from the hallway behind her, exposing the chipped paint of my bedroom walls.

"Hello, Nomi."

"Why, Caroline, are you still in bed?"

"You're not much better, you're only just having breakfast."

"This is dinner. I'm going out tonight," she said, with her words all mushed up with the toast.

"Lovely."

"I made *you* some dinner," she said, pulling the slice in two and throwing half at me.

I made it to the pub just in time. That evening I had a longer shift than usual—three other staff members were off sick, so I was covering the work of two barmaids and one of the kitchen staff. The chef was in a foul mood and kept going outside to smoke, which meant the meals were taking too long. I held a polite grin on my face as I told angry families,

"Your meal will just take a moment longer, sorry about the delay."

And they had all sorts of advice for me.

"Can't you go back there and see what's going on?"

"Could you hurry it up a little?"

"Maybe you could go back there and cook it yourself."

Taking deep breaths is the key to dealing with all that—breathe in . . . two . . . three . . . four, hold . . . breathe out . . . two . . . three . . . four.

"Are they giving you stress, honey?" Debbie the regular asked. Thankfully her husband was nowhere to be seen. "You know, I could always go over there and 'accidentally' spill my drink over 'em."

"For that you'll need another one, Debbie," I replied, pleased with what I was sure was a genuine offer. "What'll you have?"

"You know what I'll 'ave, don't come that." She smiled at me and coughed. She pointed to the kitchen. "Tell that prick to give you an 'and."

I poured her a gin and tonic.

Another customer—a middle aged man with permanent anger-lines etched into his face—stood at the bar rapping his fingers on the counter. He leered at me as he ordered his drink.

"Get yourself one, darlin'," he cooed, curling his lips and glaring at my shirt, "Loosen you up a bit."

Debbie lit a cigarette, stood up and immediately tripped herself into him, the lit end landing on his arm.

"What the fuck?" he screamed, "You total fucking bitch, fuck, you're not even supposed to be smoking indoors."

"I was just headin' outside," she calmly replied—then she stumbled through the front entrance.

"What a bitch, eh?" the awful suit man asked me. I just

smiled and headed back into the kitchen. There was no one there. I saw Debbie waving to me through the window.

"Dom," I said, before I'd even realised, I'd dialled him.

"Hey, you're finally awake then? Sorry I left without a word, you were just—at the risk of sounding corny—you looked so peaceful. Are you at work already? I bet they're giving you grief, right?"

"No more than usual," I told him, feeling somewhat ridiculous for calling him in the middle of my shift, like some distress-ridden damsel.

"I can handle it," I continued, "I just need a drink or something later."

"Sounds like a plan," he answered.

"Great," I said, feeling relief tingle through me. "I'll get us some wine."

"Shit, no, sorry babe, I actually have plans with Richard tonight—you know, the flatmate? Thought it would be good to spend some time. But the girls are in, right? You can have a drink with them?"

In fact the girls *were* in, though drinking was not the plan that evening. Nomi was stoned and lying in the middle of the living room floor, propped up on a heap of cheap Ikea couch cushions, legs and arms spread so that her body formed a giant X.

Christina, by contrast, was sat bolt upright in a metal garden chair, directly underneath the bare lightbulb, her hands placed on her knees, her posture perfect. She looked as though she was waiting for a job interview, only the pink of her eyes giving her away. She giggled at me, her high-pitched giggle, and I wanted to know why.

"What—what's funny?" I asked her. I was somewhere between the two of them, slouching into the couch with a cold cup of tea cradled in my lap.

"Drink it," she giggled. "Just drink it."

"It's cold," I answered, doing my best to keep my words from slurring. "I don't want cold tea."

At that Nomi rolled onto the floor, pushed herself onto all fours, and crawled over to me. She took the mug and downed the tea in a single gulp.

"I'm rolling another spliff," she announced, searching for her papers.

"I don't think we need another," Christina uttered, clearly trying to avoid giggling.

"Caroline does, she's been jilted."

"I have not been jilted," I told her. "Dom's allowed to spend time with friends."

"Doesn't sound like an attentive boyfriend," she said. "Zebedee would never pass up an evening with me."

I ignored her. Christina also clearly felt the need for a change in conversation.

"I saw a poster today. There is some sort of meeting, of fascists, here in the city."

"Why?" Nomi asked her.

"Probably the club. You know, the burning and all," I said, feeling much more sober. The papers had been filled with random yobs blaming the Muslim population who lived on the edge of the city centre. I hated any mention of things like that, of angry, shaven-headed men. I was always afraid of finding myself alone in some dark alley with them.

"When is it?" Nomi asked. "I won't let them get away with that shit. I mean, I'm dating a Muslim—well, a sort-of Muslim. They'd have to get through me." Nomi didn't seem a likely candidate to stop a group of skinheads, being five foot tall and extremely stoned. Her reddened eyes were determined though.

"I don't know when it is," Christina answered, "the poster, someone had torn half of it away. Anyway, we should be careful. There are angry men out there, it isn't safe. The lady I work with, she was followed by a group of men. Things are not—" she paused, searching for the right word in English, "—Normal. Usual. Correct."

"We can look after each other," Nomi stated with some certainty. "But right now, we should stop worrying and smoke some more. The door's double-locked, there's no one getting in tonight."

Christina and I nodded.

DOM

It was already bright outside, you could see even through Caroline's heavy woollen curtains, not that she needed them, she could sleep through anything. And there she was, laid over my arm, asleep next to me, some spit stretching from her perfect lip to the pillow.

And fuck, I realised, it really was bright—how late was it? I was supposed to be meeting with my best friend Zebedee that morning, and judging from the light the morning was almost over, and he'd be pissed off if I arrived when it was already afternoon.

I gently lifted Caroline off my arm, breaking the line of spit, then I kissed her and whispered that I loved her—she still didn't wake up. I brushed my teeth with the spare toothbrush I kept at her place, sloshed water under my arms, pulled on a shirt and made my way out into the streets which absolutely poured with sunshine. It would be good, seeing Zebedee, I'd not seen him in a couple of days. There was a loud pounding of a beat from some bedroom, and it was music that made me think of my first term in halls, fresh from my folks' suburbania.

It was busy, some skater teens standing on the corner, a threesome of old ladies whispering to one another, a coupla mothers with compulsory blue pushchairs but devoid of any baby boys, and on the wall by the estate agents was a poster.

NO TO MILITANT ISLAM—CYMRU DEFENCE
LEAGUE RALLY
THE BURNED CLUB, OCTOBER 11th

I pulled away at the corner, ripping off centimetres, pulling bit by bit, scattering flutters of paper over the pavement, shoving the rest into my coat pockets, pulling at it until half of it was gone, leaving an illegible smeary mess on the wall.

I was mad, I was angry, seeing that shit, and I fumed all the way to Zebedee's house up the hill, which wasn't so far from my place, where he lived with a whole bunch of people he never saw—messy people who would leave dishes on the floor and clothes in the kitchen sink, so going through his house was always like traipsing through a maze of crockery and old socks. Zebedee lived in a typical Swansea terraced house; small unwashed windows surrounded by an absolute ocean of grey pebble-dash. The door—which opened straight onto the pavement, as there was no front garden —was already open, that is, it was open just ajar.

He was in his room, surrounded by his own mess which was spread over the floor so evenly it looked deliberate.

"Alright, Dom."

"Zebedee," I said. He hated his nickname. His real name, which I'd only ever heard once, was Ahmed—which he also hated. He was squatted by the TV screen, a game controller in his hands.

"How long have you been playing?" I asked him, knowing it will have been a long, long time, and if I didn't talk about the game, I wouldn't have his attention.

"Few hours."

"Did you see the posters?" I asked him, kinda careful but also kinda wanting to know what he thought, him being a Muslim himself, or at least he was via his parents. There'd been some trouble in the city, anti-Muslim graffiti had appeared here and there. It was that fire, the club burning down—people were saying that it was the Muslims as the Muslims didn't drink, which was obviously bullshit.

"I've seen a few," Zebedee said, reaching for a mug.

There wasn't much else to say, so I asked him about his

roommates, roommates he never even saw anyway, and he asked me about living with Richard, so I told him it was great, sure, yeah, it was great. I mean, we hadn't exactly spoken much, he spent a lot of time on his computer, or reading, but he seemed nice.

"You want to get to know him a bit better," Zebedee told me, "Don't let it get to that awkward point where you're just polite to each other. I mean, look at us, look at this place. I think it's been three weeks since I even saw my housemates. They might have died. Do you think they died?"

"Probably not," I told him, but I suggested we sneak into their rooms to be safe, just to check. The first two were out, their rooms strewn with mess like Zebedee's, but the last was slumped over their bed, looking for all the world like a corpse. Zebedee looked at me, then crept over to them, hesitating before poking them in the side.

He was alive. He didn't like it.

"Just checking," Zebedee explained. The roommate swore.

"Seriously," Zebedee said once we were safely back in his own room, "I'm not sure I even remember the names of anyone who lives here. Spend some time with this Richard guy—oh, and in case you're wondering, I think the posters are a pile of shit."

I handed him the tattered shreds I'd torn from the wall. He scattered them into the chaos of his floor.

The evening drunks had gathered on the street below our living room window, occasionally clamouring with the middle-aged men from the betting shop next door. I settled down with a beer, ready to talk to Richard, to get to know him. And we chatted, we had a couple of cans, and the whole thing was mellow, and I actually felt relaxed. I liked the apartment we shared—it was shabby, and it was comfortable. The peeling green wallpaper felt like home, as did the split cushions and frayed carpets.

I was happy to spend the evening chilling in the lounge, sat in the armchair with my feet on a bucket, but Richard said we had to get me unpacked, so I said sure, why turn down an offer of free help? So we went to my room, I put on some music, and we upturned boxes and opened suitcases and got talking about this and that, and I stacked posters and pictures, posters and pictures which would eventually go up onto the wall.

We unpacked quietly for a bit, until Richard said we needed scotch and wandered to the off license by the betting shop, the one filled with teenagers, both in front of and behind the counter. An off license which managed to make me feel old, old at thirty.

Eventually the boxes were empty, and the suitcases stacked. My room was warm and smoky, I'd said Richard could smoke in there if he liked, and I let the bottle go and lay back, and he lay next to me. The flat might have been small, run-down and clawed at by damp, but it was my first home since the whole break-up thing, and the moving out, and the hassle. All the hassle. Richard took the bottle and asked,

"So why did you move in here, Mr. Dom?"

Well, so I lived with this girl, and we'd been together some time, some time like two and a quarter years, two years and three months nearly, and I was studying and she had been working at a popular chemist chain I never shopped in 'cause of what they did to helpless creatures. We'd had a house full of Ikea. Routine had hit us, and I say 'hit' but really it was slower than that, and less noticeable, and though we'd always wanted to stay interesting, to keep entertaining each other, we'd got smothered. Smothered is the right word, better than hit.

And she'd had a temper, a real temper, and she hated her job and then she started hating me. She told me I didn't work hard enough. She was a Buddhist, and by that, I mean she read trashy pseudo-Buddhist books by Americans with made-up names, so to her everything was about life lessons. I was never learning

33

mine, I was always failing to learn my life lessons, and so I was building up bad karma—that's what she'd tell me, I had all this bad karma, and then I'd tell her that I didn't believe in karma. She said that would also lead to bad karma.

She was learning her life lessons of course—she said she always tried to be self-aware, and so I tried to be self-aware too, but I'd never be as self-aware as she was. So, she told me. She was learning her life lessons so she would have a better time in the next life—and by that I suppose she meant that she wouldn't be working a shitty job in her next life, or dating a shitty boyfriend with stacks of bad karma, but I told her that I didn't believe in a next life. She said that meant I would have a bad next life.

I told her that I just wanted to be happy in *this* life, that we might as well be—I told her that the point of life was to be happy and to try and make other people feel the same way. She said that I had to face up to things, and never did—she said that I was a coward, for running away from my problems and not learning my lessons, and I guess part of me believed she was right.

I disagreed with her a lot, but at the same time I knew she was under a lot of stress so I'd tried to help, to make it better, to run her a bath, or put on music, or spend more time with her, but it all just made her angrier. My friends hated her, but I loved her, and I wanted her happy—I suppose I wanted her happy with me. But then instead I'd hear her on her phone, to her mum, to her friends, muttering shit about me down copper wiring.

And then there was Caroline, who turned up one day when the guys took me to the cinema to cheer me up, which they'd guilted me into as I'd not seen them for three weeks, three weeks I'd spent miserable. Caroline was friends with Zebedee's girlfriend, and she was fucking beautiful, with long blonde hair and—ohhhh—those curves, she was fun, more importantly she was funny, and I loved it. When I got home that night it had been late, and there was my girlfriend, filled with a fury, but she said nothing and went off to bed. I lay down on the couch and Caroline had texted, so I texted back, and back and forth and back and forth, and we did that for a couple of weeks.

It got worse, of course—she never said it, but I was racking up bad karma by being an inattentive boyfriend, and to be perfectly fair to her I wasn't being the best boyfriend, but by that point I was beyond caring. I didn't see Caroline at all, but we messaged each other over and over, getting to know each other a little better, each time in 160 characters or less. I hid my phone.

Around two weeks later my girlfriend found me naked on the couch, having 160 characters-or-less sex with Caroline. That was that. I needed somewhere to live.

And new clothes. In a mad fit of cliché, she'd cut up all my clothes.

"I see," Richard said.

"So how did you come by the spare room?" I asked him, changing the subject from my ever-so-slightly-crazy ex.

He told me about his friend Rutti, this ever-so-slightly-crazy gay guy, "—and we're still friends," he added, "Mostly. I'd like to stay friends with him, but evicting someone tends to make things a little awkward."

I could see that.

"Do you reckon you'll see your ex again?" he asked me, taking the bottle from my hand, leaning back a little to drink it.

"Fuck, I hope not. Besides, I'm with Caroline."

Richard handed the bottle back to me. I took a swig before lying back down, my belly warm and my head dizzy.

"Do you—do you have a girlfriend, Richard?"

"Not at present, no," he said, taking to bottle and tilting his head back. "Not that I wouldn't like one."

"And you're not—" I asked.

Richard took another swig from the bottle.

"I'm not. You're asking that because of Rutti, right? People would think we were a couple. Quite often. I think Rutti vaguely liked the idea—I mean, he would never correct people on it."

Richard handed the bottle back to me, his speech slurring ever-so-slightly. "We were close, I guess that's true, but guys never—well, they never got me hard if I can put it like that." He thought for a moment—a moment I took to drink and pass the bottle—before he carried on. "Perhaps it would have been easier if I had—I could have got with Rutti and he could have made all my decisions for me."

"It's not the best situation," I said. "It's what I like about Caroline. We don't tell each other what to do or anything. It's the way I like it."

"And you love her?" Richard asked, handing the scotch back to me.

"I love her. I really do." I took another drink and lay back down onto the carpet, feeling the fibres scratch the back of my neck, staring at the ceiling.

Sunlight streamed in through the open curtains, the strong light of a really hot day, and my head was thick and the room was sweltering. It stank of smoke and sweat, and music was still flowing from the tinny laptop speakers, with a small pool of scotch on the floor. The carpet had rubbed my arm and face sore over the night, and by me there lay Richard, and for a moment I felt this chill, that I'd slept by a man, but then I realised how stupid that sounded and took a swig from a glass of stagnant water. I'd go make some cereal. I'd make some for him, too.

FILIPINO QUARTER TERMINAL. PARIS
23 YEARS ON

The bus pulled free from the station. Richard had spent the half-hour break eating damp sushi, chewing everclear, and gazing at stressed commuters as they bustled past lugging briefcases and reading the news. The purr of the bus beneath their buttocks was comforting. Richard was never a fan of Paris, even just for making a transfer.

There was a loud squawking from the back of the vehicle—a salesperson had a selection of cage-bound and colourful birds balanced on the seats next to them. The driver had twice made their way to the back of the bus, insisting that the cages be kept covered. The others on the bus watched the roll of buildings from the windows—students, aunts, grandchildren. What if they knew where Richard was going—what they were going to do? Would the other passengers be horrified, or congratulatory? Of course, the students would be fine. The newer generations seemed fine with everything.

Richard reached up to the overhead storage compartment to retrieve their coat, felt their way through the pockets, and fished out their reader. It had been a long way from Abertawe, and it was a long way to Barcelona, but Richard'd had far too many coffees to sleep. Plus, they were far too nervous for sleep, even if the birds were quietening down.

Eight hours to Barcelona.

Richard checked through their notes, wondering if they should try and do some coursework. They had finally and reluctantly been convinced to study computer science part-time at Prifysgol Abertawe. They were thirty years older than the other students, but it wasn't going to bother them.

The young man on the seats opposite was watching Richard, eyes narrowed, surrounded by expertly-applied eye-liner, lips curved to a flirtatious smile. The young man was cruising them. That was another thing with the youth today—all pansexual. Almost all of them. Richard gave the young man an apologetic smile and flipped a message to them: thanks for the attention, but I'm thirty years your senior, and hetero. We could cuddle if you like.

It didn't matter: the young man had already focused their attentions on the young woman behind, who giggled and narrowed their eyes in response. Sometimes Richard felt as though they had been left behind.

Not this week though. They would be one of the first. So far it was only legal in the Catalunya Republic, but that would change. Half the states of the federation were talking about the possibility of legalising at some point in the future. It had taken long enough. They thought of Dom.

The young man was now seated next to the young woman, and the two of them kissed with matching red lips. On the streets outside the Dharmic Selassies were holding a festival, all purples and oranges, serving vegan steaks and attempting to win converts. Richard lowered the blind.

No new messages. Rutti had announced their arrival at the very last minute, with their usual affected lack of interest. Richard knew Rutti was interested. When they'd first announced the news, Richard could see Rutti trying to suppress their excitement. Rutti was a romantic at heart. There was little Rutti could hide from them, even living so far from one another.

Richard turned to see behind themself. The birds had gone to sleep, alongside their owner, whose head was already lolling around, synchronised with the vehicle.

Eight hours to Barcelona.

Richard was excited.

The time had finally come.

CHAPTER TWO

IT'S NOT GAY

RICHARD

A seagull flew over us, shrieking at the five or six gulls further down the jetty, just visible through the shrinking light. A breeze worked its way through the folds of my coat, so I pulled it tighter around myself. The sea roared beneath us. My legs ached from the shift in the charity shop, but that was the way it was—with one job you gained a headache, the other leg-ache. At least this way I felt alert—and that evening I really did. Sharp and alert, words pouring from me. I don't usually talk much, but Rutti used to say that when I got going, I was difficult to stop.

Dom had asked me how long I'd lived in the city.

"I've lived here a long time. It's what comes from not going to university. You stay home. Family winds up more important. Friends of mine left for uni, sometimes in Cardiff, or Bangor, or over in England, or Scotland. They barely even speak to their families now."

Dom nodded in agreement. My coat held against the cold, and the stone of the jetty was warm. It felt nice. I continued. He'd asked, after all.

"I didn't grow up there. I was born and raised in the Midlands. Right up until the age of five. The town we lived in was this small market town where nothing much happened. So when my mother left my dad for someone she'd met at the pub it was this big scandal. I know now that my mother wasn't the only one they blamed, either. They all talked about my father, what he must have done to drive her away—away from a young son at that. I don't know why I'm telling you this—but to me family *is* important.

"So we moved. We didn't come straight to south Wales. At first, we stayed in the area. My dad tried to make a go of things in a larger town. We moved into a smaller house, which I now know was a council house, and I went to a new school. Neither my dad nor I did very well in this new place, and we left after a few months. I was bullied at the school and never wanted to go. My dad couldn't find a job. We obviously didn't fit in.

"And then we moved north and stayed with my grandmother at her flat. It was summer so I didn't have to go to school. She used to tell me to be good—she said I had to be quiet so my father could sort his head out. I remember that he didn't talk very much that summer. I noticed because I had no way of making new friends. He ate in his bedroom. My grandmother took me to the park or for a walk in the woods, but my dad never came along. My grandmother started mentioning his headaches. He always had a headache when it was time to go somewhere."

I sipped at my beer, aware of how one-way the conversation was, but Dom was leaning in toward me, all attention, so I took another swig and carried on. I'd only ever told this to Rutti. This was new. I continued.

"I remember this one time we went to the supermarket. I hadn't been to one since I'd been with my mother. I remember standing in what I suppose was the cereal aisle. I was crying by packets of Frosties. I stopped before my grandmother found me. I knew I had to be good. I was honestly a good kid.

"Then it was the start of autumn and I heard them arguing. My grandmother said I would have to go to school. I didn't hear what my dad was saying. Then, one day, he came into the kitchen for breakfast. He was wearing clean clothes and a huge smile. He was drinking coffee. He told me things were going to get better, that our new life would start soon. We were moving to Wales.

"He had a whole new house and a new job. I went to a new school. Of course I started getting bullied almost straight away. I was too quiet, I didn't understand the games the other boys would play, and I found the lessons too hard. I didn't tell my dad though. You see, he was so happy. He wanted our new life to work. So I put up with it, placed a bubble around myself where I couldn't hear the names they'd call me. Some of the names were in Welsh and I didn't understand them anyway.

"I made one or two friends, but they wound up moving— and girls, well, there was no chance there. It was my fault really. I never spoke to them. When I was a teenager, I got into gaming forums and most of my friends were online. I had an online girlfriend, over in Canada, but to be honest that didn't work out. Aside from a few flings here and there, it was always just me and my dad, here in this city. When I turned eighteen, I got accepted into a couple of university courses to study chemistry, but they were all outside of Wales. I couldn't really leave him. I couldn't leave my dad for somewhere so far away."

And I could feel my breath quivering, my hands shaking, and that was when Dom put his arm around me.

"Family is important, but at the same time I was older, and I couldn't put up with a forty-five year old man wandering around in a dirty dressing gown all day. I told myself that we were holding each other back—I mean, if I left then he might actually start cooking for himself again. Cleaning his own clothes. Something.

"Things got better for me. After a while Rutti moved in, and I made the first real flesh-and-blood friend I had in years. A little while longer and my dad killed himself. I'd gone round to bring him the paper and he was lying in the middle of the hallway."

I took a deep breath, trying to keep it even.

"Sorry, I'm going on too much. But that's how things are, that's my life."

41

I stopped, realising how long I'd been talking for and hoping I hadn't bored him stiff.

"Fuck," Dom replied. We sat in silence together, us and the end of the jetty. I sipped at the dregs of my beer, listening to the sea smash against the stone beneath us. It was quiet.

"Are you alright, Richard?" Dom asked, his arm still around me, me leaning against him.

"I'm alright."

We stayed like that for a while, sitting in silence. By the time I'd finished my beer I noticed his breathing had grown deep and even, and he snorted into sleep. I opened another, spilling suds over my sleeve, and stared out toward the dark sea.

Things weren't so bad. Dom was a decent guy—more than that, I'd grown to like him. Really grown to like him. He was relaxed, and the way he rambled on, well, that was somehow comforting. He didn't expect anything. He didn't even expect you to listen. Rutti had always asked questions, making sure that his tirade was sinking in. Not so Dom.

I felt my phone vibrating in my pocket. I knew that it was Rutti. The reason I didn't answer, or the reason I'm going to give, is that Dom was still against my left arm, and the phone was in my left pocket. To answer it I would have to move him, and I was comfortable where he was—he was warm.

It wasn't gay. It's not gay, just leaning on someone. It wasn't— I'd lived with Rutti long enough to know what was. Rutti would have told me that it wasn't completely straight either, and maybe that was true. I didn't care. There was no one around to see, and besides, *I* knew I was straight, and that was all that mattered.

Somewhere further down the jetty a lone drunk stumbled over to the wall, throwing up into the water with a distant splash. His blurry outline leant against the stone, then slumped to the ground. I could still hear the retching sound of him throwing up over himself. Vomit, that was what marked mine and Dom's friendship. Vomiting drunk guys.

My phone buzzed again. Dom stirred slightly, then settled. I drank some more. I would have to contact Rutti, he'd be worrying by this point.

Dom buried his face into my sleeve.

DOM

Living with Richard was easy— we'd managed to get beyond the awkward-housemate-stage, and I was enjoying his company. And if I tell you that we spent most of the next several evenings together, and if I tell you that we'd often fall asleep in each other's rooms, then you need to know that we didn't even think about it. I didn't think about it. If I'm honest with you it felt cosy.

I called Caroline once or twice, hoping to see a bit of her as well, but she was busy, and then when she called me, I'd already made plans with Richard. Such things happen. It wasn't the first time that we'd missed each other for a couple of weeks—I still loved her, and when I was up in the maths building, I still waved to her. She'd wave back. I'd texted her to ask if she wanted to have lunch, but she'd already had it and had to get on with her coursework—such things happen.

Richard and I had spent the better part of a week indoors, so we decided to go out. We were both skint so Richard suggested we head to the beach—there was this jetty, a long stone jetty that juts out to sea. I knew the one.

It was late by the time we got there, and it's not the most scenic of places as it usually just sees old fishermen and thrown-away needles, and I presume people used the needles there but I never ever actually saw them. The jetty reached out into the water by the mouth of the marina, though no boats ever seemed to go in or out, they were quarantined to the harbour. It was windy over there and by us there was a single old turbine, with the flames of the oil refineries glowing in the distance. Richard was telling me about how the city had looked before,

"Before the war, when half of it was razed—though it wasn't the bombs themselves that did this city in. It was the trauma— the collective psychological trauma—the city was shell-shocked

43

and never recovered. Before the war there were grand buildings and tramlines, these beautiful bridges and shopping arcades. They could have rebuilt those things again, but Swansea can't get over what happened. It doesn't ever even try to be beautiful or interesting."

"I thought this city was first built with broken bricks. I'm not sure it was ever meant to be anything more than it is, than what it is now," I said, taking a beer from him.

"And what is that, Dom? Cheers."

I didn't have an answer, so we just knocked our beers together and faced the sea, the angry-looking sea, tinged red where it met the industry-lined horizon.

"You know I actually came here when I was a kid. On a family holiday. It seemed different. I don't even remember those." I motioned over to the distant chimneys.

Richard started to say something, but was cut short by a swarm of seagulls fighting over something—something that looked rotten—and I couldn't hear myself above their shrieking, so we watched them peck at one another until they lost interest and scattered.

"So will you stay in Swansea?" Richard asked me. "After you've finished your course?"

"I suppose I will—there are at least teaching jobs around here. I have some good friends here too, I don't know if I'd want to leave it all behind."

"You must speak Welsh then."

"Wrth gwrs. And will you stay?" I asked him. I honestly hoped that he wasn't leaving any time soon.

"Most probably. Where else is there to go? Graveyard of ambition and all."

"I've had ambitions you know," I told him, "I was a manager once, back in the day, five years ago, actually. I was the manager of a fast-food restaurant."

"You're serious?" He shivered though I don't know if it was from the cold or my revelation. "You were *manager*? That's awful. That's really awful, Dom."

"I took it seriously for about a week. In the end I got fired," I told him. "We had a party, me and the other workers, it was late at night, and we cooked a load of burgers and helped ourselves to the soft drinks to add to the vodka we'd brought along," I explained.

"So they fired you?" He seemed to relax at my misdemeanour.

"They fired all of us, every single fucking one of us and they couldn't go on without anyone to run the place, or cook, or clean or anything, and it closed. That's why it's not there, not anymore, but it was a good party though, one of the best I've had."

We didn't say anything else to each other for a while, so we listened to the water and the banter of the fishermen, slowly drinking the beer as it went warm in our hands. Lights started to flicker on in the tacky yuppie apartments over the marina as it was getting dark, and so Richard fished a wind-up electric lantern from his bag and flicked it on, gently resting it between the two of us. It got quiet—I noticed that the seagulls had gone, or at least gone to sleep, and so had all the fishermen. After a while the lantern dimmed and so Richard picked it up, the only noise around being the whirr of the motor as it was wound and the splash of the water below us both.

It was pitch-dark black and we were encircled, encircled in a small pool of light which made long shadows of the beer bottles, and finally Richard spoke, he said,

"I used to come here, too, a long time ago."

And so I asked him, "How long have you lived in Swansea?"

CHAPTER THREE

THE PET FUNDAMENTALIST

RUTTI

Of course, I used to tell the customers it was a bad idea: perfume is a notoriously difficult present. Expensive, obnoxious, and there's a 90% chance you choose the wrong scent and it's all for nothing. My manager heard me once and said if I told another customer the truth I'd be fired. I always hated shop managers with their petty ambitions and tiny kingdoms, running a loss-making branch of a chain store into the ground like a central African dictator. It was lies for the customers from then on. In fairness to my dowdy pig of a boss, most of the customers deserved it. They had too much money and too few thoughts.

An old lady entered the store and gave me a withered smile. I beamed back, ready to be polite and helpful for the first time that day.

"Can I—sorry, *may* I help you? With anything?"

May I. May I. May I. Tubby prim-faced manager says it must be *may* I. *You'wre asking someone'sh permishun*, they slurred every single hour, a pudgy snarled cuckoo popping from their dingy office. *You'wre awsking for con-sent.*

"May I help you?" I asked the customer.

The customer heard nothing, their rattled breath was too loud and their ear canals too withered. They were pinned to a tiny crucifix with a teensy-bearded anarcho-communist Jewish man pinned on to the other side. Before I had a chance to say more, the customer's elderly Romeo hobbled into the store, took them by the hand and wordlessly whisked them away. I stood by the door and watched the two stumble down the street together. I was pressed against the glass when the phone in my pocket shook, causing the glass to vibrate and cast a loud and angry buzz over the store. I glanced around. No phones in work. Another diktat. But the store was empty aside from two thoughtless women nattering nothing and spraying one another with the vile chemicals we sold, so I checked my phone. It was a message from Steph, saying they'd meet me at the end of my shift.

Three point four hours later we were on the street. Dark clouds bristled overhead, posing to end the summer with rain. It had happened the last few years, two months of sun and then rain till next year. Wet watery Wales. We took a detour to buy booze and so made our way down the crumbling high street where Swansea's last few graceful buildings were being left to collapse, the land eyed carefully by greedy property magnates and councillors desperate for a second Mercedes. We arrived at Castle Square, proudly housing a ruin which was more carefully maintained—the castle—which the odd American tourist unfortunate enough to be lost here would energetically photograph. Directly opposite the castle, across the bland fountain which was the heart of the square—the square itself a mock corporate-style plaza which had no place there—was a giant TV screen which showed the news and weather in grim silence.

The summer was trying to begin, filthy grey clouds alternating with bright sun; the occasional sprinkle of rain that dried with gusts of warm wind. Just a few people milled around, glancing into the windows of the non-boarded-up stores. A couple were dry-humping one another in the doorway of an abandoned bakery, their lips slop-slopping over one another's faces. A luminous-jacketed police officer idly watched them from the next doorway over. I was busy watching the three of them when a young man with neat brown hair and a shirt that was buttoned suspiciously far up accosted us.

Of course, it was about Jesus, the evangelicals infested the city centre. Some Saturdays there would almost literally be one on every street: at the start of town there was the van, with a loudspeaker perched on top which belched messages about Christ. There was the Baptist Church with its converts for free lunches, whilst on parallel Oxford Street, on the small stage of pavement outside an abandoned department store, two men would shriek at passers-by. By the entrance to the market was the silent old person with a sign about Judgement atop a ludicrous pole about three times their height. A further two minutes down the same street was one with Jesus films for sale. Around the corner from them was St. Mary's church, where an obese woman would sit and clutch a microphone like an ice cream cone, mumbling entertaining incoherence through pursed lips. Sometimes the all-too-earnest Chinese Christian Choir would sing opposite.

Some were even seasonal: last summer an African man with a megaphone ranted and rambled, the same spark of aggression in them as with the others, but whom disappeared come Autumn. At Halloween there was an elderly Bible Basher protesting a greeting's card shop for its tacky-yet-apparently-Satanic pumpkin decorations and Dracula costumes.

The one currently before me was younger than most and despite their crisp appearance, was vaguely attractive. They stared at me with dark, strangely serious eyes. They had a strong jawline and looked somehow familiar. I wanted to talk to them.

"God bless you," the man ordered.

"Why thank you," I replied. "And which god would you like to bless you?"

The man looked confused. "Which god?"

"Why yes." I replied. "Perhaps Apollo could bless you with reason. Or Hestia with warmth—that's the Greek goddess of the hearth, you see. Or better yet, perhaps Pan could bless you—

Pan's really good with—"

"No, no. I don't mean that," they interrupted, "I mean—"

"You mean you would like the Great Goddess to bless you instead? Well, alright then, but I don't really follow all-powerful gender-based deities myself. Fine. Goddess bless you."

Steph walked on, pretending not to hear either of us.

"But have you heard of Jesus?" the young man asked, a strange desperate glint in their eye.

"Of course, I've heard of Jesus. Who the fuck hasn't heard of Jesus?" I asked them. "Are you seriously going around asking people if they'd heard of *Jesus?* They're the most prolific mental illness the world has ever seen."

"Look, if you come with me you get some free food and we can talk. There're free lunches at the Baptist Church," the Christian said, standing in front of me, desperately trying to salvage the spiritual sale. Steph carried on walking.

"Look," I told them, "I worship many gods. None of them Jesus, or Jehovah or the teen-raping Holy Spirit. Stop bothering people." I started to hurry to catch Steph up. The Christian blocked my way.

"Please mate. We can eat, just come with me. Just come to the church." They had the threat of tears in their eyes.

"Are you hungry?"

The Christian tried to pull themself together, dragging their face into a composed and almost stern expression. "I just want to talk to you about Jesus."

"Don't they feed you at the church?"

"We eat with whoever we bring in," they said, their stoicism almost slipping. "It's not too late, you can be saved. My name is Craig."

"I'm not the one who needs saving, believe me," I told them. They had no answer, but we stood in front of one another in an awkward stand-off. Over their shoulder I could see Steph peer around the corner and beckon for me to hurry up. Instead, I said to the crazy hungry Jesus lover, "Come to my place and we'll have dinner. I don't like eating in churches as it contaminates the food. Come on, you like pasta, right?"

After one tense walk back to Steph's apartment and a quick-trip-to-the-bathroom for the nervous Christian, Steph accosted me in the hallway.

"What are you doing, Rutti? Why is he here?"

"They're hungry, so we're going to feed them. Isn't that exciting?" I gave Steph the biggest grin my face could handle.

"No, no, Rutti it is far from exciting. He's only going to try to convert us, fail, and then it'll be awkward and endless."

"Alright, look, they said they were hungry."

"We can't have an evangelical Christian staying with us, Rutti," Steph ordered, their voice a low hiss. "You're a guest here yourself."

"Why not?" I asked, ignoring the guest comment, "Is there any particular reason we can't form a refuge for wayward fascists? It'll be great, they can be a sort of pet."

"Rutti," Steph replied, their hiss growing to a growl. "He can't stay. As far as I see it, you're doing one of two things—or possibly both. Firstly, there's the possibility that this is some sort of hero complex of yours, and you want to rescue the cute little fundamentalist from his brainwashed ways. Secondly, there's the possibility that you're doing this as some sort of self-destructive melodramatic gesture, replaying the situation with Richard—who you always felt was too conservative—with someone more extreme, when you could in fact just call Richard and make up with him. Doing one of these things makes you certifiable, doing both makes you a nightmare lunatic."

"Steph," I replied, trying to ignore the possibility that any of their educated guesses might be accurate, "Craig needs our help. Not mine, ours. It's your apartment. If you want them to leave, then they have to leave."

"Don't put this all on me," Steph replied, their voice faltering. "I'm not having your psychoses played out in my own living room."

"Steph, they have nowhere else to go."

"Fuck, Rutti. We're both gay, we can't take in a fundamentalist Christian from the street. It's going to turn out horribly."

"We'll have done the right thing," I reminded them.

"We'll see about that. You're the one who's going to be sharing a bed with him, you know. Is he aware of that?"

"It'll be fine."

We gathered in the kitchen. The seal on the little oven was broken and so heat rolled over the small room. Steph's apartment had been remodelled by one of the previous occupants, whose taste bypass had been inflicted upon the entire place. It was draped in flowered wallpaper, ostentatious plastic mouldings and little mock glass chandeliers. The kitchen was the epicentre of the atrocity: every wall, along with the ceiling, had been covered in waves of icing-like plaster, giving the impression of being inside a giant cake. Steph never seemed to mind, and in fairness their apartment being up on the hill, it had a spectacular view of the tiny terraces, concrete blocks, and polluted bay of the city below.

We gathered in the baked room and set out mismatched plates whilst The Christian reluctantly told us the following: they were twenty-five, they had grown up in Gloucester but had left home at fifteen, they wouldn't say why, they joined the church, they wouldn't give a real reason why, they couldn't find a job as they'd missed their exams at school, their name was Craig, they had no fixed address.

That night Craig fell asleep quickly and easily. They didn't even snore. I lay awake on the hard sofabed next to them, watching shapes form, merge, and drift through the darkness, trying to make out the deranged floral print of the wallpaper. For the first time since I was a child I had gone to sleep wearing clothes—a slightly oversized t-shirt and boxer shorts. Craig had gone to bed almost fully dressed, as I had expected.

51

I thought of Richard. Had they even noticed that I had gone? We had shared a bed now and then, when one or the other of us had a relative to stay, and we'd always talked through the darkness. We'd never run out of things to say.

That had been a surprise. When I'd first moved in I assumed what most people assumed about Richard—that they were a boring, overly-cautious computer geek with some slightly adorable mannerisms. Against my expectations the two of us had become close friends, and we'd become close friends faster than I had realised. Sometimes they had annoyed me with some thoughtless straight-guy statement or assumption, and often I annoyed them with my sense of humour, but the two of us had always stuck together—through breakups (mine), educational failures (mine), and lost gaming tournaments (their). We'd always stuck together.

Steph was wrong. I couldn't call Richard. They didn't know, but I'd already texted Richard twice that week, seeing if they wanted to meet for a beer. There had been no response. Richard had made a break from me, and that was something I had to accept.

And there was the second surprise—accepting that was more difficult than I'd imagined. I actually missed Richard.

Craig the Christian snorted and rolled away, right to the edge of the sofa bed.

CAROLINE

When I was six years old, I liked to invent proverbs. Proverbs, I had decided, were an *excellent* way of understanding the world.

> *It's better to be sad than to*
> *be old.*
> *Cats make much better*
> *friends than dolls.*
> *Don't punch your brothers*

when you're angry: wait
until you're calm so it'll be
more satisfying.

They weren't good proverbs, of course, in fact I suppose they weren't even proverbs at all—what could you expect from a six-year-old girl? Yet one of those childish sayings was sticking in my mind at that exact moment.

Whatever you do, never
ever date boys.

I was worried about Dom. I never usually worried about relationships—in fact I tended towards independence. Does that surprise you? In fact, I've ended most of the relationships I've had. Not that I've had many of course, but it's rare that I've been dumped. It's unlike me not to see trouble ahead. My first boyfriend had dumped me, but we were at school and it was because I took some of his crayons without asking. I didn't mind—what was the point of having a boyfriend if not good crayons?

People have generally said it's because of my 'independent streak', though I imagine they only say that because I'm not a guy. It's not something you hear people say to guys very often. I was first told I had one of these 'independent streaks' when I was ten years old and didn't want to work in a group in geography class. I could draw my own volcanoes. I'd worked out that other people generally meant lower marks. I always got good marks in school.

That surprises people almost as much as the 'streak'. People hear you're twenty-seven and working in a bar and they assume that you dropped out of school at fifteen, never mind if you're doing your master's degree or not.

So suddenly I found that I was 'a barmaid'. You should know, people's perceptions of you change instantly. As a blonde bartender people make certain presumptions. I almost swore off men when guy after guy presumed I was an easy fuck. And it takes a long time of getting to know me before people suspect that I might have opinions worth listening to. I'm assumed to be pretty, and mindless, and safe. Which is why men are usually so surprised when they get dumped.

'Is it because I'm too smart?' one of them had asked me. In fact I wanted to end things between us because he was laugh-out-loud dumb, but as I had blonde hair, a vagina, and a frivolous-sounding job I, of course, must have been even dumber. I was sarcastic and said yes, he was the love child of Hypatia and Aristotle. He thought I was serious.

Most of them just looked stunned. They didn't really say anything. They just nodded or were quiet or paced the room, unable to process the fact that I wasn't happy—or more accurately, that I just didn't see the point in prolonging contact with them. It was amicable, but I imagine they're still scratching their heads.

The most recent one wouldn't accept it. He told me that I *couldn't* dump him. I told him I most certainly could. But he shook his head and sat down on my couch as though nothing had happened. I got straight on the phone and got as many of my friends over as I could manage. He looked a bit worried as they started to gather around him one by one, but he'd simply stared ahead at the television, pretending there was nothing unusual. When there were about six of us we picked him up off the couch, carried him to the street and sat him on the kerb. By the next morning he was gone.

But Dom, well I liked Dom, and it was the first time that I felt comfortable with a guy, meeting him. And yeah, maybe it was because he was so relaxed, or that his opinions were so firm. Or even that he dressed like a hippy with his hemp hand-wash clothes, but not totally like a hippy, as his hair was cropped short. He was rare for Swansea, anyway. A hippy-looking maths postgrad.

Now don't get me wrong, I found it lovely that he was getting on so well with his new flatmate—Zebedee wasn't always the best influence, and he could do with more friends. That's what I told myself for the first week, when I didn't see him but for the occasional text message. Another week and a half later, and my feelings had changed.

I tried to focus on my thesis but the words jumbled and faded before my eyes. Dom's office was just across from mine—right across in fact, and we could see each other through our windows. His was larger, being in the science tower, whereas I shared mine with three other students and Christina (whenever she could escape her call centre job). It was a nondescript academic office, with bulk-bought blue desk chairs and old school paint for the walls. Dom's was similar, though with slightly better chairs with a slightly less sickly shade of paint. I'd noticed his light was on when Christina and I had first arrived, but I'd done my best not to look—Dom was clearly busy, he didn't need me waving at him. If I'm honest, I was actually a bit angry.

"He keeps looking over at you," Christina told me, placing her hand on mine. "He's staring. He looks sad, like a puppy. Like a sad orphan puppy. A sad dying little orphan puppy with big sad eyes."

"I get it, Christina," I said, freeing my hand from hers. "He can stare all he likes. I'll talk to him when he actually comes to see me."

"So why don't you go to see him?" she asked. "You have legs and a mouth. Use them."

I looked up at Dom, who was staring with an especially forlorn expression plastered over his face. I wasn't going to fall for it.

"I have to go to work," I told Christina.

"He's cheating on you."

Things were no better back home. The whole ground floor stank of burnt plastic, with the kitchen at ground zero. Nomi had successfully mated hob and hairbrush, and was stood at the oven, surrounded by a cloud of acrid smoke, trying to chip bits off the electric stove with a pair of scissors.

"Please, Nomi, at least tell me it wasn't deliberate this time." It was the second appliance she'd destroyed with plastic hair accessories in two days. Christina would be furious.

"No," she sighed, resuming her chipping. "I just left the hob on and left my hairbrush on the hob."

"Why were you brushing your hair in the kitchen?"

"Yes!" she screeched, having just dislodged a large chunk of former hairbrush. She ignored my question and repeated herself.

"He *is* cheating on you."

"He's not cheating on me, Nomi." I opened the window in a forlorn attempt to clear the kitchen of acrid fumes, then took my laptop from my bag and balanced it at the edge of the worktop—pulling up a wobbly barstool. I tried to ignore the disconcerting whirr it had been making for the past couple of weeks.

"He's cheating," Nomi continued. "You ought to snip off his balls. Anyway, Zebedee's coming over in a bit," Nomi informed me. "We'll see what's what then."

Nomi had obviously already been talking to her boyfriend, and was relishing the notion of throwing gossip in my face. It was another hour before she got the opportunity. She watched me as she waited, only leaving to answer the door to Zebedee. I had written three hundred and fourteen words toward my thesis.

"Tell her, Zeb. Tell her what you told me." Nomi was barely containing her glee. I resisted the urge to throw my laptop at her face.

"Look, I really don't think—" Zebedee protested, before being cut off by his manic partner.

"Tell her. She has a right to know, she is Dom's girlfriend, after all."

"There's not much to tell," Zebedee began, catching Nomi's sharp, angry glare before continuing, "Well, he's been spending a lot of time with Richard."

He leaned toward me. Nomi beamed.

"Way too much time."

I could feel the annoyance welling up inside me. I wanted to wipe the smug look from Nomi's face. I shouted without meaning to.

"And you're sad and jealous that your little friend has someone else to play with? I can't say I blame you, with your tragic nutjob of a girlfriend as your only other company." I gestured toward Nomi, who glowered.

"It's not just a new friend," Zebedee told me, as calm as before. "The two of them—well, there's something not right."

I'd had enough. I picked up my laptop and made my way toward the door.

"Tell her," Nomi shrieked.

I stopped. "Tell me what?"

"Tell her."

"Well," Zebedee started with obvious reluctance. "See, I called Dom this morning and—"

"Tell her," Nomi repeated.

"I am doing," he answered, a note of irritation in his voice. "He was in bed. In bed with Richard."

"Bullshit," I told him. "So, Dom's into men, all of a sudden?"

"It's true," Nomi stated, obviously pleased with herself. "Zebedee wouldn't lie about that."

"I really wouldn't," he confirmed.

I went to my room without another word. I was angry, I don't mind admitting that I was angry, but what was worse was that I believed him. Zebedee could be a pain in the arse sometimes, but he had absolutely no reason to lie. I turned some music on and sat on my bed. What was I going to do? I could hardly confront Dom about it, the words would catch in my throat. I couldn't ignore it either. Was Dom really cheating on me with another man? He'd told me he loved me.

I didn't notice Nomi had opened the door.

"Need to talk?" she offered.

I did, I just didn't want to talk to her. But if I had to talk to Nomi, then it would be better to pre-empt her.

57

"So you think Dom's gay. Or bi, or whatever. You think he's fucking that Richard. Right? That's what everyone thinks? That poor stupid fucking Caroline has wound up with a guy who sleeps with men."

"Sweetie, it could happen to anyone," Nomi soothed, all trace of her smugness having evaporated. I knew her mind: she had been proven correct so now she could show mercy. I didn't want to give her the satisfaction.

"Well I don't believe it. There are tons of reasons the two of them were sharing a bed. And sometimes people get caught up in new friends. That's just the way it is. I'd know if he wasn't straight. I'd even know if his roommate wasn't."

"It's hard news to take, Caroline. But you don't have to take my word for it. Zebedee's going to have a talk with him, see what's what."

"That's really not—"

"Too late. He's already gone."

RICHARD

It was my one day a week off, and Dom and I had agreed to spend it together. It was actually him who'd offered, and I who'd accepted. So far we'd just mulled around, flicking the small television set on and off and checking online messages. The most I'd done was find a new splodge of grey damp on the ceiling.

"Do you want something to eat, Dom?" I called. Dom was in the living room reading, his laptop nestled in his lap, his legs crossed.

"Sure, need any help?"

"No, it's fine."

In truth I wanted to cook for Dom. I'd already been to the crowded indoor market and bought a load of vegetables, then to the equally crowded supermarket to get the ingredients for pastry. I was going to make a pie. It made sense to make a pie. First of all I was cleaning the kitchen, scrubbing at the dark patches of worktop which would never be shifted.

"You're sure?"

"Sure," I called back.

Half an hour into making the pastry Dom strolled in, standing a few inches behind me.

"You're making it from scratch?"

"I am."

"Amazing." He placed his hand on my shoulder. "Do you need anything?"

I reaffirmed that I didn't need any help. Dom strolled back into the living room. I peered around the door—he'd started reading again, something that looked like reading for his course. In the past couple of weeks, we'd talked about pretty much anything and everything—but he'd never really elaborated on his maths-studying thing. It was fairly obvious that his future occupation embarrassed him.

An hour in and I was frying the last of the vegetables. Dom's shadow loomed in the doorway to the little kitchen. For a moment he stood watching.

"Cooking takes a long time," he commented.

"If you do it right," I replied.

He strolled over to the kettle, clicked it on and started preparing two mugs of tea. I don't like drinking tea whilst I'm trying to cook—I find it distracting. But I didn't tell him. When he handed me a mug I took it from him and smiled in thanks. He stumbled back into the other room.

Two hours later and I brought the plates through into the lounge. Dom suggested taking them through to his room, where he'd downloaded a movie. His room had remained spotlessly neat ever since we'd unpacked his things. His bedspread actually looked ironed. I perched on the edge of his ironed-looking bed. Once we'd done eating, he started rolling a spliff, dabbing at the green with his fingers and carefully flattening the paper. I'd not smoked since I was a teenager. Dom slowly spread the tobacco, then haltingly rolled, dabbing at the paper with his tongue. He took two heavy tokes before handing the joint over.

I told him I didn't really smoke. Dom nodded and placed it to his mouth again.

I stopped focusing on the film. Had I been focusing on the film? Dom's eyes had tinted pink. I wanted to smoke—what was stopping me? Wasn't it being rude not to? Dom didn't seem to mind, but I'd talked myself into it. If he was getting stoned then I might as well, too.

"Actually, can I have a drag?" I asked him.

"Sure thing." Dom clumsily handed it over, our fingers jumbling together in the effort to transfer it from him to me. I took a drag.

"Hold it in," Dom said, covering my mouth with the palm of his hand. "It'll have more of an effect."

I spluttered, smoke burning through my nostrils and tugging at my throat. Dom handed me a glass of water from his bedside table. I took a swig and held the spliff out to him.

"No, no—try again," he instructed. "Just take a deep breath and hold it there for as long as you can."

I did. I think I did it right. The room grew hazy. I did it again. I was falling off, perched at the edge of the bed like that. Dom made space for me, and I pulled myself to his side. He lay next to me, his head on his pillow, no longer focusing on the film. I did the same, taking the joint as he handed it to me. I could feel the blood pulsing through my ears.

"How're you doing?" Dom asked. I don't know if I responded.

I woke up as Dom switched the light off, tugged off his shirt, and pulled the covers over us both.

"Goodnight."

It was morning when I woke up again. A phone was ringing. It was loud.

"Wuh—hello?" I heard Dom exclaim into the receiver, his voice deep from sleep. "Zebedee. Hi. No, I'm still in bed. Already? Shit, I thought it was still early."

My lungs felt as though they were burning. I coughed.

"Who? No, that's Richard, Richard, you know, my roommate—yeah, I'm in bed. What's up?" Dom sounded more alert. "You're pretty heavy on the questions right now, you know, I don't ask you what you're doing in bed at one in the afternoon."

I sat up, feeling dizzy but awake. Rain was beating against the smeary window.

"Why are you so pissed off?" Dom asked, his voice growing to a growl. "What could possibly be the fucking matter? You've crashed over at mine before, I never—sure you stayed in the bed, didn't you—the floor?"

His voice grew quieter. He glanced back at me.

"To be honest I really don't see what difference it makes, who cares where—oh come on, you're making a weird thing about this—"

It was time to leave. I pulled myself free of the duvet, stepping as quietly as I could from Dom's room. I pulled off my clothes, grabbed a towel and took a shower. I heard the front door close as the water beat against my neck.

"Dom?" I called. There was no answer. Trailing steam from the bathroom I stepped into the hallway. He was gone. I tried calling him but still no answer.

I could feel my throat tighten.

Had we taken things too far? Why would that even matter? We were both adults, and we were both twenty-first-century straight guys. Even so, I could feel a lead weight in my stomach. I went to my computer, ready to play something, *anything*. Instead, I found myself staring at the blank monitor, hoping that nothing was wrong.

DOM

I looked out the window over to Caroline's shared postgrad office, I mean the office that Caroline shared with her Spanish roommate, hoping to get a glimpse of her, hoping she might see me as well. There she was—sat at her desk, like always on a Tuesday evening, with her roommate opposite. But she didn't look up, she didn't see anything of me. So, I watched her, I watched her from the window, waiting for her to look at me, until she did, until she glanced up at me, so I waved to her, I waved like I always did when we'd seen each other through the windows. But she just glanced at me and went back to her work.

Fuck. I was really fucking things with Caroline. She'd always waved back, that was what we did, that was how we knew everything was OK, but it wasn't OK, it couldn't be OK, not if she didn't wave back. She was angry, she was angry with me, and I knew why, of course I knew why—she was mad that I'd spent so little time with her. I'd been too wrapped up in hanging out with Richard, and it was going to mess everything up. Perhaps she'd even spoken to Zebedee, got some wrong-headed idea about me.

I was going to make it up to her, I would clear it all up—I picked up my phone, ready to call, but no, I thought, no, it would be better coming from me in person, in the flesh, so I flicked off the harsh overhead lights and I made my way to the elevator. I'd wait for her, outside her building—when she came out she'd see me, and I could apologise for being such a negligent boyfriend to her and we could have a long talk about it, then maybe a film, or maybe dinner, or maybe sex. Or maybe all of the above.

So I waited outside the entrance to the humanities tower, which faced the tower for mathematics and physics. I stared up at the two buildings, hers crumbling concrete-grey with rattling windows, mine a tidy but bland-looking corporate blue, with new windows that wouldn't open. It had gone dark by the time I realised she wasn't coming, and that I realised her building had a back door which she sometimes used. So I sent her a text telling her I loved her and made my way home, home to Richard.

I reached the door of the flat, hearing voices from inside—slow, careful voices, and as I got nearer, I could hear those voices making small talk. The door was unlocked, so I walked straight in to find Zebedee sprawled over the lumpy sofa, with Richard perched on a stool awkwardly responding to him. I hadn't spoken to Zebedee since he'd caught me in bed with Richard, except 'caught' is the wrong word as we'd not been doing anything.

"Richard here's really into open-source software," Zebedee said to me without greeting, "Open-source software and multiple personality gaming."

"Massively multiplayer online role-playing games," Richard corrected, his face scrunched in discomfort. I felt bad for him— Zebedee was picking on him, and I could feel myself cringe, but at the same time I wanted to join in with him, to pick on Richard too.

"Right. That." Zebedee nodded, grinning at Richard, who responded to him by staring at the floor. "I can understand why you two are getting on so well." He gave me this hostile look, a look like I'd done some wrong to him.

"Why not come through to mine, Zebedee, I'm sure Richard has stuff to do without you bothering him."

Zebedee followed me into my room without a word. The door was sticking, so I had to shove a couple of times to get it closed, which it did with a slam.

"Shall I get into the bed?" Zebedee asked, his lips curved into a sneer. I decided to ignore the comment, so instead I asked him,

"What's up?"

"Don't ask me 'what's up?' like nothing's the matter. Like nothing's weird." He went and sat on the laundry basket opposite my bed, picked up a coat hanger from the floor, and swung it between his fingers.

I was kinda taken aback to hear him so upfront—the two of us had never really had a problem before, and though I'd seen him angry, it had never been at me, so I just stood by the door without anything to say to him.

"Nomi's been telling me about your girlfriend," he said,

making sure to hold eye contact with me, still swinging the coat hanger. "Caroline's kind of upset."

Fuck.

"Not that you'll have noticed, of course," Zebedee continued, "holed up here with *that*." He gestured to the other room. "Your new boyfriend."

"So you're a homophobe, now?" I asked. I could hear myself shouting. Zebedee remained calm, perched on laundry.

"I'm not being homophobic, Dom. If you came out to me as gay, right now, that'd be fine. But you're lying to me." He dropped the coat-hanger.

"I'm not lying to you, Zebedee," I told him, slowly and surely as I could manage, "I'm straight. There's nothing going on between me and Richard."

And the more I protested, the more I wondered how much of what he said was true, and the more uncomfortable I felt, and though I tried to shake them, I couldn't, so his words stuck, they stuck to me like an itch.

CHAPTER FOUR

HAPPY FUCKING BIRTHDAY

RICHARD

I watched the couple in the apartment opposite, from what looked to be a fairly severe fight—complete with arm-gesturing and reddened faces—to bashful recriminations, to the start of make-up sex and the closing of their curtains. It was the night before my birthday, and I was trying to keep my mind off things, but I'd finished work (where no one knew it was about to be my birthday as I'd deliberately kept quiet on the topic) and had already prepared for the party. There was little left to do.

Something was definitely wrong with Dom. I tried talking to him as we cleaned the apartment, then as we lugged the old fold-out table into the living room. I even tried talking to him as he fiddled with a screwdriver when one of the legs broke free.

Each time he'd remained monosyllabic. If he answered at all.

"Is everything alright, Dom?" I asked as he righted the table again. He failed to give an answer as he sloped off to his room.

I went into my own room and sat down on the bed, going over the past hours and then days, trying to imagine what I had done wrong. At some point things had got confused. I didn't think that Dom was gay, but things between us—well, they weren't exactly simple. Something was broken, and I forced myself to breathe deeply. Blood pounded through my temples. I ached.

I realised I ached. From my chest to my fingertips.

I focused my attention on the shelves above my bed. Board and brackets. Breathe deeply.

What did I feel? I was given no clue aside from the dull ache, from the leaden pain of his not speaking to me, of whatever I had broken. I imagined Dom moving out, the feeling intensifying, growing sharper, growing clearer.

Dom.

I said his name, quiet enough to not be heard, loud enough to sound strange.

Dom.

I didn't want him to hate me. I didn't want him to leave. I wanted things to be as they had been, beer and spending time daily. Talking. Him being there. Something else too, something intangible. Something I couldn't figure out.

Dom.

I needed to stop saying his name. It wasn't helping anything.

I heard the front door slam once more. He'd gone out. My heart plummeted. I had to talk to someone.

I reached Rutti and Steph's apartment and peered up at the house, searching for life in the upstairs windows. They stared blankly at the dirty clouds.

I pushed the buzzer. No answer. I pushed it again.

The door clicked open without a word. I'd never actually been to Steph's place before, though I'd met Rutti outside a few times. It was worse than my apartment. I'd have taken the faded green wallpaper hanging limply from my hallway over the artex monstrosity of Steph and Rutti's any day. The carpet was splattered in a floral pattern and smelled of dust. At the head of the stairs stood an anxious-looking man in his early twenties, wearing flannel pyjamas forty years too old for him.

"I thought you were the postman," he stated, giving me a glare of suspicion.

"Where's Rutti?" I asked.

"How do you know Rutti?" replied the stranger.

I answered him quickly, doing my very best not to get annoyed.

"He lived with me for four years. I evicted him for threatening a random girl with the head of a sex doll."

The stranger nodded in recognition and stepped aside, beckoning me in.

"I'm Craig, with the Living Hope Baptist Church," he said. "You must be Richard."

I nodded, looking around for some sign of the other two. *Baptist church?* Surely Rutti hadn't lost the plot so completely that he'd stumbled into Jesus.

"So how did you two meet?" I asked him.

Craig from the Living Hope Baptist Church gave an overly detailed account, accompanied by a series of disconcerting hand gestures. "And so now I'm staying here. Rutti got me the pyjamas. He said if I sleep in my clothes one more time he's going to wrap my face in cling film. This is just until I find something more permanent."

So that was it—Rutti had adopted him. It was a game. I was already bored of it.

"Do you know when he'll be back?" I asked the increasingly animated individual.

"Not exactly, no. I'd like to ask you—does Rutti really believe everything he says?"

"Of course he does," I answered. My patience with Craig from the Living Hope Baptist Church had all but evaporated. I left as he was half-way through making us a cup of tea, slipping down the stairs and out the door before he noticed I was gone.

I sent Rutti a message.

"Hello, replacement me."

It was the following night, the night of my birthday, and I'd not

67

seen Dom. I suspected he had been at his girlfriend's, a point proven when he'd stumbled through the front door with his arm around her. Rutti had just arrived, and greeted Dom with an unnecessary kiss on the mouth, thrusting a bottle into my hands. "And Mrs. replacement me," he greeted Dom's girlfriend Caroline. Dom at least seemed to have cheered up a little.

"Is this your girlfriend?" Caroline asked, greeting Steph who stood to Rutti's side, her hair a violent shade of lavender.

"I don't have girlfriends," Rutti commented.

"Single, then?" she asked. "Not seeing anyone?"

"I suppose I'm seeing you two right now, and if I turn my head to the left, I could see Stephanie. If you're asking whether I'm currently having regular-but-gradually-diminishing sex with someone within those regulated social confines that people refer to as a 'relationship', then no. No, no."

Steph smacked him on the arm, but he didn't seem to notice. Instead he turned his attention toward me.

"Happy birthday, Richard. I bought you a gift. I noticed you were lacking one of these." It was the toaster he had stolen as 'alimony' when he'd left.

"How kind," I answered. "And you brought some budget vodka."

I'd told him to bring wine.

"No one was going to drink enough to take their clothes off on red wine," Rutti stated, reading my expression. "You're terrible at planning parties. They're terrible at planning parties," he informed Dom and Caroline. Caroline gave me a polite smile.

"You didn't bring your Christian then?" I asked him.

"Oh, so you met Craig? Aren't they cute? They're coming later—Craig's the one who's going to get undressed."

"I do hope you're kidding."

Caroline thrust a glass of vinegary sparkling white wine into each of our hands, before picking up her own glass.

"To Richard, happy birthday," she grinned. Dom nodded briefly, avoiding eye contact. I in turn tried not to look at him.

"To Richard, congratulations on getting ever so slightly

older," Rutti toasted. "Come with me," he added, gesturing to the hallway, "I have something for you."

Once we were alone, he handed me a real gift, wrapped in newspaper and old string.

"What is it?" I'd be lying if I said I wasn't suspicious, but Rutti made a motion signalling me to open it.

It was an extended guide to *Myst Legends III*, one of the games I'd been obsessed with just before he'd moved out. It was sweet. It was genuinely sweet. I hugged him. He hugged me in return, and I held onto him, longer than was appropriate.

"What's wrong, Richard?" he asked over my shoulder.

So, I told him. Firstly, I told him I didn't know exactly what was wrong, but I knew how I'd been feeling. Things had gone sour between myself and my roommate, and it was bothering me more than it should have. Rutti listened patiently until my rambling dwindled.

"We'll find out," he stated. "We'll find out what's going on."

"Thanks, Rutti. Does this mean you've forgiven me for kicking you out?"

"Never." He planted a kiss on my cheek. I wiped it away.

I could hear Dom laughing again.

RUTTI

The bar was the same as every Friday night: drunken giggling queens and their mouthy fag hags, the hallmark of every provincial scene. If you weren't camp you weren't one of them—it meant you were straight, or worse, bisexual. My friend Paul—who was in reality somewhere between 'acquaintance', 'occasional friend', and 'drunken fuck'—was the only reason I was tolerated. In turn I tolerated them. I could see them over at the bar, flirting with the princess bartender.

I was waiting by the entrance—waiting for someone to leave with. Leaving by myself wasn't exactly safe, especially not with the mood the city had been in since the club burned down.

69

The number of homophobic skinheads seemed to have increased dramatically. *Waters* was in a deserted part of the marina, and angry guys had a habit of stopping by from the even shittier straight places to put one of us in hospital. Last month it had been Paul. Their cheekbone was still a raw purple.

No one looked as though they would be leaving anytime soon. Of course, Steph had refused to come to *Waters*. They would never lower themself so far.

Paul returned from the bar clutching two cocktails, both bright blue, before leaving for the small and overly-sticky dance floor. They were instantly joined to an overly plucked young man with no shirt or visible body hair. I took a sip of the cocktail and felt it warm me.

Are you coming to my birthday tomorrow?

It was a message from Richard, apparently received five hours beforehand. We'd been speaking tentatively, text-by-text. I was about to respond—

"You're a fucking liar!"

There was a commotion by the bar. Two guys I vaguely recognised were hysterically screaming to one another. I tried to hear them, but their words were drowned by the wail of a cheesy pop song. A bored bouncer strode over, uttered something to one of them, then led the pouting partner on past me and out through the exit. As those two barrelled by, a group of four men entered, a drunken haze clouding their expressions.

I'd never seen the men before, which was unusual for Swansea's scene. They'd be visiting from Cardiff, or the valleys. I hoped not the valleys. One stood out: they looked casual, clad in a battered hoody among a sea of high-street shirts. They were hot.

The man broke away from the group. I downed the syrupy blue drink and stalked them. Were they going to the bar or to—

The toilets.

The man pushed their way in five seconds or so before I

entered. The door was sticky. Then there was the second question: will they go to a urinal or a cubicle?

Urinal.

There was no one next to the man. No one blocking them.

I went and stood by them. I unzipped my fly, and stared straight ahead. The tiles were stained a filthy cream.

I glanced. A glimpse of pink.

I stared ahead again. The lines between tiles were black with dirt.

I glanced a second longer. More than a glimpse: I saw them whole, long and slender.

Ahead again. I watched from the corner of my eye. Dark-pink skin, light-brown pubic hair splayed in tufts around the base.

The tiles once more.

The man belched. I looked over. They were swaying. They were drunk, with one hand against the wall for support. They wouldn't notice, so I watched. I watched as they finished, as they shook themself—not for long enough—then as they pulled themself into their trousers, a few dots of urine landing around the crotch. They stumbled away without washing their hands.

Paul accosted me outside the toilets.

"We're leaving," they hissed. "That guy was all hands. I mean, I *have* a boyfriend, I was just being friendly. You'll never guess what sick things he wanted to do to me."

"I bet I could, given enough time."

"Shut up and let's leave."

I was halfway home when Richard called. Paul strode on ahead.

"Rutti, are you coming to my birthday or not?"

"Of course, I'm coming. Why are you asking? What's wrong?"

There was a breath-long pause before they answered.

"No reason. It would just be nice to know, that's all."

I'd lost sight of Paul.

"Well, now you know."

"If you could come early, I'd like that," Richard pleaded, their voice wavering. Something *was* wrong.

"Are you going to tell me what's up, Richard?" I asked, putting on the firmest voice I could manage.

"I'd just like to see you," they replied.

I told them I'd do my best.

In reality I managed to get waylaid by Steph, who insisted on coming with me but who also needed to trek around every shop in the Uplands looking for the right cat food. We reached Richard's party only ten minutes before they'd officially told people to arrive. We introduced ourselves to Dom and their girlfriend, each of whom I'd only met briefly at the burning of the mediocre nightclub—and to be honest I'd been paying greater attention toward the fire. Dom was actually quite handsome, in an unknowing, hetero-male kind of way, and their girlfriend— Charlotte?—was equally attractive. Steph was openly eyeing the nervous-looking woman.

I was more concerned with Richard, especially after I took them to one side and they told me their anxieties over Dom, and Dom's strange behaviour. I told Richard I'd keep an eye out. Of course, I would, but it didn't take any special effort to realise something was wrong.

An hour later and the small apartment was half-filled by a few small pockets of different social groups, clustered away from one another, each with their own clothing and gestures, which could be made out even in the too-dark living room: I recognised some of Richard's dull colleagues from work, clad in bland high street shirts and blouses with overly clunky jewellery. The group kept their arms mostly to their sides, talking in quiet, subdued voices which were drowned by the rest of the room. In the dim light their skin looked grey, or slightly transparent, as though they were slowly fading from our dimension.

Some women were clustered together, presumably friends of Dom's girlfriend. These women were more boisterous—taking moments from talking only to gulp at red wine, passing the bottle back-and-forth like panicked divers sharing a single oxygen tank.

Some men were seated near Dom, presumably their friends. The man had been almost as animated as the women nearby but had started to grow more subdued as their attention was drawn to Dom—the men looked worried: Dom was sitting hunched over, cheeks clamped around the smoky plastic rim of a bong. Dom inhaled and rolled back. Their face was scrunched in agitation.

"What's with everyone tonight?" Steph asked. "With one or two exceptions, there's no one here I really want to talk to." Steph was wearing dungarees, which was almost fancy-dress considering their femme status. I liked their new hair. I wasn't going to tell them.

"No idea," I replied. "How's the lesbian power league?"

Steph slapped me across the face—not too hard, but enough to redden and sting.

"What's that for?"

"You'll get that every time you call it something other than the Women's Circle."

"That's not fair. You call gay bars 'fag cages'."

"Do you disagree?"

"That's not the point."

But I lost Steph's attention—they were looking across the room at Dom. Dom was enclosed in a commotion: while taking another bong hit, Dom had been interrupted by a young Middle Eastern-looking guy making attempts to take the bong from their grip. Dom was growling anger in return. They reeled back, smoke spilling from their lips, their grip on the bong as tight as ever. By that point even the girls had noticed, watching intently as they passed a wine bottle back and forth between them.

"Where's his girlfriend?" Steph asked.

73

At that moment the girlfriend and Richard spilled through the front door together, clutching carrier bags full of booze and snacks. Richard seemed to have relaxed—they were actually laughing and joking, but both faces froze when they saw Dom. Richard wandered over to me, their expression one of concern.

"How're you doing, Richard?"

Richard just nodded.

I'd drunk enough to melt at the edges of my surroundings when Paul came in from the kitchen. I had invited Paul at the last minute, half-hoping they wouldn't show up—I was used to seeing them on Swansea's gay scene, not in a human place. Paul had pretended they might be too busy to come. Paul always did that.

I asked where their boyfriend Tim was.

"We had a fight," Paul mumbled, their eyes watering.

I didn't really want to get into it but there was no way I could avoid asking.

"A fight?"

"He's moving out, he says," Paul whimpered. They scrunched their eyes closed and finished their bottle of Citrus Breeze Cranberry. Then opened another one.

"I'm sorry to hear that."

"He cheated on me," Paul replied, still on the verge of tears.

"Oh." I didn't know what to say to that. I wasn't the biggest fan of monogamy, but it was hardly time to bring it up.

"Well, he said that he couldn't stick it out, but he'd also said that he'd try—" Paul couldn't finish. Tears rolled down their face. I took them to the bathroom, being careful to block any view of them from the rest of the party. The room was small, so we sat two fingers-width apart. Paul perched on the edge of the bath and I granted them a tissue. I squinted to see them—the only light was from a small candle.

"So, what happened?"

"Well, he slept with someone. I don't know who. He told me—he said he was sorry. He said he couldn't do it. He said he was too young to just be with one person for the rest of his life." Paul sniffled. "If I can do it, why can't he?"

I had no answer, aside from 'monogamy isn't in our nature', but it would have been less than supportive.

"Is it me?" Paul asked. "It's me. He just doesn't love me, if he did—"

"No, it's not you," I told them. "You'll find someone else."

I sat with Paul for a few more minutes but we didn't say anything further. They whimpered between gulps of their drink. Eventually they stopped wiping their face and stood up. "I have to go. I should go home."

I gave Paul a hug and returned to look for Richard. I noticed Dom's door was open, so I poked my head around, hoping they might be inside. The scent of patchouli curled around the air with no identifiable source, with wafts of Dom's body mingled in. It was surprisingly neat—I had imagined piles of underwear and fag-ends mounted about the floor, but the used laundry was piled into the basket, with only a single sock threatening to jump to freedom.

I'd noticed the floor first, but my eyes drifted to the grimy walls.

Hundreds of women stared down, twisted and contorted, their faces draped in flashy false-fake smiles or childy pouts, the expressions of tiny kids who were beyond reason. Beneath their baby faces were the engorged breasts of new mothers, nipples wide and swollen, ready for suckling, or barely hidden beneath scraps of man-made fabric. The walls were plastered in these posters, overlapping, spilling across one another, each pressing forward for space, for visibility. Nipples were stacked above thick brown thighs and corpse-white elbows, here a flicker of eyelash, there an expanse of skin. Some posters were almost entirely obscured, just a peak of colour marking their presence. Beneath the women were the monosyllabic markers of lads-mags and sometimes the porn-star names of the girls, if they deserved them. A zoo. Plenty of posters had two girls together, pressing themselves to one another, prodding or pinching or pecking on the lips, but with their eyes on the photographer, their play for the benefit of the grown-ups watching. On Dom's walls was Sex stripped down, shaking and exposed but smiling, then packaged and sold for someone else. Sold to magazines which were sold to newsagents which sold to teenage boys who spewed spunk over those pouts and smiles, those bulging breasts and knowing eyes, adding their own mark in the process. On Dom's walls was Sex sold. Here was Sex restrained.

I left the room, wanting more than ever to talk to Richard. Things were no better in the party proper. The atmosphere was frozen. The music had stopped, the glaring overhead lights were on, laying bare concerned—and one or two amused—expressions. People were talking in hushed gossipy murmurs, whilst the girlfriend stood amongst them looking horrified. Dom was on the couch with their face in their hands.

Richard was gone.

"What the hell's happened?" I asked. "Caroline?"

CAROLINE

It had been a quiet evening at the Tail and Tugboat, an evening of checking inventory and tearing beermats into squares. I had been given the shift at the last minute, but I would still be done in time for the party.

I'd felt better since talking to Dom—he'd come over, apologised profusely, then made me dinner followed by perfectly satisfactory sex. Things seemed to be going well again.

"I've missed you," he'd whispered into my ear as we'd lain in bed together.

"I've missed you, too," I'd told him, feeling the last of my reservations about the last couple of weeks melt away to nothing. "I hope everything's been going well," I added, hoping he would give something more by way of explanation.

"Look, this is my fault," he'd said, kissing me again. "I fucked up, I got caught up in my own stuff—stupid stuff, worrying about work and everything—and I neglected our relationship. Well, it won't happen again. I love you, Caroline."

"I love you too, Dom," I'd replied. So, it wasn't Richard, Zebedee had just been his usual, paranoid, slightly weird self. Still, I couldn't exactly blame him for any paranoia—Nomi had told me how he'd been getting random abuse recently, how his mum had had stuff shouted at her as she came out the mosque. I couldn't really blame him, especially as for the first time in days I'd felt myself relax. We'd even gone shopping for Richard's birthday present together—it would be from the two of us, a sort of peace offering.

I looked around for Debbie the regular, but she didn't come in all evening. There were one or two older couples, an elderly lady who I thought I'd seen before, and a tubby man in a suit downing whiskey. By the time my shift ended it was already dark. A text message from Nomi told me to meet her at the supermarket: for once she had noticed we were out of food. I was supposed to be going to the party that evening, and figured I'd grab a bottle of wine. I couldn't afford it, but it was a one-off thing, so I told myself it was allowed.

I checked myself using the cracked mirror in the toilets before heading out through the main bar. The man in the suit was drunk. He stood up as I made my way out the door and into the marina. It was quiet—the marina was always deathly quiet. People lived there, but you never saw them. I suppose they drove from their underground car parks to their offices and to the supermarket, you know? There wasn't much there—a dingy gay bar, and a museum further down. I made my way through the bland red brick alleyways.

You can feel it when they follow you. He was following me and I knew it was him. I walked a little more quickly, but not too quickly—I didn't want him to start running or anything. It was fine, it was fine, I told myself. You've been followed before. It's not the first time. They see you working and smiling at them, and they think that you want to fuck them in some alley somewhere. I had long ago made sure not to have sex with anyone I met whilst working—you get a reputation and that can wind up pretty dangerous.

"Fuck off fuck off fuck off," I muttered to myself. My skin tingled as I started to sweat. I glanced around, but we were alone. He was just a few metres behind but his face was bright red with the effort it took to keep up with me. I felt a bit better—I could probably outrun him—but I reached into my bag and gripped my rape alarm as hard as I could. I turned the wrong way, leading back to the pub, just to see if he really was following me. Hopefully, hopefully this time I wasn't being followed.

He was following me. I had to make my way as quickly as possible to the supermarket—at the supermarket there would be security guards. I held my breath as I went into the dark tunnel which led out from the marina. My footsteps echoed behind me. He was still a little way back as I reached the main road. My armpits were sticky with sweat. There was nothing but cars, no people at all. I reached the crossing and pressed the button. There were too many cars to be able to run across. I pressed it again and again. I could hear him getting closer, I could hear his panting, I pulled the alarm out of my bag and clutched it.

The light turned green, and I sprinted over the road to the supermarket. I ran through the car park. It was empty but there was Nomi—beneath the bright lights, there was Nomi.

"Jesus, Caroline, are you alright?"

I nodded. "I was just—this man from the pub was—"

Nomi nodded and looked over my shoulder. "I see him."

"Is he still coming?"

"He's still coming, but don't worry."

I held my breath and turned around. He slowed down and walked towards us.

"Ladies," he snarled, clearly trying to keep his balance.

"What do you want?" Nomi asked, coldly and firmly.

"I just want to talk to you—to her," he pointed at me.

"She doesn't want to talk to you," Nomi said.

"I don't," I told him. He didn't hear me.

"She does, she does really, we were just in the pub together." He took a step toward us. Nomi shouted at him, thrusting her face toward his, standing on tiptoe.

"Piss off. Just piss off. She doesn't want to talk to you, I don't want to talk to you, and if you keep bothering us I'm calling the fucking police."

He took a step back.

"Sure, alright love, calm down. You and your fucking little girlfriend can fuck off an' all." He started walking away. "Fuck you both," he shouted back to us.

"Come on," Nomi said as she took my arm and leant her head on my shoulder. "I'll buy you some wine. Don't worry about him, what's the point in worrying about him? Fat old fuck couldn't hurt anyone. Look at him, waddling away. His arse looks like two bin bags filled with custard. See, you're smiling already. Listen, I'll pick us up something nice to eat from the supermarket. Nothing for Christina though, she's been getting on my nerves. What do you fancy? And I'll run you a bath when we get home."

My feet were already killing me. After the evening I'd had I just wanted a quiet night, so I called Dom, asking if it was all right if I didn't go to Richard's birthday thing that evening.

He was strangely insistent. "Ahhh, you have to come," he said. It was sweet that he wanted me there so badly, so I said yes. His voice sounded odd—he was really bothered at the prospect of my not coming. I told him not to worry and stopped the bathwater running.

I had just slipped into the warm water when Nomi wandered in: the door to our bathroom had a broken lock. Nomi acted as though nothing at all was wrong with her being there and I knew that it would be useless to tell her to get out.

"I hear there's a party tonight," Nomi mentioned, pretending to be casual and smearing cream all over her face. She was in her tatty dressing gown which I was pretty sure had once been mine. "Do you think it'll be okay if Zebedee goes? It is his friend's housemate's birthday. That's practically family. And I'm his girlfriend."

"So that makes you Richard's aunt?" I asked. Nomi tutted.

"I'll tell Zebedee we're going."

I didn't ask Nomi why she wanted to go to the party of the guy she'd been convinced my boyfriend had been having an affair with, nor did I want to. She had probably simply decided everything was fine and that a party was a party.

"Are you in there, Caroline?" Christina called from the hallway.

"Yeah, come in," Nomi called back. I tried to cover myself with my arms.

"Caroline," Christina gasped at me when she entered, "why don't you lock the door?"

"The lock is broken, Christina," Nomi told her. "Besides, Caroline doesn't mind, it's just us girls."

"Caroline does mind," I said.

"So, you wanted something, Christina?" Nomi asked.

"I hear there's a party tonight."

"There is, if you must know," Nomi relented. "Come along, but it's close friends and family only."

It wasn't going to be a relaxing bath. I stepped out of the tub and wrapped a towel around myself. I padded wetly down the hallway, dripping onto the scratchy cheap carpet. They followed me to my room. Nomi perched on a chair by my desk in front of my mirror, whilst Christina stood in the doorway. Nomi was listing the things about Dom that she found annoying: it was a good sign, it meant things were back to normal.

"He just rambles constantly," Nomi moaned. "It really does irritate me," Nomi said. "Does it irritate you, Car?"

"Don't call me 'Car'. And I never noticed," I answered. "Anyway, I'm leaving."

Nomi pulled a face.

"I need to get there early," I explained. "I promised Dom."

"Well, I won't be too far behind," Christina cried, "I am having such a week, I need to do some drinking."

I peered up at Dom's building, tilting my brolly back to get a better look. It was the same as all the others on the street—all of them attached to each other, little peeling grey faces looking out at the narrow road. Aside from the tatty old betting shop next door, this was the only one in the row that didn't have dirty net curtains hanging in the window. I stepped to the side and climbed over the little wall into the garden so I could peer into the building. What was the harm?

An old woman glared at me from the other side of the glass.

Of course. Dom lived upstairs.

The front door opened.

"Hi, darling, erm, try to avoid standing in the neighbour's flower bed, she won't like it." Dom gave me an enthusiastic and somewhat inappropriate kiss, slung his arm heavily over my shoulder, then led me inside.

It was only the second time I'd seen the apartment—the first had been when I'd been helping Dom move in. He'd answered the ad because the place was cheap, though it wasn't really any worse than most flats in the area. The ceiling was lined with smudgy grey patches of damp, but the bathroom walls were newly painted. The lounge was small with a window that didn't open, but most of the furniture could pass for nearly new.

Dom was being strangely clingy, which was sweet on the one hand, but also struck me as a little odd. Anyway, when Zebedee arrived, I took the opportunity to go for a cigarette. His roommate Richard joined me—I mean, as Dom's girlfriend it was right to get to know him, and all the gay rumours had been figments of Zebedee's demented mind. I figured I should at least see what he was like.

Richard told me that he doesn't often smoke, and we smoked

quickly as the night had turned cold. On the phone box opposite was a perfume advert—the model was staring at me.

"So how old are you?" I asked him. He was sort-of good-looking, in a sort-of geeky way. I figured he was nearing thirty, something along those lines, but more mature than aged, if that makes sense.

"Twenty-two," he said, blowing smoke into the face of the model. It didn't stop her staring. I was surprised by how young he was.

"People don't usually seem to guess my age right," he added.

I nodded. I realised I'd left my drink inside, but it didn't bother me—I wasn't a fan of neat vodka, and I'd drunk more than I wanted. I wondered if I should head to the shop to get something else. The wine I'd brought along hadn't lasted.

Richard finished his cigarette and placed it carefully into the drain by the kerb, before turning to me. "I'm going to head to the shop for something else to drink—do you fancy coming along?"

"Sure."

I was feeling the effects of the vodka, and I reckoned that Richard was too. Once safely inside the supermarket—the same I'd escaped to earlier that evening—we'd taken turns predicting the contents of different shopping trolleys by examining their owners, then took to covertly swapping their items as they waited in the checkout line. The crowning moment was the switch between a bottle of value gin and baby formula. There was almost a fight between the two customers, with the two of us stood behind them trying to keep calm. We giggled almost the whole way home from the supermarket. The only thing that stopped me even for a minute was checking the time on my phone and seeing—shit—that we'd been gone almost an hour and a half.

"You've been missing your own party," I told Richard, but it only started us laughing again. He offered me a drink from the wine he'd already opened, and which he'd insisted on paying for.

"We can't drink that here," I told him. "It's not legal." I hadn't stopped laughing and I could feel my chest hurting like little knives stuck into me.

"No one will see. Anyway, only the police would care."

I took the bottle without saying anything. We walked the rest of the way home in silence, but it was comfortable. In terms of roommates, Dom could have done a lot worse.

"Caroline?" Richard said as we neared his apartment. He said my name with an effort, as though he'd been building himself up to ask me something. I suddenly felt cold. I didn't want to hear it.

"Richard," I replied, handing the bottle back to him.

"Is everything okay with Dom? He seems to have been a little—"

"Oh, he's just been distracted, I think," I quickly explained to him, wondering what he'd noticed. Why should Richard care?

I told myself to stop being so paranoid. Fucking Zebedee.

"Dom can be a little odd at times," I said. "It's part of his charm."

We returned to the apartment with the bags—the girls had already arrived, along with half a dozen other people. I was sure they would be mad at me for having been gone so long, so I planned on offering them a bottle of wine. It was then that I saw Dom. It actually took me a moment to realise that it *was* him— he looked angry, really angry, angry like I'd never seen before. He looked like someone else. Zebedee stared at me helplessly. I turned to ask Richard what was going on, but he was off talking to that weird friend of his.

"You have *got* to get a grip on this," Nomi ordered from over my shoulder. I hadn't even seen her. "Zebedee's been trying, but your boyfriend's acting psycho."

I turned around to see Nomi's face frozen with barely suppressed anger. Christina stood by her.

"It does not look good," Christina added. "What's bothering him like this?"

"He's a fucking nut job, Caroline," Nomi spat. "If he carries on like this, I'll be having words."

"There's no need for that," Christina said, placing her hand on Nomi's arm. Nomi shook her off. "Look, Caroline," Christina continued, "maybe have a talk with him. See what the problem is."

"I'll come with you," Nomi stated, before anyone had chance to refuse.

We made our way over to the battered sofa where Dom was sitting and staring into nothingness. Despite her mood, I was glad Nomi was with me.

"Dom," I said. "Dom?"

He looked up at me, his eyes reddened. I wondered if he'd been crying. I couldn't think of what to say.

"We still need to give Richard his birthday present." It was all I could manage. I hoped Richard liked the gift, though I couldn't help thinking I'd have got him something better if I'd realised we'd get on so well. I hope that doesn't sound too mercenary.

Dom leapt up, marched out of the room, and came back with his bag, which he slammed down onto the room's only table, rummaging through it and then he took the present out, a pair of headphones we'd seen on sale, wrapped in red paper.

I brought Richard over. What else was I to do?

Richard took it. He looked as nervous as I felt. Something was wrong.

Richard thanked Dom. Then Richard went to hug Dom.

But Dom shoved him, he shoved him away, causing Richard to fall backwards, and I called out 'Dom' from surprise, and so he turned to me for a moment, his eyes wide with rage. I tried to take his arm, he looked at Richard in a panic, who looked at him in a daze, a hurt, scared, confused daze, and Dom muttered 'sorry' before running out through the living room doorway.

"Dom, Dom, what the hell? What the fuck was that?"

"Let him go."

CHAPTER FIVE

FAGGOTS

We stood there in the dark, facing them. One was nearer us, with a beer in their hand. They were scowling. They were six others, maybe seven, but it was hard to tell—the only light was from the marina on the one side and the distant refineries on the other. The sea surrounded us. I felt cold.

"Faggots."

And we didn't say anything back to them. The air caught in my throat as I tried to speak, and I wanted to say something to make them leave. Something to get us out of this situation. What could you say though, what response could you give to that? Faggots. Faggots. All I could hear was the rush of water and the roar of blood surging through my ears.

"Fucking faggots. Look at'em, look at'em, they're actually scared."

We did look scared. I gripped onto the stone wall. Caroline and Nomi were huddled together.

Dom stepped forward. Richard grabbed at their arm. Richard missed. Dom stepped forward and told them that we would never be afraid of some chavvy little fucks like them. Dom told them to fuck off, and then turned back toward the rest of us.

A bottle burst against the wall. Nomi screamed.

CAROLINE

What the hell had just happened?

I heard Dom's bedroom door slam closed. I leant against the kitchen wall. What was wrong with him? Okay, I've always been a bad judge of character, but Dom had never seemed psycho. And violent men, I always swore to avoid violent men: I'd had friends who'd gone out with guys like that and it never—it just *never*—ended well. Katy, a friend of mine from school, she'd wound up in the hospital after her boyfriend thought she'd cheated on him. You'd see them, those women, being battered around town on a Saturday night. I'd made myself a promise to never get involved with a guy like that.

The party had ended, and one or two people started to leave. Someone was rummaging through the mass of coats piled on an old armchair. Nomi took me by the arm and led me into an empty corner of the room.

"What was that?" I asked. "Why did he hit Richard?"

"Perhaps he's on his man-period," she said.

"Nomi."

"Fine, look, why don't we ask Dom himself?"

She was right—I'd have to talk to Dom. Talk to Dom and sort the situation out. After all, Dom lived with Richard, it wasn't like they could just stop speaking to each other, and I didn't want an unpleasant atmosphere every time I went to my boyfriend's flat. On top of that, well, Richard seemed like a nice guy and if there was any confusion then it was best sorted out.

I went to Dom's room, opening his door without knocking. He was stood by his desk. I asked him what was wrong, but he gave no answer—he simply stared at the floor like a naughty child. I told him, as firmly as I could, that he should go apologise to Richard.

Dom was actually quite reluctant, but he followed me out of his bedroom and into the kitchen. Richard was gone.

"Where is he?" I asked.

No one knew. No one knew where Richard had gone. I said we should find him.

"I didn't mean to cause any trouble, Caroline," Zebedee called after us.

❖ ❖ ❖

Dom and I stood in the street awkwardly looking in different directions. Rutti and Nomi stood with us, having followed us outside.

Dom spoke. He said he might know where Richard was. He wasn't sure, but he might know.

And so we walked through the deserted marina, where I could feel my skin tighten at the memory of being followed earlier that evening. We walked right over to the stone jetty at the far side. The jetty plunged out into the sea and into darkness, but we could see there—over there, half-way along—there was Richard.

I felt pleased with myself. Was I not, after all, being a bloody good girlfriend? I was patching things up between my boyfriend and his mate. His housemate no less. I was certainly due some positive karma for that.

Dom nodded to us before heading down along the jetty toward Richard. We watched him approach. Richard didn't move.

"What're they saying?" Nomi asked.

I strained my ears trying to hear them, but the sound of the waves breaking against the stone walls drowned out their conversation. They were stood facing each other for a while, two dark shapes we could barely see, and then the two shapes merged into one. They were hugging. I turned to Rutti and was about to talk about how glad I was when—someone shouted something. Richard and Dom drew apart, two separate shapes again.

Then there were other dark shapes. There were at least five.

"We should see what's going on," Rutti said, but I was already walking toward them.

As I got nearer, I could see it was a group of guys, drunk-looking guys, and a couple of them were shouting.

"What's wrong?" I asked, though I don't know whom I asked, Richard, or Dom, or the group of men.

87

"Nothing. They think we're lovers," Richard told me, "Dom and I, they think we're together."

"Why would they think that?"

"We just want to talk to you guys. Are you gay or what?" one of them asked.

"Look, we should just go," I said.

"No, don't go, we just want to ask you a question. A simple fucking question. Do you hear what I'm saying to you? Are you two gay?"

"We're going," said Rutti.

"Faggots."

I froze. For a moment it was quiet. It was quiet and dark. We didn't say anything back.

"Fucking faggots. Look at 'em, look at 'em, they're actually scared."

I felt for the phone in my pocket. I could call the police. If anything happened, I could call the police. Dom stepped forward, and Richard tried to stop him, but Dom still stepped forward.

"Like we'd be afraid of some chavvy little wankers like you. Just fuck off."

"Dom," I said, I wanted to tell him no, don't say that, just let it go, but it was too late. Dom took my hand and told me not to worry. For a moment nobody moved, and nobody said anything, there was just us and the jetty and the sea. Then there was shouting. I couldn't tell what but there was shouting. Something flew through the air and broke on the wall next to us—

There was screaming—

Dom's hand let go—

They shouted; they shouted something else—

Something else was thrown thudding to the ground—

Rutti to one side, throwing something back—

Nomi's face shouting something to me—

Her hand squeezing my arm—

A burst of glass—

Then they were running, running past us, they grew smaller and smaller—

"RICHARD! RICHARD!" Nomi was shouting.

"RICHARD! RICHARD! RICHARD!"

I looked where she looked . . .

And there was Richard sitting on the ground his head in his hands and blood between his fingers which dripped down his wrists and there was Dom holding him holding him and crying with his face pressed against Richard's head and his arms wrapped around him.

I just stood there—unable to move, not sure what to do. Nomi and I stood there watching the two of them as Rutti ran over, taking off his shirt and pressing it to Richard's head. Dom cradled his friend, and someone made a phone call, all of us rooted in the same position until the sky was lit with blue lights and the paramedics moved Richard away. Tears ran down Dom's face.

It was then that we moved forward.

CHAPTER SIX

BEWARE OF ROOMS WITH PLASTIC PLANTS

CAROLINE

Oh god, Dom was crying. What should I do? What was the right thing to do? I wanted to be a good girlfriend and help, but the sight—the very idea—of my boyfriend crying like that, weirded me out. I know it probably shouldn't have, but it did. I couldn't help wondering if he really was crazy. In the hospital I did my best to chase those thoughts away.

The waiting room felt as though time had gone completely still. The flickering light above us and the obnoxious white of the walls were seeming to crawl under my skin, though I was doing better than the others. Dom's eyes were red-rimmed, and Rutti was pale, leaning against a wall and staring into space.

It was quiet, and we were only interrupted by the occasional nurse scurrying from one door to the next. There were three other people in the room—an old man whose drunken wheezy snoring marked each slow moment, and a familiar-looking couple, the woman in high stiletto heels and a sombre-looking man who kept dozing, only to be jolted awake every few minutes by his girlfriend's elbow.

I'd only come because Dom had. Nomi had gone home. I promised I'd call her, forgetting that the hospital makes you turn your phone off. I was worried for Richard too, of course. Should I have mentioned that first? How could he have deserved a bottle to the head? I'd asked the doctor all the questions I could, but he didn't really have anything more to say; they'd keep him overnight and see.

I wanted someone to talk to, so when Rutti asked if I wanted to join him for a cigarette I accepted. Anything to be away from the plastic pot plants and the smell of cleaning fluids.

"Will you be alright here alone for a minute or two?" I asked Dom. He nodded so I kissed him on the forehead and stepped outside. I noticed it was cold. Colder than an evening in July should be.

Rutti's hands shook as he lit the cigarette. I placed my hand on his arm. I didn't exactly know him, but it seemed like the right thing to do.

"They'll be fine," Rutti said, his voice trembling.

"He'll be fine," I repeated to him. The doctors'd told us that. They were going to keep him overnight, but he would be fine. It had been a shock, that was all. An awful shock.

We stood there in silence. Every now and then though, Rutti would look in through the glass doors at the waiting room. When we returned the couple had gone, though Dom and the old man were still locked in the same position. Dom seemed to barely register our return.

After an hour or so I said we should leave. It took some coaxing, but Rutti agreed—we weren't doing any good there in the hospital, and they wouldn't let us see Richard anyway. I stroked Dom's arm and told him it was time to go. He wouldn't move.

"We can come back in the morning," I told him, gently squeezing his wrist, whispering in his ear. He just stared straight ahead, eyes red-rimmed, mouth closed. Mute.

Rutti put his arm around me, glancing back at Dom as we left the waiting room, and then the hospital.

I didn't sleep well that night. I lay in bed and listened to the girls making their usual noises—doubtless they were still discussing the evening's excitement. Eventually I heard Nomi go to bed, and then later still I heard Christina's footsteps on the stairs. She had some anonymous person with her, and she was giggling. I heard her bedroom door close.

When it got light, I went and sat on a bench in the scraggly little park near my house—it's a good spot to watch people. I like watching people when they're just going about their lives. The park might have only been around the corner but, well, it was enough space to be able to relax. So far, the girls had never found me there—their various routes home took them elsewhere. I used to sit by the beach, but Nomi kept joining me.

I'd made myself sandwiches with chocolate spread and had brought along water in a metallic bottle Dom had once given me. I'd already dropped it and dented it but it still worked perfectly well. I pretended to read my book whilst watching the usual joggers and dog walkers underneath the pink sky. I noticed that the joggers were almost always overweight—was jogging something they gave up on quickly or was it just an ineffectual method of exercise? I recognised some of them but not others: there was a puffy middle-aged lady in a lilac tracksuit who was listening to music so loud I could make out the individual words as she passed.

When we'd first met, things had felt easy between me and Dom, possibly because he'd told me that he already had a girlfriend and so he was safe. He had been off-limits, I suppose. We'd laughed a lot and his friends had seemed to like me, though I knew that was only because they'd disliked his girlfriend so much. As soon as she and Dom had officially broken up we'd got together. We'd barely even discussed it. It was never a matter for discussion. It had just happened. It was simple.

There were two students carrying boxes: a boy and a girl. It was the end of term, and they were obviously going back to stay with their parents. They were both looking melancholic, which meant that they were at the end of their first year of studying. They wouldn't be seeing each other for the summer. Perhaps each was worrying that the other would forget them.

I tried to understand, to figure out what was going through Dom's head. So, he'd reacted badly to Zebedee calling him gay— it was stupid, but he wouldn't be the only straight guy to act like that. It wasn't fair and it doesn't excuse it, but perhaps he had just freaked out. Zebedee had given him strange ideas.

But then why was he still at the hospital? Why was he so upset? Why wouldn't he leave?

Some teenagers on rollerblades sped past. There was nothing especially unusual about them and they laughed as they passed me. Some people walking their dogs came from opposite directions, and they greeted each other as the dogs sniffed one other from their faces to their arses. Then they carried on their respective ways. When I was little, I was convinced that dog owners had their own secret codes and I had wanted a dog so badly, so I could join in. It's actually not so far from the truth— dog owners do seem to have their own special way of talking to each other.

I found an old bar of chocolate in the far corner of my bag. It was already melted and so I scooped it out of the wrapper as best I could. I let a terrier lick my fingers. Her owner seemed annoyed at that—she yanked the poor dog away by its chain. I wiped my hand with a tissue.

"Do you want another one?" A guy leaned over me. He smelled like hair gel and deodorant. His hair was neatly combed. He looked unusual.

"I think I'll be fine," I told him. I hoped he'd walk on. He sat down next to me.

"So why are you up so early?" he asked me.

"I have things on my mind," I said. He nodded.

"Me too."

"I'm meeting someone in a moment," I told him, willing him to leave me alone. He nodded again.

Neither of us said anything for a little while. In fact, I

pretended to read. He was watching people pass us by. Finally, he leaned toward me and spoke.

"I never went jogging and I don't have a dog. It's difficult to find an excuse to go to the park. I'm not as good at pretending to read as you are."

"What makes you think I'm pretending to read?"

"Well, you haven't turned a page."

"Perhaps I'm a slow reader," I said. "Why *do* you come to the park then?"

"To tell you the truth I don't really know. It's nice to just be by yourself sometimes, isn't it? I never went to the park when I was a child, so it's not memories. In fact, the first time I even remember going to a park was when I was a teenager. I got stoned, that's why everyone went there. It was a long time ago."

He looked thoughtful. "There weren't many joggers there, but there were dogs—Alsatians, Rottweilers, all the horrible ones. I shouldn't say that though, no dog is really horrible. Owners can be. Dogs generally just respond to how they're raised. They're a monumentally passive species."

"I suppose you're right," I said, before holding my book back up to my face.

"You're thinking," he said. I wasn't. "So, what is on your mind?"

"Well, if you really need to know, a friend of mine is in the hospital. A friend of my boyfriend. My boyfriend's pretty upset right now."

"I'll pray for them both," he said. Of course—the hair, the shirt. It was a pure white short-sleeved shirt. He looked like a Mormon.

"That's very kind. Thank you. I have to go and meet my friend though. It was nice meeting you." I stood up to leave.

"It was nice meeting you too. My name is Craig."

I smiled, I nodded, and I walked away, checking my phone as I went. It was still only half eight so none of the girls would be up yet. I could have whatever I wanted on the TV whilst I pretended to watch it.

But I couldn't keep my mind off him, my strange hippyish boyfriend who was keeping vigil in the hospital. What was I going to do? What exactly was up with Dom?

DOM

Alright, alright. What I need to do is, I need to tell you a story. When I was smaller, and by smaller I mean younger, when I was smaller my mum and dad had this friend. Well, he was my dad's friend really, not so much mum's, but they'd both see him and they both seemed to like him in a middle-middle class pleasant way. And I liked him. His name was Ron and dad would call him Ron-the-Man and acted like we all knew why, and I didn't, but I called it him all the same, little six-year-old me who had yet to grasp the politics of private nicknames.

Ron would come by every other day as regular as anything in our neat and tidy household, and let me tell you, he fitted in: everything in our house was ordered, Mum saw to that. Everything had its place and Ron-the-Man had his place, my dad's friend and drinking buddy, my mum's hello-how-are-you pleasant acquaintance. Tuesdays at six he'd knock at the door, Thursdays at six he'd knock at the door, and Saturday evening he'd knock at six-thirty as it was the weekend. So that was how Ron-the-Man became a sort-of uncle to me and mum would call him 'Uncle Ron', even though I never let go of 'Ron-the-Man'.

And as dad would get ready—it was part of the routine, he'd have to do his taking-out-the-rubbish and tidy-the-bedroom chores just as Ron-the-Man got there, and as dad got ready, Ron-the-Man would tell me all sorts of things I never heard from my folks, stuff about life and the way that people acted, stuff that people hide from the utopia they try to build for six-year-olds. I loved every conversation we had, even when he told me that Santa and Jesus were fictional. He told me that people are trained in school, that they try to train women to lie and cry and manipulate and they train men to shout and punch and dominate, and that that was the true function of school. So, I still studied and learned but I tried to ignore the other stuff, the education you get from the others your own age, all because of Ron. If I saw boys picking on other boys I'd call them on it, if I saw a group of girls giggling and teasing other girls I'd call them on it. Somehow it won me friends, all because of Ron.

He told me other things—he told me about what people get up to together in bedrooms and what those needles just lying around the street are really for. He spoke to me like I was equal, like I was an adult too, and of course I appreciated it, what six-year-old wouldn't? He taught me how to keep my balance on a bike when I was seven and he taught me how to do all sorts of things my parents didn't have time for; when I was eight he taught me how to play chess, when I was ten how to draw, when I was twelve how to play the piano, all in the half-hour chunks it took dad to get ready and go down the pub.

And I still say that Ron-the-Man taught me most of what I know about the world and when I was fifteen, I smoked my first spliff with him.

So I was still fifteen when Tuesday came round and there was no knock from Ron-the-Man, then Thursday was the same and by Saturday—by Saturday I asked my dad what was going on. He said that nothing was going on, just that Ron—he said 'Ron'—hadn't been by, and that no, no, he wasn't sick and that no, no, nothing was wrong and that I should stop asking stupid questions. As I asked my stupid questions his face got redder and redder until he stood up and marched out the room. Mum saw the whole thing and her voice was low and quiet and she said that Dad and Ron—she said 'Ron'—weren't going to see each other anymore, it didn't matter why, that was just the way it was. I was angry and I was confused, and I wondered what could be so bad that they would stop seeing him, I wondered if he'd hit on Mum or killed someone or something, but I knew whatever it was my folks would never say, so I didn't ask any more questions.

It was a year and a half before I saw Ron-the-Man again, shopping in a supermarket in town and he said it was lucky I caught him, lucky I caught him as he was moving to France, and as soon as he'd said that all the questions I'd saved up stormed out, and I rambled at him, asking him where he'd been and why he hadn't seen Dad, what could have happened, did he kill someone, did he hit on Mum?

Not your mum, no.

And stupid-as-hell I asked him what he meant, and he said that he'd had feelings for my dad for ages, that he was gay and that he'd thought my dad was wonderful, that he wanted them to have a future together, that was what he'd said, and we swapped contact details, and I wished him luck with his whole new life. As I left the bright hell of the supermarket I wondered if that was it. Was that it? All he'd done was hit on Dad and their long, long friendship had ended forever? Outside the tacky place I made a vow: I'd never shun someone for liking me, whether they were a man, or a woman, or anything. What did it matter? Why had my dad been so stupid?

Why had I been so stupid? It should never have mattered, what Zebedee had said, but he'd got to me somehow, and after he'd said that Richard and I were gay I'd spent the whole day with it buzzing round my mind, I'd spent the whole day thinking about everything we'd done together, whether he'd been eyeing me up when we'd shared a smoke or whether he'd been thinking about fucking me while we watched downloaded shows. All Richard did was go to hug me, but I could hear Zebedee's voice and I could see Ron-the-Man and I couldn't handle it, I couldn't handle him having his arms round me, so I pushed him.

Of course, I was fucking ashamed, I was straight away, and I did want to apologise, to apologise to this guy who was my friend, to tell him I fucked up, but I barely had time to say I was sorry.

And then he was hit by a bottle and surrounded by glass and all I could think was, he might die, he could die and the last thing I did was push him when he tried to hug me on his birthday. Over and over, the same thought, the last thing I did was shove him, the last thing I did was shove him, the last thing I did was shove him and I held him tight, I held him as tight as I could, I didn't want to push him away again, I wanted him to know that I'd never do that again.

The hospital was awful, just really awful, and I didn't want to leave him there, in that place where the air was still and thick with chemicals and where the plants were made of an unnatural shiny plastic, where there was an endless hum that made it feel like you were stuck inside a giant dishwasher.

I spent the night there alone. I needed to be alone, I needed to sort out my head—what I was doing, what I was thinking, and I couldn't do that with anyone else there. But sitting and lying and kneeling and pacing under the fluorescent light it came to me, bit-by-bit. I knew I needed Richard. I knew I needed Richard. Minutes went by as I thought about how I wanted to be there for him and hug him and not push him away. I drank lukewarm coffee from a half-filled cup. I wanted to spend more nights talking to him, whole nights talking to him and chatting with him, about useless, stupid, important things, I wanted to hear what he had to say, about anything. I ate cheap shitty chocolate from the vending machine and hours went by as I thought of him, how I liked living with him, I liked coming home and knowing he was there. There by myself in the hospital I thought of him in the next room, probably sleeping, definitely alone, and I wanted to be with him. Not fucking him, I didn't want to fuck him, but I wanted him to see me when he woke up and know that I was there for him, that I would always be there for him. That I needed him too.

The night was almost over. And I knew I loved Caroline but, sat there by myself in the endless light, it came to me. I was in love with him as well.

❖❖ ❖❖ ❖❖

The sun came up and they wouldn't let me into the ward to see him, they said I had to be related to him, or married to him, or at least *something*, so I told the night staff that I cared about him, wasn't that enough?

It wasn't enough.

By that point I couldn't even go out and breathe in some fresh air, by then it felt like cheating— I had waited for him all this time, if I went outside now, even for a moment, it would be abandoning him. I went to take a piss, staring at the blank tiles and trying to keep my eyes in focus. I was tired. I was really tired.

I came out of the hospital toilets and there he was.

"Richard."

"Dom," he almost shouted, looking pretty fucking surprised. He had a dressing on his forehead, a tiny speck of red in the centre where the blood had seeped through, and I couldn't help myself, I walked right on over and put my arms around him. I could feel that my eyes were starting to burn, and I blinked, I blinked as hard as I could.

I asked him if he was okay.

"I'm fine, it's nothing serious," Richard replied, giving me this really strange look. "You're here pretty early in the morning."

And I just looked right back at him, and my eyes must have been bloodshot red because his expression changed, he must have realised that I'd been there all night.

"I'm sorry, Richard, I'm so fucking sorry," I said, and I had to bite my tongue to keep from apologising again, over and over. "What I did, that's not how I feel, it's not how I feel about you, it really isn't."

"I know that, Dom. But I can give you space, I know that we've been spending a lot of time together and—well—it's made you uncomfortable, I can see that. I mean, I don't like it, but I want you to be comfortable, I want you to be happy."

"I am happy, Richard."

99

And maybe that would have been all, maybe that would have been an end to the night, but I couldn't hold back, my eyes were stinging, and I felt like every single vein in my body would burst, so maybe that why I took a deep breath and I said, very quietly,

"I'm in love with you, Richard."

I'd said it.

"What do you mean you 'love me'?" he asked, looking at me like I was nuts, the fucking lunatic who had waited all night for him at the hospital. "You're straight, aren't you?"

And what could I say to that? I was scared, I didn't know if I could get it all out right or make him understand, especially when I didn't really get it myself, so I told him that I was straight—that I *am* straight, at least I only really like girls sexually, and if they weren't born a girl at least they should look like one.

"My cock likes girls, Richard. But I love you."

And he took all that in, and I was just standing there, needing to pee again and hoping he understood. He was just quiet for a long time, sitting there staring at the wall of the waiting room, the same wall that I'd been looking at all night, the same wall that I'd been watching when I realised that I loved him. And he was looking at that wall when he said,

"I know how you feel. My cock doesn't like you either," and then he looked right at me and he said, "but I love you too."

"I love you, Richard."

"I love you, Dom."

And I gasped and pressed my face into my hand, both of them wet, and I think I laughed or choked or something, and he placed his hand on my arm, then put both his arms around me and pulled me into a hug. I put mine around him too. I held him tightly, and he held me tightly, but he felt dry, and I was absolutely fucking dripping with sweat.

"I'm absolutely fucking dripping with sweat," I said.

"Don't worry about it," Richard said, and I could hear him smiling as he said it. My throat and chest and gut felt tight, and I could see the room grow hazy with water, and I smiled and swallowed and coughed and did everything I could, but I couldn't stop the water running down my face and I hoped he couldn't hear, but if I could hear him smile then he could hear me cry, and he said nothing and he held me tighter and we just stood there, in the middle of the waiting room at the start of the day, hugging each other, an overly inquisitive nurse watching us from the corner.

THE NORTHWEST PASSAGE
23 YEARS ON

It had only been three days and already Dom was tired of it—they had explored the boat a dozen times over, and already spoken to a good third of their fellow travellers. The boat had one bar, which was too modern—it gave off the impression of trying too hard—and there was little else by way of entertainment. It was going to be a long and cold journey from the Cascadian Territories to the Catalunya Republic, but it would be worth it.

As Dom looked out from the deck to the crisp horizon where ocean met cold sky, they couldn't help but smile to themself. They glanced around. An old woman watched them warily. The salty chill air seemed to find its way through the gaps in Dom's clothes, but they preferred it to being below deck. Dom'd never much enjoyed being trapped indoors, even if there was nothing above but a surface of melting ice, where the strangely bright sun burned their eyes.

Though Dom conferenced with his partners almost daily (with their new reader they could even feel and smell the two of them) it had been a year and a half since they had seen either Richard or Caroline in the flesh. It had been the one downside to the job. Cascadia had been in desperate need of teachers—teachers in the sciences especially—and so pay and conditions had been decent. Being whisked between Vancouver, Portland, and Seattle had been inconvenient, but it was also true that not settling down had made things simpler. At least now they were leaving.

An arm wrapped its way around Dom's waist, a gloved hand on their hip.

"You're pretty forward," Dom uttered, turning their head slightly, not far enough to see the fellow traveller, but far enough to feel breath on their cheek.

"You can talk," the woman teased, "for a man on the way to his own wedding."

Dom stuck their tongue out.

"You know it's not like that. I've even told Richard and Caroline about you."

"We only met three days ago," the woman exclaimed.

"I tell them everything," Dom informed them, face flushing with light irritation: Dom hated having the same conversation with every woman they ever slept with. The wind grew fiercer, and the woman drew Dom closer, placing their fingers into Dom's coat pocket for warmth.

"I hope you said good things," the woman replied.

"I told them you were pretty," Dom teased in return, the annoyance ebbing, "that's the most important part. They were both interested."

"As long as I live I'll never understand polyamorous people," the woman replied, withdrawing their arm. "Yeah, yeah," they continued before Dom had chance to respond, "you don't need jealousy and all that. You live perfect little lives where you share everything, don't have secrets and have mostly decent sex with strangers you meet on boats."

"So what's the problem?" Dom asked.

"It's not real. When you love someone you should want that person all to yourself. I mean really love someone."

"Enough to marry them?" Dom responded sharply, irritation flooding through them once more. They were bored of that accusation, too—they'd heard it enough times over the years. By now it was even old-fashioned. Dom loved Richard, Dom loved Caroline. They didn't need a borderline stranger telling them otherwise.

"I'm going to get a drink," Dom said.

"Don't be like that," the woman replied, reaching for Dom's arm and drawing them close once again. Dom stumbled, balancing against their body. "I didn't mean that. I just don't get it. But you love your fiancées. Fine. I didn't mean to suggest otherwise."

"Good." Dom blinked, the sting of salt and sun still on their eyes. They would head back below deck soon and call the others.

"There's just one thing I still don't get," the woman continued. Dom held their breath.

"If you guys have been together for so long, and you're happy, why do you need a piece of paper from Spain to prove it?"

"Catalunya," Dom corrected. In truth Dom didn't really know—

Richard had first brought it up, and Caroline had agreed. They didn't mind the idea, but it made little difference to them. It made little difference legally as well—they'd done their research: the three-way marriage wouldn't be valid anywhere except Catalunya, Nepal, and Brazil. Not Wales.

"It makes them happy," Dom replied. It was true.

"Then I think you'll be a good husband," the woman said, kissing them on their cold earlobe.

Dom certainly hoped so.

CHAPTER SEVEN

FALL IN LOVE WITH ONE GUY AND EVERYONE THINKS YOU'RE SUCKING COCK

RUTTI

"Well, there's a party tonight, down in Neukölln. It's nothing special, just some people I met at Morgenrot. But I'm going to go, they told me there's this roof terrace with all these art works that's supposed to be amazing, so I thought I might as well check it out."

"Have you been going to anything other than parties, Stephanie? Is anything else happening there in Berlin?"

"Well, no one has a job here, so pretty much no."

"No one has a job here either, but there still aren't parties."

"People get drunk in Swansea all the time."

"They're mostly homeless and passed out on the pavement. It's not the same. Besides, I've not got drunk in a while."

"What about Richard's birthday? How is he, by the way?"

"*Now* you're interested in little old Wales? It been days since you phoned. Stuff's been going on I suppose."

"Stuff? It's not like you to be unspecific, Rutti."

"But it's exactly like you, Frau Steph, to be nosey."

"Tell me."

"Fine, but don't mention to Richard that I told you about

what's been going on. I'm not even sure how they really see the whole thing and—"

"—Whole thing?"

"You won't hear anything if you keep butting in. Do you promise to be quiet for five minutes?"

[Silence]

"Good. So, did I tell you what happened at the hospital? Just before you left?"

[Silence]

"Fine, well so anyway I was worried sick. It was one of the worst nights of my life, and I didn't sleep for about a week after that. But sure, Richard was alright. I went round to see them to make sure. I went around to the old apartment a few times, bringing stuff I'd cooked, just making sure that Richard was getting by. But the thing is, I noticed that something was going on between them and Dom. The two of them were spending a titanic amount of time together, and, you could see them— oh fuck, what's the word—well just enthralled by each other or something. I mean, you could watch the two talk for hours and not get bored. I mean, I got bored, but they didn't. [Slight pause]. Where was I?

"Ah right. So, it turns out the two of them are in love. Richard told me after I wrangled it out of them, though it didn't exactly take much work. They seemed happy at that time though—I guess they were smitten, and by the look on their face, Dom was too. It was actually kind of cute to see the two of them, really.

"But Dom has this moronic hetero friend—Zebedee— and I can only guess because Zebedee was jealous, they'd been picking on Dom about it. Apparently, this friend doing that is what caused trouble between Dom and Richard in the first place. I didn't see any of this from this Zebedee person of course, but it was upsetting Richard. I think that's why they told me about it. Anyway, this Zebedee was saying that the two of them *were* homo after all, which is ridiculous. I mean, if Richard never slept with me, they certainly wouldn't with some patchouli-rank hippy. I mean, come on."

[Silence]

"Yeah, you're right, that's not the point, whatever. So, Dom tells Caroline—I heard this from Richard themself—and the shit really hit the fan. Dom and Richard told Caroline they were in love, but that they weren't fucking. That both of them were hetero. I mean, I get it, love's not always about sex, right? But by all accounts, Caroline certainly didn't. Next thing you know, Caroline and Dom have broken up, and Dom's all heartbroken and so that leaves Richard to pick up the pieces, and so they ramble on about it to me. Not that I should give Richard the time of day, what with them evicting me. By the way, I forgot to feed your cat, I think it's dead."

[Silence]

"Yeah, yeah, it was a joke and it's not funny. But that's the long and short of it. The two hetero boys are in love, which is quite remarkable for south Wales, and now they seem sort of lost. Dom's upset and that means Richard is too. In all seriousness I'm being as helpful as I can be, but what can I really do? And most of the time Richard is out of contact anyway, and I can hardly offer them advice via telepathy. Anyway, when are you coming home? It's pretty boring here, and the Christian seems to be away most of the time. Steph? Stephanie?"

[Silence, then a female voice]

"Sorry Rutti, I really had to go and pee. So, what was that about Richard and butting in?"

"Fuck."

RICHARD

I woke before Dom and checked for the scab on my forehead. It had shrunk considerably just over the past night. Dom was still asleep, but his lack of consciousness was doing nothing to curb his stress—his face was contorted, his lips curled, and forehead furrowed.

We had taken to sleeping in the same room after Caroline

had broken up with him. Dom had spent the hours after she'd left in silence, his eyes shimmering with tears. Now and then he'd come over and hugged me, and I had asked if he wanted to talk. He'd simply shaken his head and held on tighter. That night I had slept alongside him, listening to his breath shuddering in the dark. He'd been crying. There was nothing I could do about it.

I loved him.

I'd loved him before he'd told me the same—but what I felt hadn't had words, it didn't have any sort of frame. I could have gone on and on being in love with him and never even knowing what it was. But seeing him in the hospital—sleep-deprived, desperate, and shaking with fear—my heart thudded. He told me he loved me, and I knew that was what it was. I loved him. He said he was straight, and I told him I was too. We were two straight guys in love.

It had been laughably simple, and it would have stayed simple if not for Dom and Caroline. She'd left and taken a part of him with her. He'd gradually grown a little better over the next days. He didn't cry again, but he looked washed-out and distant, like a grey net had been draped over him.

I didn't know what time it was, and the white-grey clouds of Swansea's summer hung outside the window, hiding the sun and any hint of how late it was. Dom's breathing was light and long, until he gave a snort and opened his eyes. His expression softened for a moment as he woke, then hardened once more.

"I love you," he said, smiling for my benefit.

"I love you too, Dom," I replied. "Good morning."

"Good morning," he muttered, rolling over and going back to sleep.

I decided to make him breakfast. I had to at least try and cheer him up. Somehow. I even went to the corner shop and bought eggs and flour to make pancakes. When I returned he was up, sitting at the rickety table and staring at the wall, his hairy shoulders sagged.

Breakfast wouldn't work.

"Give Dom a break, they've just lost their girlfriend."

Rutti was sympathetic as ever.

"I'm not complaining, I'm just worried," I answered, delicately holding the handleless mug by my fingertips and sipping at the weak coffee. The place was in one of the shabby arcades, broken tiles and a dingy, brown-stained glass roof. I preferred the arcades in Cardiff, with their Victorian brick and ironwork. They'd been like that in Swansea, once. I'd seen the grainy black-and-white pictures. They were a far cry from the place in which we were now seated. The little café was Rutti's favourite place based on price alone, though I had wanted to go to a chain that had cups you could actually hold. The woman behind the counter hadn't been too friendly either, glancing up from her magazine with disdain and taking our orders with exaggerated weariness. The place stank of re-fried meat from the greasy spoon next door.

"Occasionally he seems a little better", I continued, "and he smiles at me, so I think I at least make him happy sometimes. But then he's down again, and it's like he can't see me."

"Surprise. Guys can have mood swings too," Rutti replied, chewing on a biscuit with his mouth open. "You need to know these things, now that you're dating one."

"We're not dating," I corrected, knowing that Rutti had only said it to wind me up.

"You're right, you've done all the dating and now you've won them."

"We're not having sex," I stressed, exasperated.

"I swear to the gods, Richard, if you repeat that one more time, I'm going to throw this mug at you."

"Go ahead, it's lukewarm anyway," I responded. Rutti burst out laughing. I couldn't help but join him, laughing for the first time in days. Once we'd calmed down Rutti leaned toward me and spoke again, his breath smelling like cheap coffee.

"Honestly, Dom just needs time. I wouldn't worry—if they were willing to risk their relationship for you then they must love you. Break-ups are hard. Give them time. Just give them some time."

Rutti was right—he could be the most irritating person in the world, but on the rare occasions he wasn't trying to direct me toward a stress-induced heart attack, he was good at making me feel better. I relaxed. Even the coffee tasted better. At least, it tasted less terrible.

No, no, no, no,
I ain't gonna show,
Ain't gonna show you babe,
Not without,
Not without a ring babe . . .

I knew the song—it had been played endlessly on every station. Rutti groaned.

"I come here to avoid shit like that," he complained, slamming his coffee cup down on the chipboard table.

"I think the song is fine," I told him, grinning a little and carefully watching for his reaction. It was fun to annoy Rutti back.

"If you consider women being bought 'fine'," he argued, glaring at me.

"Marriage isn't being bought, Rutti, and you know it. Even feminists are pro-marriage now." I was enjoying this. I tried not to smile.

"Did the gods of feminism tell you that, Richard? Tell me, what are they saying right now? Are they screaming?"

"I think it's romantic. Besides, what do you know? I mean, men can't really be feminists." I knew that would get at him. It worked.

"You don't need a vagina to be a feminist. Feminism is really about not having your genitals control your whole destiny."

"Well maybe some people's destiny is to find themselves a

110

husband or wife." I was sure that I was openly grinning by that point, but Rutti didn't seem to notice. The woman behind the counter glanced at us.

"Spoken like a true closet member of the far-right. So, Richard, tell me about the market of human bondage."

"Are you going to start on some pseudo-communist rant again? Because I believe the free market happens to—"

Rutti cut me off. "Free market bullshit. Tell you what—I'll believe in a free market when you show me one."

I laughed at him. He punched me on the arm, then leant back and started mouthing along to the final lyrics of the pop song.

"How do you know the words?" I asked him.

"I have to listen to it at the perfume store. It's reprogramming. My boss thinks it will make me more normal."

"It's not working."

"I know."

DOM

Richard snored next to me, his face pressed against my arm, which felt sort of nice—it was nice to feel him close. The lights were off, and the only illumination was the sickly orange street light shining in through the open curtains. Richard had fallen asleep first because he always fell asleep first, but I'd lain in bed awake for hours, hours until I decided to get out my laptop. I was flicking through pictures of Caroline, and pictures of Caroline and me.

It had been difficult, and by that, I mean it had been *fucking* difficult, and any happiness I felt toward Richard was smothered by the total misery of losing Caroline. And I'd had to tell her, I'd had to—I'd called her one afternoon and said I needed to speak to her, urgently if she could, and she'd sounded worried as Caroline could never hide what she was feeling. We hadn't spoken, and it'd been three days since we'd come back from the hospital.

"How's Richard?" was the first thing she'd asked me, as soon as she'd walked through the door, so I answered her, because I needed to be honest, and so I said,

"It's Richard we need to talk about."

And she'd just nodded and walked straight through to the room, her arms clutched around herself as she was already in pain—like I say, Caroline isn't very good at guarding her emotions. I could feel little beads of sweat tickling my forehead, and Caroline looked not only hurt but also confused, confused at the situation.

"I'm not gay," I told her, and she looked at me in disbelief, confusion and disbelief, so I continued. "I'm not—but you need to know that I'm in love with Richard. Those sound like contradictory statements, I know that, I do—but it's true. I need you to know that. I need you to know everything."

She just looked at me, her arms still folded, glaring at me—she was getting angry, and then I'd have run out of time. I felt myself panicking, I had to explain things properly, I had to explain them quickly. But I couldn't. Instead, I managed to ramble on, saying nothing.

"What do you want, Dom?" she interrupted, unmoving but now visibly furious.

I want to hold you, I should have said, I just want to hold you.

"I want you both," I told her, "I need the two of you, I couldn't do without either of you."

Caroline unmoving.

"You can't have the both of us, Dom. You're in a relationship with me."

And what could I say to that? What could I say? I was new to all this, I barely had a grasp on things myself, and here I was expected to explain things, to make them clear, but how could they be made clear? I said nothing, I just looked at her, I watched her knowing that I'd lost her, and she said nothing to me, her arms staying folded until she stood and said,

"I'd better go."

"Don't go," was all I managed, in a tiny croak which I'm not even sure she heard. She was nearing the front door when Richard had come home, his arms laden with a torn carrier bag of groceries.

"Well look who it is," Caroline said, her voice rising, her anger seeping through at the sight of him. She turned to me.

"In love? Fucking in love? How could you have fucking hidden that from me? Oh poor stupid fucking Caroline, not even realising that her boyfriend's gay, not having any clue that the whole time he's been fucking a man behind my back. And stupid me with everyone knowing about it, with your friends and my friends talking about it. How stupid have I fucking looked?"

I told her we hadn't been fucking, it wasn't like that, it just wasn't, but I still loved him, I was still in love with him.

"Oh, right, of course you haven't been fucking. Do you think I'm so dense? Do you really think so little of me? And you," she cried, turning to Richard, who stood dumbfounded, "you've a fucking nerve pretending to be nice to me when all the time you were having sex with my boyfriend, right behind my back. All the while you were cheating and I'd trusted you, I'd trusted both of you." She turned to me again, her voice sharp but lower, her eyes on the floor.

"God and it was me, I'm the one who pushed you two back together. You two fell out and I'm the one who made it right between you."

"We haven't been fucking," Richard said, his voice a murmur to Caroline's bellow.

"I'm leaving," she'd announced, "I'm not sticking around for any more of this. Thanks Dom, you've hurt me, and you've made a complete fool of me. Great."

She'd slammed the door behind her.

"Are you okay?" Richard was awake now, his hand on my arm,

113

his eyes bleary. He glanced at the laptop's screen, at a picture of Caroline supporting a drunken me, so I closed the laptop, lay down and placed my arm over his shoulders.

"I will be," I said, feeling a flicker of happiness from the way he looked at me, from the set of his eyes and the curve of his mouth, looking at me like he loved me. Then the sickening lurch of losing Caroline returned, and I closed my eyes, hoping to close out everything—lose Caroline, keep Richard; lose Richard, keep Caroline—pain in any direction, with nothing I could do. I loved them both. I loved them both.

CAROLINE

"It is a commonly known *fact* that romantic comedies are the very apex of shit. Total, meaningless shit. That's the way it is these days, everything is about love. Every story, every song, every form of entertainment. And I know why it is—love is easy. It's safe. Music labels, or film producers, or publishers, they all know that love is a safe subject. You don't want to get people thinking—thinking leads to politics, and people disagree about politics. Disagreeing alienates people, and if you alienate people, they won't hand over their money. Money is conservative, and so love is conservative. Do you see?"

"What—what the hell are you going on about Caroline? 'Money is love'? What do you mean?" Nomi stared at me, intent and confused.

What had I meant? The words had come out wrong. I wanted to try again—whatever I had said was important—but the train of thought was gone. Vanished. I had a mostly eaten box of brownies in my hand. Nomi was perched next to me on the bed, still looking at me for an answer. Her hood was pulled down partly over her face, obscuring her reddened eyes. She was always embarrassed by how she looked when she was stoned.

We were lounging in my bedroom. The main bulb had blown and so we were gathered by Nomi's lamp, which she had plugged in and then thrown down in the middle of the bedspread. Strange shadows were cast over the walls—coupled with the haze of smoke it felt like some sort of mystic temple, or pre-smoking ban bar.

A hand thrust up out of nowhere. It was Christina's—she was slumped to the floor by the side of the bed. I put the box into the hand. It vanished.

"Caroline was talking about capitalism," Christina's disembodied voice confirmed, muffled by the cake crumbling between her teeth. I was pleased; Nomi was the stoned one. I was merely mildly buzzed. "Capitalism and love."

Nomi was undeterred. "Bullshit," she slurred, her shadow oddly doubled on the wall behind her, two heads and four arms. "People like hearing about love, that's all. Capitalism, com—communism, wouldn't make a blind bit of difference. Love is love. You're just thinking about Dom."

"Oh come off it, Nomi." She loved going on about my so-called heartbreak. My views were hardly new, I'd done my share of activism back in uni, and Nomi knew it. Evidently Christina knew what I was thinking as she chimed in.

"She's winding you up, Caroline. How do you fall for it, every time?"

As always, I didn't answer.

I hadn't felt anything about the break-up, not at the time. It had been like watching some tragic play which I wasn't really following. In fairness, both Nomi and Christina had been relatively supportive since I'd broken up with Dom—or he'd broken up with me by declaring his love for another guy, or however you want to see it. She'd endlessly rambled about how she'd never liked him, how he was a terrible boyfriend, and how anyone could see he was gay from a mile off.

"Except you," I'd said, which had shut her up for ten whole minutes.

Christina had been more subtle. She had told me once that if I needed to talk, then she was there—but otherwise she wouldn't mention it. So far, I hadn't needed to talk at all—what was there to talk about? My boyfriend was in love with someone else, and was in the very least bisexual, if not gay.

"Are you—are you thinking about Dom?" Nomi mumbled, her stoned face looming into view once more.

"No," I lied.

Christina made her way to the bathroom, and Nomi took the opportunity to lean in toward me.

"You need to get through to his friends," she whispered.

"What?" I asked, trying to focus on her too-close-up face, lit from below by the lamp.

"You need to get through to his friends. Dom's friends."

"I'm not doing that, Nomi. I'm going to let it be. Anyway—" but she continued before I could distract her with another topic.

"What you need to do is, you need to talk to his friends," she repeated herself, as though neither of us had said anything. Now she was leaning closer to the source of light there were four shadows on the wall behind, each mimicking her.

"No."

"It's a—fool-proof plan, he won't even trace it back to you."

"No."

"And Zebedee is my boyfriend."

"I know."

"And Zebedee is, like, best friends with Dom."

"I know."

"So, I could talk to Zebedee—"

"No."

"—and I could get him to confront Dom—"

"No."

"—and I could get him to see sense."

There was no point saying anything further, so we sat there not saying anything—I pulled a duvet over myself (an acquisition of Nomi's from Christina's bedroom) and closed my eyes, feeling myself gently floating away.

Water. Cold water. On my stomach. Water. I jumped up,

dripping all over the carpet. Nomi and Christina were giggling. There was an upturned washing-up bowl in front of them. It took me about three seconds to realise they had decided to put my hand in warm water to make me pee myself but found the kettle too much effort and used cold water instead, spilling it over my stomach before they could reach my hand.

"You two are pathetic," I groaned at them, but it only made them giggle more.

The breakup hit me when I woke up the next day. Day One. It was still dark. I must have been dreaming about Dom, or about Dom and the fight, and I woke up feeling sick. So then I was sick, into the washing up bowl next to me. We'd broken up, that was it, it was over. It didn't feel as fine as it had earlier. It felt awful.

I heard a snort to my left. I turned around to see Nomi sleeping next to me. To her other side was Christina.

I lay back down. My stomach cramped and I throbbed with the thought of never being with Dom again. I told myself that I knew it would be like this, that I knew it would hurt and in the end it was for the best. Even so, I didn't leave the house for three days. For three days I called in sick to work, watched terrible films I borrowed from the others, and came downstairs to eat pity meals from them. Christina cooked me a meat-free lasagna the first day and salmon on day two. The third night I ate with Nomi. We had cereal.

By the fourth day Nomi convinced me to go shopping with her. The intense stabbing in my stomach had subsided to a dull overall ache. So, Nomi marched me around the mall, around cheap, ethically-dubious clothes shops, the probable human-rights violations in a cardigan making me think of Dom, who would never have gone there. I didn't buy anything. Then she took me to a fast-food chain, and I stared at my fries, thinking of plundered seas and bleached coral reefs. We went to a music store which sold albums distributed by evil child-suing record labels, we went to a department store promoted by a racist tabloid newspaper, and then to an ice cream stand that was owned by a criminal corporation that mostly manufactures cleaning products. It was entirely his opposite, but the whole mall made me think of Dom. Child labourers, depleted ozone layers, and melted ice caps.

CHAPTER EIGHT

THE CUCKOLDESS

DOM

The night was free of clouds, so free that a hundred-hundred stars lit up the sky above us, and it was warm, warm enough to sit in t-shirts. It would have been warm enough even if we didn't have the fire. In front of us was the mouth of the cave, the rush over the underground river spilling from the dark inside, the smell of damp rock tumbling out with it. Richard was at my side, poking at the ground with a stick. We hadn't said much to each other since we'd left, and I hadn't figured out if we should have or not. My mind was on Caroline, of course, though Richard did his best.

We'd spent three days wandering through the dry twigs of the woods, washing in inexplicably cold streams and wallowing in the rush of the equally cold sea. It had been Richard's idea, he'd sussed that I like camping, and I had enthusiastically accepted; there are few things the city was good for, if not being perched on the edge of the Gower.

There were noises, over through the stumps of trees behind us, bursting now and then, noises like the wild sobbing of someone out of all control, and each time the two of us would swivel our heads to face the mysterious sounds, and now and then Richard would edge a little closer to me—he was an indoors type, after all, though I can hardly talk—in fact, I'll admit, I was anxious to avoid whatever made the awful noises somewhere in the land behind. Then I'd carefully settle back, back with his head rested on me, back with me leaning against the bags with the glow of the fire flowing over my face, and I'm not sure when I drifted, but then it was morning.

On the way back to ours we stopped by one of the rural pubs, each ordering an ale and enjoying the small and cosy front room, watching the empty fireplace, and trying not to think of the world outside, of life back in the city, the one we couldn't pretend to escape.

Thankfully we couldn't; we were mobbed by Zebedee almost as soon as we got home, worn out from two burning bus rides, the apartment a mess of cans and pizza boxes. There behind Zebedee was Caroline and her friend Nomi—Caroline—but Zebedee spoke first, his eyes full of what he knew, and his face twisted into this mockery of a smile, some sort of cruel joke playing over his lips, one he had yet to tell us, yet before we even swapped a 'hello,' he said,

"Have a good time, you two?"

"Sure," Richard replied, making a moment's eye contact with me.

"Well, that's nice," Zebedee said, his voice thick with sarcasm. For a moment I hoped, and I'm sure Richard hoped, that that was the end of it, but then Zebedee added, "It's probably not nice for your girlfriend though, is it?" As he said it he thrust his finger at me, making these violent jabbing motions at the air, his face shifting a tinge of red.

He was determined to have a fight with me, but Caroline was with them, Caroline and her friend, Zebedee's girlfriend, who looked as though she was chewing glass. Richard stood by me, close enough to hold hands but not quite, not quite close enough for that. I nudged a beer can with my foot.

"We want to talk to you by yourself," Nomi said, standing by Zebedee and gesturing at Richard. "Not with him."

I told them that 'he' lived here, and 'he' was staying here.

"Look," Zebedee said, as stern as he could, "It's fine if you're gay—"

"I'm not gay."

"Seems pretty gay to me," Zebedee's girlfriend chipped in, her arms crossed.

"It's fine..." Zebedee trailed off for a moment, but then grew angrier, "It would be fine, if you'd just be fucking honest with us."

"We are being honest with you, Jesus Christ," Richard said quietly.

Zebedee raised his hand like a prophet and said, "Be decent about this to Caroline, she deserves to know the truth. If you're gay and you two are a couple, more power to you, but at least tell *her*. Show us you have some respect for at least one of us."

I looked over at Caroline, but she was shaking her head, and she looked beautiful, like she'd just got out of bed, her hair was messy and she was wearing an oversize shirt, she looked beautiful just like that.

"She's worth ten of you," Nomi spat at me.

"Enough of that, Nomi," Zebedee told his girlfriend, and he stepped towards me, like he was trying to be friendly, he put his hand on my shoulder, but the gesture was awkward and unnatural. "You two were great together, Dom, it doesn't have to end like this. If you're not gay then you're throwing a great relationship away. Caroline loves you. Don't be mad. Look, you can stay with me for a bit, get out of this flat, get your head straight. Richard will find someone else—"

I took his hand off my shoulder and I told him, "Don't talk about Richard like he isn't here."

"He can talk about Richard how he likes," Nomi said. She'd sat down on the couch and dragged Caroline to sit with her, scattering papers to the floor with a flick of her hand.

Zebedee looked hurt, and I regretted pulling his hand away. He carried on talking, he said, "We all waver sometimes, we all have our moments where we lose our minds, we don't have to mess up our lives over it."

"Dom," Zebedee continued, and he was perfectly, perfectly calm, "Just come with me, get some space, get some time to yourself, have some time to think. Yeah? It's the best thing to do, you know it is—he's a distraction, the two of you obviously just have things confused right now. Richard would be better off with some space as well. It's better all 'round."

But Zebedee didn't notice Richard, he didn't notice Richard all ablaze, his cheeks a fierce kind of red, his own hands pulled into fists, his whole body trembling, and for a moment I started to speak, to diffuse the situation, to try and keep some sort of calm, but it was too late.

"Who the fuck do you think you are? I'm right here. I'm right here. Talk to my face."

"Alright then," Zebedee bristled, his eyes narrowing on Richard, "I'll talk to your face. What do you want me to say? That you're breaking up two people who are right for each other? Dom says he ain't gay, so why are you doing this? He's not gonna fuck you, you know. He likes women. Women. You're better off looking elsewhere, you'll get over it."

"You don't have a clue what you're talking about. Listen to me. I'm not trying to fuck him. Why is this even any of your business? I do love him though. That's not going to change if he goes and stays with you. It's you who isn't fucking wanted here, Zebedee."

"You're getting in the way."

"I'm not getting in the way of anything. Not anything. I would love it if Caroline and Dom would work things out. Do you have any idea how unhappy Dom is without her? And you think you're helping? You think any of this is helping?"

"It's Caroline who deserves pity, not Dom," Nomi said, "And you are in the way. God, what an absolute freak show. Zebedee's being nice to you."

"Dom loves the both of us."

"I say Dom loves himself a fair sight more." Nomi replied. "Come on, Caroline, we should go."

"We've both been honest, and Dom still loves Caroline, of course he fucking does, believe me, and I don't want to take him away from her. He loves her, he really does," Richard tried.

There was a moment's pause, all eyes narrowed on me—I

was expected to say something, to end the scene, to give them a reason to storm out. I just said what I felt—I was being honest. I loved Richard. I looked over at Caroline, whose eyes refused to meet mine, and I wanted to wrap my arms around her and tell her that I loved her and that it was fine, it was fine really. I told her I still loved her. I told Zebedee that he was still my friend—of course he was—and that I still needed a friend, but as I was speaking, I could tell they weren't listening, that they wouldn't or couldn't or felt they shouldn't listen, and that if I was to be with Richard then I'd have to do without them. They left, taking Caroline.

CAROLINE

Two days later and there had been another attack near the seafront—this time on a woman who had only just escaped with a black eye, managing to get away before worse had happened.

"We just need to make sure to stick together," Nomi stated. "There's not much else you can do about it."

"Actually, there is," I told her. "There's a women's group that meets in the Uplands. I'm going to go. There must be something I can do."

"Sounds like a waste of time to me," Nomi replied, baring her usual level of support in a falsely sing-song voice. "What're you going to do, Caroline? Change the world by sitting in a circle and talking about your period? Because I already know everything about you. I'm your menstruation expert."

I left the room.

The next evening, I found myself wondering if maybe Nomi was right. Not about the period-talk—Nomi was easily the most sexist woman I'd ever met—but maybe there really was nothing I could do. I'd been sitting in the fluorescent yellow room in silence for almost an hour, amongst a dozen women confidently throwing their opinions at one another. So far, I had managed to tell them my name and the fact that I was a geography postgrad, and I'd only managed that because a small and familiar elfin woman with green hair had taken the trouble to introduce me. I was thinking about leaving when the green-haired woman asked,

"So, what do you think, Caroline?"

"Sorry," I confessed, "I was miles away."

The woman smiled at me. I liked her. "Don't worry about it, I tune out sometimes when Kitty's talking too. We were just discussing the attack at the beach."

"Oh," I exclaimed, doing my best to gather up my thoughts as quickly as I possibly could, before realising that I actually did have something to say. "Well, I don't think it's a one-off thing, and I don't think it's limited to women either. A Muslim friend of mine has been getting all sorts of abuse recently, and someone I know was put in hospital because some thugs thought he was gay." My stomach tightened as I thought about Dom and Richard, but my comment kicked off a rabid discussion around the blue plastic chairs of the circle. Amongst the clatter of voices, I noticed that the woman with green hair was still smiling at me.

"It's been worse ever since that shitty club burned down," she announced. This drove the debate into what seemed to be a good-natured frenzy. I stared at the ratty linoleum floor and the scratched legs of the chairs.

The green-haired woman and I were the last to leave.

"I'm Steph," she said, holding her hand toward me in half-handshake, half-salute.

"I'm Caroline," I replied. Steph smiled as though I'd said something witty, then guided me through the front door.

Richard's friend Rutti was waiting there—Steph seemed to recognise him.

"I'm busy right now, Rutti, I don't have time to hang out," she ordered. Rutti looked dejected.

"But I've been waiting for you an hour," he complained. "I have things to tell you."

"I've only been back a day. Besides, you've already had a glorious three seconds with me," she replied. "Go see if you can find some new homeless people to move in with us."

He pulled a face and walked off.

We went into the Uplands Tavern across the street. I'd never really spent much time in the Uplands Tavern, and it was more crowded than I would have liked. A band was playing, a group of young guys with identical haircuts, their eyes partially hidden by their hair. The speakers blasted the pub, deafening everyone into paying attention. I kept having to lean in to hear Steph, and she would lean her ear toward me when I said something back. After a while I suggested we sit outside. The air was a little cold, but we were protected from the summer drizzle by the pub's oversized umbrellas.

"Did you hear a word I was saying?" Steph asked me, pulling her jacket tight against the breeze.

"No," I answered.

She leaned her pint glass toward mine. "So, you broke up with your boyfriend?"

I was about to ask her how she knew about that but thought better of it. I nodded instead.

"Better off without men, I say," Steph replied. "Mind, I'm somehow lumped with two of them at the moment—a weirdo and his weirder Baptist pet."

I nodded again, whilst Steph peered at me with obvious curiosity. "So why did you break up with him?"

"Don't you know already?" I answered, my voice unwittingly edged with a hostility which Steph outright ignored.

"I want to hear it from you," she stated, keeping her gaze locked on me as she sipped at her beer.

So I told her. I told her about Zebedee's suspicions, Nomi's taunts, and Dom's assurances. I then told her about the party, the hospital, everything. I told her how I'd trusted Dom, only to be proven wrong.

"Proven wrong?" Steph asked.

"Well, Nomi and Zebedee were right. He is gay. Or bi, whatever."

"Did he tell you that?" Steph asked, her eyes narrowing, her gaze intensifying. I felt pressured—she was small, but I could feel her surrounding me, staring at me, demanding answers.

"No," I said, defensive to the point of shouting, "He told me he's in love with a man. A weird, geeky, supposedly-also-straight man. I suppose you're going to tell me that doesn't make him gay? That I should stay with him, in some weird little totally *heterosexual* trio?"

"If he didn't tell you he was gay or bisexual then he probably isn't," Steph replied, as calm as though we'd been forced into small talk. "I mean, he told you he's in love with a man. What else would be left to hide? It seems to me that there are two important questions here: do you love him? And could you accept him loving someone else at the same time?"

I nodded once more and changed the subject, but Steph kept her gaze on me, fierce brown eyes under dish-liquid hair.

At mine everything was entirely normal. Christina and Nomi were in our cheap Ikea kitchen and—according to Christina's open laptop—trying to bake hash brownies. Of course, neither of them knew how to bake, and were firing the opening shots of an argument when I came in. Both changed their expressions when I entered, a misplaced concern I didn't want.

"Caroline, where have you been?" Christina asked, throwing an assortment of uncake-like ingredients into a mixing bowl.

"I'm fine," I said, feeling the urge to block everything out and just relax, "I'd like to help you two bake. You're not going to manage it by yourselves, anyway."

"If you're sure..." Christina said, before turning and handing me a potato masher.

"I'm not going to need that."

So that's what we did, and Nomi shared gossip and the three of us ignored my break-up. I managed to guide the two of them into making something approaching cake, and the floor and walls coated themselves in flour and egg. But by the time we got

126

to mixing the batter I could see it was taking a real effort to keep Dom off their tongues. The glances they sent each other were shared more and more often.

"I've made my peace with it," I insisted. The two glanced at one another again.

The cake was cooling, and Christina had gone out when I heard Nomi call me into her room.

"Hello, Caroline," she chirped, picking up a top from her floor. "Does this smell clean to you?"

"What do you want? And no, urgh, fuck, Nomi, what is that?" I threw the top back at her.

"Fucking Zebedee," she growled, "he's been using my clothes to wipe up again."

"Wipe up what?" I asked her, moments before I realised the answer. "Gross."

"Will you fetch me something else to wear?" Nomi asked, gesturing toward the wardrobe like I was her maid, though she also winked at me to let me know she was being cheeky. I deliberately picked out the gaudiest thing I could find and tossed it over to her, but she didn't seem to notice.

"You're coming with me," she ordered.

I told her I'd already been shopping with her.

"We're not going shopping. We're going…" she hesitated for a microsecond, "out to lunch."

I didn't believe her, but I was bored and there was at least a hint of sun out the window. I wanted to know what the hell she was up to.

We started heading toward town. Very few people were on the streets, bar the odd pensioner, drunk, or drunk pensioner, so I saw Zebedee from miles away.

"Nomi, what is your boyfriend doing here?"

"He's coming to lunch."

"Nomi." I stopped and stared at her.

"Look, you'll feel better after this."

"After what?" I asked, but Nomi didn't reply and started walking. I followed. "We're going to Dom's flat, aren't we?"

"Look," she stated, "Zebedee is Dom's friend, he just wants to talk to him. And we're Dom's friends."

"No, we aren't. I'm his ex and you're—I don't know, you're his friend's weird girlfriend."

"We're going for moral support." She grasped my arm and pulled me forward.

Zebedee seemed just as surprised to see me.

"Why are you here, Caroline?" Zebedee asked me.

"She's here because this will be good for her," Nomi told him.

I felt weak. I knew there was no way I was going to just turn away and go home, so I just nodded. We all started walking toward Dom and Richard's flat, but no one said anything, so I was left wondering what the hell they were planning.

Apparently, what they were planning was some sort of fight. The door to the flat was unlocked (and strewn with camping equipment), so they marched straight into the lounge. By that time, it was just too late to leave. I stood there passively. And I stayed standing there as Zebedee tore into the one who was supposed to be his friend, and as Nomi threw in the odd comment for good measure. Then I sat down and remained wordless and motionless as Dom tried to reason with them, but I listened. I listened to him tell them that he wasn't gay, he just loved a man. Zebedee gestured toward me, displaying me as the prize Dom had missed out on. I watched as Dom looked at me with a faint glimmer of tears in his eyes. I heard Richard tell them that Dom still loved me and that he didn't want to steal Dom from me. There might have been more shouting, or it might have gone quiet, but after a while Dom told them that he didn't want to lose any of us, not his friends or his girlfriend. He looked at me again. He told me he didn't want to lose me. He said it didn't matter how he felt about Richard, it didn't change the way he felt about Zebedee. Or about me.

Nomi said we should leave. I watched Richard beg them to stay and talk so they could sort some things out. I saw Zebedee turn away and head for the door, then I felt Nomi snatch my arm and lead me out behind them. It was so cold in the street.

All of a sudden, I felt awake. Things felt clear. I knew what I wanted.

"They've really got a nerve," Nomi shouted, but I wasn't going to stay and listen to her rant. Dom loved me and I loved Dom. I felt tense, I felt stiff, and more than anything I felt determined. We loved each other, and maybe Richard would change that or maybe he wouldn't, but I couldn't just leave it, I had to find out.

I turned and ran back into the apartment, and somewhere behind Nomi called out in surprise, but I didn't stop. I ran into the living room and faced the two of them.

I'd made up my mind. We were going to try and make it work.

CANOLFAN. ABERTAWE. CYMRU
23 YEARS ON

"You'll have to leave soon," Steph reminded their friend. "You don't want to be late to your own wedding. Especially when there are two grooms to disappoint."

Caroline made a face. They wouldn't be late.

Music trilled from the table, through Caroline's bones. They and Steph were sharing the same track. A particularly high-pitched note brought them to a simultaneous shudder. The street outside filled with smartly clad young men and women, herded from the convention centre opposite. It was nice to see the city with a lot more wealth these days, but with the wealth had followed a hoard of obnoxious suited-up business-types, who spent their time in the more upmarket coffee houses lodged in the towers of the marina. Caroline always did their best to avoid them.

"You should be grateful for my company," Steph continued. "Catalunya's a long way away. Still, at least we're taking the boat. I couldn't stand to sit on a bus for so long."

The music picked up pace, bouncing through their bodies, moving up to the ribcage, each beat rushing up the neck, to the jawline.

"I thought you didn't believe in marriage," Caroline stated, sipping at a mocklassi.

"That doesn't mean I'll allow you to be late. You wouldn't even be packed if I hadn't stood over you." Steph gestured to Caroline's case. Caroline pulled a face again.

"You're not getting cold feet?" Steph asked, eyes narrowed. Caroline flinched. They hated it when Steph tried to analyse them.

"You've spent too many years in discussion circles," Caroline reminded Steph, flicking a few drops of lassi in their friend's direction.

The truth was that Caroline was a little apprehensive. They had never been one for marriage—well, not since they were six and imagined marrying Bugs Bunny, whom they'd had a particularly lengthy crush on. But they'd also gone over the arguments a thousand times over the past few months—this was different. This was different. Sure, Caroline didn't relish the thought of being anyone's

130

wife (although the idea of two husbands did have its appeal), but this was more than a wedding. It was a political statement. Who knew who long it would take before the poly marriage law was repealed? And there had been murmurs of legalisation in the Welsh Parliament. They had to lend their support—the first Catalunyan group weddings were to be uploaded and viewed across the globe. They felt their throat tighten.

"You know I'm kidding," Steph said, trying to maintain as disinterested a tone as was possible whilst keeping their gaze locked on Caroline. "You're doing the right thing. Stick it to the man and all that."

Caroline flicked more lassi at them. It didn't do to speak in ancient clichés.

The music thudded low through the stomach, a slightly queasy but not unpleasant sensation. Caroline looked over at the conference centre, which had finished emptying and was deserted, but for the legion of street sweepers who had appeared from nowhere, an army of orange suits replacing the grey, black, and trendy browns which had stood there five minutes before. Coffee cups and sandwich bags were swept away. Returning their attention to the table, Caroline noticed that Steph was still eyeing them.

"What is it now, Stephanie?"

Steph smiled, glad to have their attentions noticed.

"I was just wondering if you'd invited Sandra. It would make sense, given the theme."

Caroline hadn't invited Sandra, as Steph knew quite well. Both Steph and Caroline had each found themselves dating the same woman for a whole two months before they'd realised. After that they'd pledged to speak more often, if only to avoid such future calamities. This had led to a single degree of sex separation between Caroline and Steph, something which Steph had teased Caroline about numerous times, their elfin fingers poking at Caroline's sides.

"We could have formed our own trio," Steph said airily, making their fingers into a triangle.

Caroline pulled a face. The music spread down to their legs, in short, sharp hypnotic movements which were unusual for a café.

131

Caroline had never thought of Steph sexually, and Steph had never noticed them in turn, or at least not as far as Caroline could tell. Caroline preferred to keep it that way.

"Would you guys like a mood enhancer?"

They hadn't noticed the overly confident server approach, a colourful array of tabs balanced on their arm. Steph took one, Caroline didn't.

"Staying sober for the journey, eh?"

It was going to be a long one.

CHAPTER NINE

FLEE THE SCENE

RUTTI

"... I don't have time for this, Rutti."

"You won't make time for it."

"That's not fucking fair—"

"You want to know what's not fucking fair? I was there for you when things were looking bad with Dom. I've been there for you whenever you needed me. Am I wrong?"

"No, but I'm there for you too, you know that."

"Like hell you are. Now you're with Caroline and Dom that's it. When did we even last see each other? It was before you started playing trios, that's for sure."

"Rutti, I'm going to keep my patience. Will you do the same? I know I've not been about much, but if you really needed me—"

"Really needed you? Fuck, Richard, I've been needing you for months. I don't know where I am, Steph's hardly reliable, and now I can't even see you. Stop telling me you'll see me in a couple of days when it isn't true."

"Talk to me now, then."

"What?"

"Tell me what's wrong."

"I hate this city. I'm lonely. I feel like I'm going mad. I feel like the two of us have drifted so far apart we can barely even see each other anymore, and I fucking hate the scene, but I don't know where else to actually meet friends. I need to get out, but I have no idea where. And what if I feel exactly the fucking same elsewhere and the problem is me? What the fuck do I do then?"

"Rutti—"

The bar was tired, lumpen queens slumped over their cocktails whilst thonged dancers cruised the strangers they'd fucked a hundred times before. The same game, the same pseudo-anonymity, the end results identical every time, unless they were lucky enough to fight. Even the fag hags looked tired, cigarettes melting between their fingers as they watched their overweight gay husbands cavort. The scene digested itself. A man sat alone at the bar, good-looking and looking nervous, but I was tired of pulling closet bi guys. The last had walked right up to me, their first words "You wanna jerk off?" And they say romance is dead. I'd been on my feet for eight hours at the perfume store, and I was as exhausted as everyone around me.

Not Paul though. Paul was in their element, spirits and cocktail-filled hands raised high.

"A toast," they cried. "To my reunification with Tim."

"So, Tim's not going to cheat on you again?" I muttered, remembering Paul fleeing Richard's bathroom in tears. Paul ignored me, spotting the object of their reunification coming through the doors of the bar. Paul left to greet them without another word.

I awoke in the middle of the night. Craig the Christian was sitting up in bed, their eyes a faint glimmer in the dark. For the first time Craig wasn't in their pyjamas—the duvet covered their waist, but their upper body was bare, a goatee of hair in the dead centre of their chest, two moustaches around the nipples. I made

134

sure to look at Craig's face. It was then that I realised who Craig reminded me of—it was in their eyes. They watched me with a serious, intense gaze. I knew why I'd invited them to stay.

Like Richard I'd never been very popular in school—we'd bonded over that, a long time ago—but unlike them it wasn't because I was new. I just didn't fit, and never made any friends—right until I met Peter. I was almost a teenager by that point, and I'd grown used to things. Peter didn't make fun of me—*they* even defended me once in front of the brainless sport-obsessed boys. Peter was tall and had dark black hair with serious-looking eyes. Peter was popular and so by spending time with me I was that-little-bit-less unpopular. I was only bullied every now and then.

I wanted to hug Peter. I wanted to kiss them and press my body to theirs. We'd have sleepovers and I'd lie awake watching the rise and fall of their chest, wondering how it would be to sleep cuddled close. I didn't know what any of this meant or why any of it mattered, I just knew how I felt. I didn't even consider if Peter felt the same things—I believed they must have done.

One day they came round my house. We were watching cartoons on the sofa together. Peter was watching them with the serious look they had. I don't know why I did it then, but I leant over and kissed them. They didn't kiss me back. They just kept watching the television with their serious eyes.

The next day people stared at me in school—more than they usually did. I heard the girls whispering and then stop when they saw me. In PE the other boys changed with their backs to me. No one said a word.

Then I'd had names shouted at me. They were strange and alien and I had no idea what they meant. I just knew they were bad. Something terrible. Sometimes, when a teacher would hear, they would send the boy out the class. But it didn't stop.

One day I saw Peter in the locker room. I tried to talk to them, but they looked away, staring at their bag. Their loud, heavy breathing. Without saying anything they grabbed my neck and smacked my head against a locker. I was surprised. I pushed them. Peter punched me then pushed me down, then kicked me. One of the teachers walked by and found me on the floor. They asked me what had happened, so I said Peter hit me. I didn't say why.

I was called into the headteacher's office. I missed all my classes that day. The balding headteacher stared at me until the armpits of my school shirt were soaked. The headteacher asked me over and over about Peter. They asked me what we did together. They asked me what had happened when Peter was at my house. All I knew was that I'd done something terrible. I was terrified and told the headteacher nothing. For hours I told them nothing at all had happened. The headteacher said they had been in the military—there had been 'effeminate' men there. I didn't know what 'effeminate' was, but I didn't ask. They asked more questions, if I had been friends with any other boys. I told them no. There was nobody else. They told me that I wasn't to do anything like that again, that I was lucky worse hadn't happened. They would overlook it, just this once. When I was leaving, I saw Peter's mum and dad standing outside the office. They glared at me.

Unlike the other fights, the other jabs and kicks that went on in the school, Peter never got suspended. They never even got detention. What Peter had done was a natural response to the awful thing I'd done. I had attacked them first.

"Are you happy, Rutti?" Craig asked me, voice hushed.

"Are you happy, Craig?" I asked back. They simply stared back at me, a small movement of their hand somewhere beneath the sheets. I made sure to look at their face. A minute churned by before I spoke again. "Why do you ask?"

Craig sighed, focusing their eyes somewhere on the ceiling, gathering their thoughts. I leaned in toward them. Craig returned their gaze to me as they spoke.

"Rutti," they said slowly, "I want to thank you for having me stay here. You and Stephanie. It's been really nice of you. Of you both. I was planning on cooking you guys dinner actually, when you're both free. Honestly though, I don't know how to cook much."

"Well, we could see if Steph is around tomorrow," I suggested. "Food is food."

"The thing is," Craig started speaking slowly again, before picking up the pace, "I've needed to talk to you, on your own. No, I don't mean anything by it, I just noticed you've seemed kind of—kind of sad. Ever since I've met you you've seemed sad. It's there in the way you stand, the way you hold yourself, and you can see it in your eyes, in your expression when you're thinking. Is everything okay?"

So, they'd asked me if I was okay. They said I'd looked unhappy. And it might have been their posture, their body language, the look in their eyes-eyes or their expression, or maybe it was just me snared in a weak moment. But I told Craig everything.

I don't know why but I told them about my fears, about my concerns, about the terror I felt at turning twisted and bitter, about being shunned by guy after guy, about being alone—why I went back years, why I told Craig how I missed Richard, how I missed Richard more than I ever could have expected. I told Craig about Peter. I don't know why I did that. I just wanted—for that moment—to voice my loneliness. And it didn't matter who heard. Just that someone did.

Craig listened with patience and looked concerned. When I finished talking neither of us said a word. That was fine.

Then Craig leaned forward and hugged me. Their skin felt cool against my own. When they pulled away, they said, "Do you know what I've been doing earlier today?"

I shook my head.

They leaned over to the bag at the foot of the bed, pulled out a leaflet and placed it into my hand.

I read the title out loud. "*The Real Family*. I see homosexuality is mentioned." I felt sick.

"I know that you're unhappy," Craig said. "You can't find a connection with someone. It's because you're looking in all the wrong places."

I took a deep breath.

"Really? Because that sounds like a bunch of god-pushing bullshit, Craig."

"I'm just concerned," Craig answered, half-naked and serene. I could feel a tickle of rage forming in my gut.

"You'll not find love the way you're going."

"Did Jehovah tell you that?"

"Rutti, this isn't about God, or about my religion, or what you think about society. Those things are important but that's not what I'm talking about right now. This is about happiness. It's about fulfilment. And yeah, it's about love. You're never going to find those things if you carry on the way that you have been doing. You know you're unhappy, but you don't really know why. You think you do, but you don't. Do you reckon everyone else is as unhappy as you are? Do you think all those people who got married—those husbands you haven't been sleeping with—do you think they're as unhappy as you feel right now? Those people with kids, those people who have structure to their lives—do you think they're as miserable?"

"Yes."

"You're angry, I can tell. You're angry because you're hurt. You're hurt because you're hurting yourself." Craig paused for a moment. When they spoke again their voice was harder.

"I know I've not been here long, but I want you to think of me as a friend. And I know I come across as old-fashioned, but sometimes that can be a good thing. Not everything needs to change. Not everything needs to be different. Joy is important, and family is important. Yes, families come in all shapes and sizes—my own parents are divorced—but again there are those limits. You've got some weird notion about being different. And I don't just mean being gay, it's more than that—you make it more than that. You want to be different. The sad thing is, being different doesn't make you better than everyone else. It doesn't bring love."

"Love?" I interrupted. "I've been fucking born-again, Craig, and believe me, you have no fucking idea about love. All you know is fear and blind fucking obedience. You're obsessed with other people going to hell but really you're just afraid you're going there yourself. That's not love. That's self-loathing."

"It's love. Jesus loves you, and He loves me. I know He loves me because despite what's happened in my life He's been there and always made sure I made it through. That's love, that's real love. That's something you've forgotten, Gareth, but you can find it again. You can."

"That was all you. That was just you." The rage in my gut twisted into pity. "That's something to be proud of. But it's not love to hate people because they live their lives in a way you don't like. Some people are perfectly happy as they are."

I realised as I said it that I was guilty of the same thing. That same judgement. In that moment I saw things clearly. Some people are perfectly happy as they are.

Craig slowly stood up—they wearing their pyjama bottoms—and started to get dressed. "It's not too late. It's not too late for you. Just think about it." They picked up their bag. "Thank you for giving me somewhere to stay."

So, they left.

I was awoken the following day by my phone angrily buzzing against my bare leg, the space in the bed next to me strangely empty. It was Paul. They and Tim had already re-broken up, and it was my duty to spend the evening at the bar again consoling them. I relented, reasoning I could in the very least tell Paul about the drama with the Christian.

But when I pushed through the double doors to the bar, neck wet with 'I'm late' sweat and legs aching, I saw that Paul was already surrounded by a small court of followers, each of them paying rapt attention to every one of their hand movements, to each of the dramatic rolls of their eyes. I needed at least one drink before dealing with all that. I ordered a cocktail and took a place in the corner of a booth at the darkest, furthest edge of the bar.

I quickly finished the cocktail and ordered two more from the tired and slightly manic-looking bartender—the fewer trips I had to make to the bar the less my chances of being discovered. I wanted to see how long I could remain hidden. Over at the other side of the bar Paul gave a histrionic swoop of his arm, face contorted in an impression of pain. I kept an eye on everyone around me—a drag queen had ascended the stage and was busy taunting various patrons, so I placed strangers' coats about myself in an attempt at camouflage. In the booth next to mine a young twinky couple were engaged in heated discussion. I strained my ears, sipping at my sour drink.

"Fine, we can invite Philip for a threesome but—and I mean this—no kissing him for more than five seconds at a time. More than five seconds and it's like you're in love with him. He needs to know you're in love with *me*. No extended eye contact, no licking below the balls, and no face-to-face fucking him. Fine, if you have to then I want you to keep your eyes on me as you do it. And I swear to you if it lasts for more than thirty minutes we're never doing it again. I don't care if we've cum or not, pants are on after half an hour..."

The drag queen was mumbling into the microphone, lips curled into a smile, finger extended toward an irritatingly attractive guy preening themself at the end of the bar. The man's face flushed slightly and they pretended to fiddle with their phone. There was a clap of laughter from Paul's table, and Paul was looking wryly pleased with themself. Now and then I would duck into the toilets, following the occasional attractive guy inside, though each cock—foreskin, circumcised, foreskin, stubby, long—had failed to excite me.

I left via the fire exit, without waiting for someone to walk home with.

Rutti stared at the cock. This person wasn't too bad, almost the same age as themself, their penis short and stubby, satisfyingly thick. The man gave Rutti a shy glance before hurriedly zipping and leaving the bathroom. Rutti returned their gaze to the screen in front of their face. The advertisements were hard to understand these days, and harder to avoid. Rutti zipped up, grabbed their stick and stepped into the street, knee aching. This was their one concession to ageing: having a bad knee at forty-eight. They checked the time.

A wedding. Why would Richard be so thrilled about a wedding? Hardly anyone bothered getting married these days. More importantly, why had Rutti agreed to go? Certainly the fact that Catalunya was now performing legal polyamorous weddings was interesting—a term Rutti used to convey decidedly mixed feelings—but only to a point. It was a formality. All marriage was formality.

Rutti still had two hours to kill before taking the train—that was the real reason they'd agreed to go to Barcelona—they were excited to take the new direct Barcelona-Berlin maglev. They'd even told Richard that was the only reason they'd agreed to go and be best man. Best man. The very words made Rutti want to be sick. Rutti was neither. Rutti would order coffee.

The street outside the stained glass window was almost empty: Berlin was quiet these days. Rutti still remembered the chaotic, trashy city they'd first moved to. Don't be bitter. Don't be bitter. Cities are like any other organism—they change, they adapt. Berlin had simply adapted to an influx of wealthy, vapid rich wankers. Rutti had watched it painted, rents climbing, queer bars closing. Everyone else—everyone important—had already fled to Sarajevo, the newest 'poor but sexy' city of Europe. Rutti had stayed behind. Berlin was home. They'd built the Temple here.

The café was as quiet as the street outside: an old woman ate an americaner by the window, a well-do-to young couple were drinking lychee lattes behind. The only activity came from the dark room at the back, from which escaped a series of groans. Rutti took their coffee *from the counter and peered inside, to see four young people entangled together, arms and legs shared. Rutti made eye contact with one of them, and was tempted to go in, but instead decided on claiming the nearest table and drinking the coffee to the sound of the young, ecstatic moans.*

The coffee was good—no one would ever give up on coffee being shipped from the other side of the world, no matter how good the Latvian growhouses became. This was Rutti's concession to middle-class gentrification—the coffee. They didn't have coffee so good in Sarajevo. Rutti checked over their messages again.

Don't you not forget to give a righted speech. Keep it tory.

A speech of all things. Richard had also demanded Rutti wear a suit. A suit of all fucking things. The foursome groaned in sympathy. Well the speech wasn't 'tory' (Richard using English slang ten years out of date) and they'd just have to cope. Rutti had made enough in the way of compromises—the most excruciating being their tolerating Richard's thinly-veiled and deeply patronising sympathy.

"Don't you not worry about—about—" Richard had stammered, unable to even mention the names of Rutti's two lovers. Gods, it was only a break-up. It was sweet, in its own way, but Rutti had resented Richard's sympathies. Richard had never even had a break-up.

The foursome left. Rutti followed them.

Rutti would check in on the Temple. They made their way through the bitterly cold streets.

"A very fine day to you, Rutti," greeted Elia's reader. Elia didn't speak a word of English: they spoke into the reader in Estonian, beaming at Rutti. "Things are quiet, today."

"As always then," Rutti commented. They smiled back—it was impossible not to be cheerful around Elia.

"There's a ritual in the back. Some Belgian witches. They're in Berlin for the weekend."

Belgian witches. Last weekend it had been Dutch druids. These days the only visitors to the Temple of Intemperance were weekend tourists. Rutti and Elia headed to the bar together. Elia sat at the counter, Rutti went behind and served each of them a glass of wine, poured from the mouth of a life-sized effigy of Pan.

"Do they need anything?" Rutti asked Elia, motioning to the ritual room.

Elia shook their head.

"Won't you miss your train?" they asked.

"Probably."

"Rutti." Elia barked, the reader following. Elia looked at their friend impatiently. Rutti was always pleased to pull this reaction from them.

"It's not so important," Rutti replied. "It's just a little ego trip. Richard's making me dress formally. They're doing it just to torture me."

"You know that isn't true," Elia replied. "You know that this is important to them. Besides, you always talk about Richard. Richard Richard Richard. You wouldn't let them down. You know how it would hurt them."

"Maybe."

"Get going."

"Fine."

CHAPTER TEN

GIDDY AND STRANGE

RICHARD

It was the longest day of work I'd ever had. I was on the phones as always (for a long time they promised me something else but it never happened), and as always the room was loud and hot and too dry. The customers seemed angrier than usual. One woman even threatened to break my neck. "I will," she said, "I'll snap it right in two, you see if I don't."

"Madam," I replied, "We're an Internet Service Provider. We can't do anything about the fact that you've been barred from matchdate.com."

"Sir, I can only help with problems relating to your internet connection. I can't help explain how to upload pictures of your dog to your web page. Please sir, there's no need for that kind of language. If you can access the internet you're not having a problem with your internet connection. No, no, the breed of dog doesn't matter—"

By the end of my shift I was more than ready to leave. I arrived home to find a leaflet pushed through our front door. There was a black-and-white image of the burning club, with red lettering above and below.

FIGHT FIRE WITH FIRE

STOP ISLAM AND SUPPORT THE WELSH DEFENCE LEAGUE—BURNED CLUB, OCT 11th

"Dom?" I called. There was no answer. I found him in his room, lying face down on his bed. I sat down next to him and hesitated before I ran my fingers over his hair—it was a gesture I wanted to do, but some part of me was reluctant, and I couldn't quite put my finger on why. Dom rolled over and wrapped his arm around my waist, smiling up at me, his eyes red and puffy.

He'd been happier since Caroline came back, though of course he would have been. And I'd been happier as a result. In reality though, nothing felt especially settled—I had a strong feeling Caroline would leave, and Dom would be worse than before.

Dom sneezed into a roll of toilet paper he had with him in the bed.

"I'm not feeling well," he croaked, holding me a little more tightly before letting his arm go limp. I went to make him some tea, shoving the obnoxious leaflet into my pocket. I absent-mindedly wafted my hand through the steam as the kettle boiled. If things didn't work out with Dom and Caroline, then they couldn't carry on between him and me. I wasn't being pessimistic, I realised, that was simply how it was. It wasn't that I hadn't enjoyed the time we'd spent together during the breakup—the long nights talking, the company. But without Caroline things between us didn't work—without Caroline things between us *wouldn't* work.

I put my thoughts on hold for the moment and brought him the tea.

"Where's Caroline?" Dom asked me, looking helpless and confused.

"She's still at work," I told him, then left him to get some sleep. I went to my room and sat at the computer, ready to play something, the screen remaining blank. I nervously tapped at the enter key, finding the rhythm of the click-click-click somehow

145

soothing. I'd decided that if Caroline left, then I would follow her. I didn't want to hurt Dom, but if she didn't understand then what girlfriend ever would? How would I ever get a girlfriend myself if Dom's—who was already in love with him—couldn't handle it?

I thought about calling Rutti but decided against it. He seemed to have enough problems at the moment without me adding to them, and he wasn't the best person to go to for advice on straight relationships. He'd tell me to stick it out, to be a martyr to being different. He was lonely himself.

As soon as I thought it I felt bad.

Click-click-click.

The answer lay with me and Caroline. There was no one who could make Caroline comfortable with me better than I could myself. The thought brought me into a cold sweat, and I tapped at the key harder, pointlessly, dreading the thought of talking to someone who may very well have hated me. And beyond Dom, what did we have in common? There was no evidence that she liked computer games or board games—in fact I had very little clue as to the things she liked.

But we'd got along before. Perhaps we could again.

Before I had a chance to chicken out I picked up my phone and messaged her.

RUTTI

"This is your punishment," Paul informed me. I had not been there in Paul's hour of need—or rather, I had, I had simply been hiding in the back drinking cocktails by myself. I hadn't told Paul that—though it was hard to imagine the 'punishment' being any worse. A straight bar during a rugby match—if it wasn't hell then it was at least purgatory.

The pub was choked with the stench of cheap deodorant. There was some sort of testosterone-bleeding ball-kicking contest spewed out by the numerous large screens and eardrum-pounding speakers, and gangs of lager-soaked men were standing in groups howling at one another, all dressed in the same cultish colours.

"Mate," one shouted, "If our team win we're gonna get so bladdered we have an excuse to wank each other off and pretend not to remember."

"They better fucking win," another called, "My ego can't take another lost match. Sport is all I have left after squandering my life having kids and working a dead-end job. They'd better win or I'm fucking offing myself. Come on you, come on, kick it!"

Paul and I stood out like a severed head in a playground.

"Isn't this punishment for you as well?" I asked. Paul nodded without saying anything more. They seemed to take the point.

The next 'punishment' was actually quite nice, though I was careful to hide that fact from Paul, who was eyeing me triumphantly. It was one of the old-men-and-real-ale pubs, which were getting rarer and rarer, but this one held on, albeit with the addition of the obligatory big screens and expensive lunches. They were showing the same game, but at least it was on mute. We were the youngest customers in there, aside from a small group of black-clad Wiccans having some sort of meeting. I was tempted to leave and join them, but I was always more generally Pagan than specifically Wiccan. The whole god-goddess thing was much too hetero.

So instead we sat at either end of a lopsided oak table, sipping at our drinks—mine an ale, Paul's a vodka and lemonade—as elderly gents enjoyed their own grim silence and the young bartender fiddled with their phone. Paul tired of it before me.

"Fine, I think you've suffered long enough," they sighed, motioning me to follow with one hand and texting with the other.

We walked through the doors of the usual bar, to be mobbed by a gaggle of Paul's friends from the scene. I'd never really spoken much to any of them, and in turn they tolerated me as a quiet pet of Paul's.

We occupied a booth near some windows in the bar below

the club. I sipped at the tap water I'd ordered as the others compared the men they'd met there. I kept an eye on the toilets, but didn't see anyone worth following inside.

"Hello there guys, how're you doing? Is anyone sitting here?" I hadn't noticed the older man until they'd spoken to us. The older man gripped at the only empty chair at the table. They looked at us with a hopeful smile, but I could see the others assessing them: a belly, small wrinkles around the eyes, wrong clothes.

"Yeah, my good friend Piss Off," Paul cackled. One of the others threw their head back and guffawed.

"Yeah alright, fuck you too," the man said. I watched them go. They left the bar.

"The last thing I need is *that* hanging around me like a bad smell," Paul said, waving their arms to the words.

"He wasn't that bad," one of them said, "I've seen far worse."

"You've fucked far worse you mean," Paul responded. "Rutti, where the fuck are you going?"

I made my way to the toilets without replying. They were empty. I stared into the mirror and wondered if I looked old. *What was I doing?* I couldn't stand the people I was with. For a moment I looked into the mirror, past my own image. I felt the sharp scratch of a fingernail on my neck.

It was a drag queen. They didn't have their wig on, their short hair slicked back over a ton of make up. They were thrusting a glassful of dull brown liquor toward me. They were tall.

"Here, you look like you need this more," the drag queen hushed, before turning to the mirror and removing their make up, every wipe met by a small sigh.

"Thank you. I think. Do I look so bad?"

"No more than most in here," they said, turning to me. "You look fine, you just look sad."

"That's not the first time I've heard that this week," I confessed. "Besides, I'm pretty sure drinking won't help."

The drag queen laughed. "It doesn't hurt as much as most people make out, I'm sure of that."

"I'm Rutti."

"High Hopes. You know, I'm tall. I need to change it, I hate having to explain it to people. Anyway forget about my name, did you like the performance?"

"Sure," I lied, having not even noticed there was one. I downed the foul brown drink, making a considerable effort to force my face straight. They noticed.

"I'm guessing you prefer mixers."

I nodded.

"Well, then let's get you one," they offered.

"Look," I started, feeling exhausted, with visions of a late-evening awkward rejection bursting into mind. "You seem really nice, I'm just—"

"Oh no, no," the drag queen replied, "you're not really my type." They pulled me toward them, peering down my shirt. "Nope, not hairy enough."

I was relieved. I was offended.

"A drink it is."

"First though," Hopes uttered, pulling a lipstick from their handbag and guiding it toward my face, "You might actually smile if you have decent lips to show off."

I'd never worn lipstick before but I let them, staying perfectly still as they expertly smeared it over my mouth. What did I have to lose?

CAROLINE

I lay with my head on Dom's chest, feeling his fur against my face whilst gently circling his nipple with my fingernail. I could hear Richard in the other room making breakfast.

I won't lie and say that I knew what I was doing. I was worried. My boyfriend might have loved me, but he was in love with someone else at the same time—what the fuck *was* I doing? I could hear Nomi's voice in my head, telling me to leave.

You've gotta have some self-respect Caroline. Call yourself a feminist? Your boyfriend's got his own little harem.

But then there was the other voice, the one that told me I had nothing to lose, this one sounding like Christina.

Caroline, life is short. Live it. Experiment. If it doesn't work, well, you know you tried. You can only try.

I hadn't gone home. With the two of them doing battle in my head, it would have been too much to actually see them. And my confidence in my own decision was far too weak to stand up to sustained assault from Nomi. I'd sent her a single text, telling her not to worry, and that I'd contact her soon. I'd heard nothing back. I hadn't even gone into the postgrad office.

There was a clatter from the kitchen. Richard had dropped something—it sounded like plastic, not breakable. Dom stirred next to me, edging closer toward waking up.

If I'm honest, I felt guilty about not going back to the girls' house. The home the girls and I had made together had felt safe. We'd carried it with us. When we went out at night, we went out together—and we'd be a little safer when a man at a bar didn't get the hint, or would get angry when he did. We'd be a little safer when a drunk followed us home, calling at us and telling us to lift our skirts. If we saw a guy hit his girlfriend on Oxford Street we would hold hands as we called the police. We never stopped calling the police even though you would see it every Saturday night, some poor woman sprawled on the floor or being dragged by the wrist or even thrown against a wall, her skull hitting concrete with a crack. When the police came the woman would almost always deny anything had happened. The four of us would go home and make each other tea and drink it in silence. But we knew if we had each other then we wouldn't wind up like that.

So a part of me felt guilty—like I'd abandoned the girls and left us all a little weaker. And this situation—it wasn't safe, I didn't even know what it was. I loved Dom. Was that enough?

Yes.

No.

❖ ❖ ❖

When I woke up again I was late for work. As soon as I walked though the heavy doors to the bar, my boss cornered me and asked, with an aura of cold anger, where I'd been the last week.

"Caroline—Caroline are you even listening to me?"

I apologised to my boss and said that I'd be happy to work longer this week to make up for it. My boss looked less than satisfied.

"Give 'er a break yuh mean sod," Debbie the regular berated him. "She works 'erself to the bone for you, you're lucky to 'ave 'er."

I gave her a free drink.

On the way home I stumbled through the rain and stopped into Oxfam to buy some more clothes—and therefore more time before I had to return home and face Nomi. I noticed I had a text from Richard, asking to meet for something to eat. I was about to object, with the excuse of rain, but the sky was already clearing. Swansea was like that—filled with passive-aggressive weather. I couldn't think of a reason not to and so twenty minutes or so later we were at the chip shop. It was the only place we could find that we'd be able to afford.

Richard made me laugh. He had a way of relaxing you, of making you feel at ease, but gradually, in some way you might not notice. They brought over our food and Richard suggested taking it to the park to eat it in the temporary sunshine. The waitress scowled as she tipped our food back from the plates and onto paper.

"Do you get chips often?"

"I used to."

We made our way to my park, the one where I liked to sit and watch people. We sat there together for a while, watching the people go past and commenting on them, avoiding one another as the subject of conversation until I couldn't any longer, and I asked him a question I wasn't sure made sense.

"Is this how you expected things to go, Richard?"

I half-thought he'd look at me baffled, wondering what the hell I was going on about, but instead he just looked thoughtful, before giving me his answer.

"No. Not at all."

"Me neither."

And the two of us sat there slowly chewing chips, each of us in love with Dom but with no guide as to how to be with each other. What were we? He was my lover's lover. Sort of. There was a cold breeze blowing in from the coast, though there weren't yet any flecks of rain.

"Her, there," Richard uttered, his voice low, his head thrust in the direction of a jogger. "She's either thinking about—or currently having—an affair."

"Bullshit," I said, glad of the distraction. We'd both stopped eating.

"Honest to god. Quick, look—there, the way her hands are clenched, her whole body looks like she's angry—but then—her face, her mouth—look—does she look angry?"

"She looks tense," I said, not following him. She had almost reached our bench.

"Her mouth," Richard explained, his voice even lower. "What about her mouth?"

From her mouth she didn't look tense at all, even though her eyebrows were furrowed, and she was squinting. I said as much to Richard.

"Exactly. She's not unhappy. She's not—" he paused, waiting for her to pass by, "—not angry. Whatever she's thinking about is stressful but not unpleasant. Quite the opposite."

"Or maybe she's exhausted from the jog and thought of something funny," I countered.

"Maybe so," Richard replied.

"So when did you start reading so much into people's bodily gestures?" I asked, gently teasing him but also wanting to know something about him—Richard himself wasn't an easy person to read.

"Rutti. Who I used to live with. You met him, right? We used to do it all the time, though it was his idea. He's not as good at it as he thinks though, he presumes too much."

"You spend much time with Rutti?"

"Not these days. I mean, I did, when we lived together."

He started eating again, and I followed. He then stopped, chip in hand, thinking.

"I'd like to. It just seems awkward now. It doesn't quite work the same way. Maybe it was him moving out—which he'll probably tell you is my fault but was his, believe me—or maybe it's—" he paused, glancing at me for a moment, then resumed eating.

"It's what?"

He looked at me. He looked shy.

"Dom. I mean, Rutti's always been the closest guy in my life. And he liked me a lot. I don't think he'd have minded the idea of the two of us getting together. Then the second he moves out I fall for the new housemate. I doubt he'd admit it or anything, but maybe he feels he's been replaced. And maybe he has, who knows. Things aren't the same. I'm not even sure I'd want them to be. I do miss him though, and that feeling doesn't go away when I see him."

"Have you told him?"

"Fuck no," he answered. "What about you, anyway? You've not been home since—well, you know. You bought new clothes." He motioned to the bags by my feet.

I didn't think he'd noticed.

"You're afraid of going back?" he asked. "I would be. That friend of yours is frightening."

"She's protective," I replied, defending her despite myself.

"Very."

"I *will* talk to her," I told him. Suddenly it seemed very important to convince Richard of that.

"Make sure you do. If she's important to you, I mean. Gaps grow. Once you're distanced from someone it can be hard to gain the ground back. Don't get me wrong, I like having you in the apartment—just don't lose out on other stuff that matters."

We didn't say any more and we ate while the sun went down. The chips were cold but they tasted good.

"I do—I like you, Caroline," Richard stuttered, the chips and sunlight almost gone.

"I like you too, Richard."

It was a start.

DOM

I woke up with a full and very, very cold cup of tea by my bedside, my head pounding and my nasal passages on fire. I was sick, which was rare for the summer, but I was also very, very hungry, so I decided that the best thing to do was to get something to eat. With the cupboards bare and neither Caroline nor Richard anywhere to be seen, I decided to go and get something from the corner shop. On my way from the apartment I found a leaflet for the fucking fascist defence league, and I wanted to talk to Zebedee about it, he was the one I would always go to, so I decided: first food, then Zebedee.

The sky was a mix of clouds and the streets were wet, but thankfully it wasn't raining, or at least it had stopped—and I stopped into the shop and bought a soggy sandwich, limp inside its cancer-leaking plastic case. I'd just finished stuffing it into my mouth when I arrived at Zebedee's door. It took him a while to answer, and when he had I was left with the strong wish that he hadn't.

"What do you want, Dom?" he asked, staring at me coldly, colder than I'd ever seen him look at me.

I wasn't sure how to respond to him like that, the friend of mine I'd trusted and was always used to having an easy time with. So I simply stuttered out that I wanted to see him, to spend some time with him. You know, to hang out.

"We're not hanging out, Dom," he replied.

"Because you think I'm gay?" I asked him.

"You know it's not about that," he stated.

"Can I come inside?" I asked.

"Do as you like," he said, stepping to one side to let me in.

His apartment looked strange. Well, most of it looked normal—the kitchen was covered in pans furry with old food, and I could just about see into the bathroom down the hall, the once-white floor tiles now grey with grime. What was strange though, was Zebedee's bedroom—the floor wasn't covered in socks and plates, like normal—the floor was bare, barer than I'd ever seen it. It was clean. His bed wasn't a storage centre for old magazines and dirty laundry—it was neatly made. His desk wasn't covered in overflowing ashtrays, his cupboard wasn't in disarray, everything was neat and tidy, and it caught in my throat, this alien place, it scared me. It smelled of disinfectant.

"You tidied," I managed to get out, sort-of motioning over the space.

Zebedee sat at the edge of his bed and started to speak.

"I know you think I'm a homophobe—"

"I don't know what to think," I interrupted.

"I know you think I'm a homophobe," he repeated, "but I'm not. I'm not pissed off at you for being gay. I've told you that before. I'm pissed off at you because we've been friends fucking forever and you won't even tell me about it."

Why had he been cleaning so thoroughly?

"I love a guy, it doesn't make me gay, I mean, come on, I love a girl too. Both of them are important to me and they both want to be with me," I replied.

"For now," Zebedee said, his words clipped short, one hand clenched around his phone.

"What's that supposed to mean?"

Zebedee looked sheepish, though still somehow also bullish, like an indignant kid, and so he said, "I've been talking with Nomi. She says Caroline won't stick this out, she has too much sense. She'll come home sooner or later."

He let out a deep sigh, letting his phone drop by his side, before continuing.

155

"What're you doing, Dom? I feel like I can't talk to you at all. There's the Dom I knew, my regular mate, a bit too much of a hippy but who loved girls and loved his girlfriend, and then there's stuff as it is now, which isn't that. I don't know what it is, but it's not what it was."

I was going to say something but I didn't know what was right—I didn't know whether to agree or disagree. Was everything so different? I was still the same person, still the same guy Zebedee was always mates with, and I was still into women—but yes, something had changed, something was different, and I guess that—though I wasn't gay—I wasn't as straight as before either, whatever that meant.

"I just want you to go, Dom," Zebedee uttered, his shoulders hunched and his head sagged. I wanted to make things right, so I placed my hand on his shoulder, trying to comfort him, but he jerked back, his head snapped upwards, his face stern, almost snarled.

"Fuck off, Dom."

And so I did, I left Zebedee, I left his strangely clean room, and I slammed his front door behind me, my throat tight and my gut sinking, shaking with anger or hurt, or who the fuck knew what, and when I stumbled down the hill home and through our front door there was Richard, who saw my face and hugged me without a word, my head swimming, then he put me to bed and started making soup.

CHAPTER ELEVEN

OFF-WHITE FEMINISM AND LOW-FAT FASCISM

CAROLINE

Steph was seated among the others, under the harsh show-evcry-line lighting, her now-bronze hair declaring her the head of the circle. She looked triumphant, as the women around her chatted angrily, voices everywhere.

"Look," a large woman with short brown hair declared, pushing her chair back a little with a clatter over the tiled floor, "I don't know what your game is right now, Steph, but the Women's Circle is not for discussing relationships, not unless there's a serious political point."

Several of the other women nodded in agreement. Steph didn't seem put off in the slightest—in fact she shone as though everyone in the room was, in fact, praising her.

"No offence to you, Charlotte," the woman continued, getting my name wrong as everyone always did. "You're more than welcome in this group. I'm sorry Steph's put you on the spot like this."

I looked at Steph for help, but she didn't even seem to see me.

"This is political," she said, her voice slow and light, as

though she was making considered small talk. As though she were stoned. "Caroline is dating two men. Or rather, she is seeing one man who is seeing her and another man. She's worried about it, from a woman's perspective—from a feminist perspective." She paused to look around the room. The large woman looked thoughtful, taking a moment to glance at me. I cringed. It wasn't what Steph was saying—she was right, though I'd never expressed it in quite so many words—but to have a whole room full of people discuss my love life? What the fuck? What had I agreed to?

"Caroline came to ask me about it, but we should all be here to support her," Steph continued. "To give her our advice. What she's doing is *political*, we just have to find out what that means."

"Bigamy is patriarchal," cried a small, thin woman in an oversized hoodie. "He's a man with two wives—or a wife and a husband, though that doesn't make any difference—"

"We're not married," I said, but no one seemed to hear.

"—he's having his cake and eating it. He's taking everything for himself."

"Steady on," Steph countered, gesturing toward me. "Isn't monogamy also patriarchal? The whole point of monogamy was—is—to ensure the male bloodline. It's not really questioned though—we just get so-called feminists wearing a cream-coloured wedding dress instead of a white one, like it makes a difference. Sexual exclusivity is unnecessary in cultures following a female line. After all, we always know who the mother is."

"I don't go in for history—" the large woman began.

"It's not history—"

"But," the large woman continued, "Even if that's true, that doesn't make Charlotte's situation equal, does it? It's not *her* with two boyfriends. It's a man. It's she who has to share, not him."

I thought about that for a moment.

"I would never share my girlfriend," one of the other women declared. "Love is about fidelity and honesty."

Steph looked like she was about to speak when another woman joined her side.

"It sounds like the situation *is* honest. Besides, you're spouting opinion, you're not making a proper argument. Love isn't necessarily about anything. What love *is* is decided by society. If Charlotte's happy—"

"Even if she is happy, is she as happy as she would be with just him?" the woman in the hoodie replied.

"What do you mean?"

"I mean, there are degrees of happiness. It sounds to me like she's compromising so she doesn't lose him. She'd be happier in an exclusive relationship, but she's taken the option that makes her less happy in order to avoid short-term misery."

"No," Steph replied. "We can't know what will make us happy until we do it. It's not possible to make a conscious choice between degrees of happiness. What if this makes her more happy? Besides, half of you are socialists, the other half pretty much anarchists."

"So?"

"So," Steph continued, resuming her firm decorum, "What sort of world do you really want to see, anyway? Isn't it a little hypocritical to complain about property and ownership and then demand to own the person you love? Isn't sharing what it's all about? Kitty, you're a vegan—is it wrong to own animals, but okay to own people?"

"That's different," Kitty replied. "People can consent, the ownership is mutual."

"But uninformed consent isn't consent," Steph stated, growing a little wild. I didn't know she felt so strongly about all of this. "Most people don't know there's any other way. What if there is?"

"I wouldn't take that risk," the woman in the hoodie announced. "I wouldn't want to be an experiment for some man, like Charlotte here."

"She can make her own decisions," Steph stressed.

"Let's let Charlotte speak for herself, shall we?" the larger woman said, raising her hands to take control of the situation. "Tell us how it happened, tell us what you want from all this. In your own words."

I took a deep breath. I knew what I wanted, I knew what I had to do. So I told them, starting from the beginning—they were right, the situation was uneven, but I had a good idea of how that could be resolved. By the time I was done speaking even the woman in the hoodie was giving a small nod of agreement. My back ached from the cheap plastic chair.

"If you think that's best," she said. "I'm sure you know what you're doing. But be careful. If you're not going to look out for yourself then who is?"

RICHARD

I stood outside clutching a large holdall of leaflets, not really sure on what to do next. The meeting to organise the counter-demo against the defence league had been a good one—the people there weren't as militant as I'd imagined anti-fascists to be (not that I had anything against them). We sipped coffee and sat on wooden chairs from the 1950s in the old Quaker meeting house. They seemed down-to-earth and said sensible things about protecting Swansea's multicultural heritage. In fact, everything was fine until they went around the circle, with each person offering to fill a different position, to accomplish a different task. What could I do? I had no idea, and I could feel my face burn as they reached me.

"Just do what you can," the meeting's chair had told me. "Can you cook? Hand out leaflets?"

I chose the second one, and was one of the eight people who had been placed in charge of promotion, of handing out the 'keep Swansea racism-free' flyers. Thanks to us there would be two demonstrations at the blackened shell of the burned club. I'd attended the meeting for organising the counter-demo because I'd wanted to do something. It hadn't occurred to me that I might actually be able to. Where was I supposed to start?

I called Rutti, waiting in Castle Square for him to show up.

Dark leaves whirled about the ground, carried by an increasingly-chilly wind. I realised that the summer had mostly passed me by.

I tried handing out leaflets, but the few which people actually took were dropped straight to the floor, and picked up by the breeze, scattered around with the leaves. After a few dozen averted gazes, Rutti arrived, with Steph in tow.

"I see you brought an extra pair of hands," I told Rutti, greeting Stephanie with a brief hug. Her hair was a metallic-orangey colour.

"We have much more than that," said Steph, taking a stack of leaflets from me.

I asked her what she meant, but she was already bustling toward a young family wrapped in bulky, oversized coats, alluringly holding out a leaflet to their child.

"What does she mean?" I asked Rutti.

"Something good." He kissed me on the lips and took another stack.

It wasn't long before a woman in a hoodie arrived and took a stack, followed by a female couple, followed by a larger woman with short dark hair and an *OutRage!* t-shirt.

"I'm Richard," I introduced myself to each in turn. Each told me their own name, but I'd never heard of them. They strode around like missionaries patrolling a heathen land. I was amazed to watch them at work—each of the women seemed to have a knack for getting rid of leaflets, churning through a stack and then hurrying back to the holdall for another one.

"Come on, get stuck in," the larger woman ordered me. She watched as I held a leaflet out to a young man in a long black leather coat and goatee (who refused to take it), then to an old woman, (also refused).

"No, no," she instructed, as brusque as an old-fashioned school headteacher. "Wait. If someone sees someone reject a leaflet, they'll reject it too. People copy each other. If someone refuses to take one, wait until every single person who saw that is gone before you try again."

"Isn't that a waste of people?" I asked.

161

"Of course not. They'll reject you in an endless train otherwise. People are pack animals. Try again."

I walked up to a young couple and held a leaflet toward them. They glared at me.

"It's not working," I told the woman. I saw Steph return for another pile.

"It's easy," the woman explained. "Make eye contact as you approach them. Make sure not to break it. Smile at them, keeping your eyes locked on theirs, and swoop the leaflet into their hand in a clean motion. They'll take it every time, believe me. Go on, do it now."

I walked up to a woman dressed in a purple pullover with an oversized daisy on the front. Smile, eye contact, hand. She took it and wandered away.

"There you go," the stranger who was guiding me whispered. "Now to the next one, they've seen her take it."

It worked, though I didn't do as well as Rutti, Steph, and the others. Things were tense as a lone sick-looking skinhead tried to grab all the leaflets from the hands of one of the women, but the others quickly converged and drove him off, laughing as he fled.

"They're useless on their own," said Steph, "Scared little thugs. No one takes the full-fat fascists very seriously. The ones you have to look out for are the low-fat fascists, the more respectable-looking ones who sound a bit less racist at first but still believe all the same bullshit. They're the ones we have to look out for."

Rutti overheard and reminded her of the skinheads on the jetty. I could feel my body tense as I remembered the confrontation. *Faggots.*

"Don't get me wrong, they are nasty and dangerous," said Steph, "but they're not the ones who'll change people's minds."

"All right, ladies," leered a young man in a tracksuit as he went past. Steph motioned to him, as if to prove her point. The sky had darkened, and the breeze was starting to carry a drizzle.

"Well, I think we're done for today," called Steph. The

woman each motioned their goodbyes and scattered in different directions. Rutti and I sheltered underneath the awning to one of the grimy abandoned store fronts, taking cover from from the rapidly-thickening rain. It wasn't until the last of the women had disappeared that Rutti spoke, raising his voice against the bombardment of rain on the mould-stained canopy above.

"You know, I'm surprised at you, Richard."

I felt annoyed. I might not have been his level of socialist but I was hardly a fascist. Why shouldn't I help fight them off? I ignored the comment.

"I don't mean any offence," he said, obviously noticing the offence I'd in fact taken. "It's good to see. How is everything with you, anyway? On the Dom and Caroline front?"

I told him that I had no idea. If Caroline left, then I would leave too.

"Touch and go then?" Rutti asked.

Things felt far less 'touch and go' that evening, when I arrived into the warmth of the apartment to find Dom cooking and Caroline pouring wine into three glasses, each perched at the edge of the coffee table. We decided on a film. At first the politics of seating froze us once again into indecision—the sofa had two seats. We stood and looked at one another, just waiting for the whole scenario to collapse, for someone to storm out, for shouting. Instead I offered Caroline and Dom the seats, then as we sat down I rested against Dom's leg, sitting on the floor.

We barely stayed that way for half an hour. We were talking so much, the excited, frantic, nod-heavy talking of the newly-reacquainted. We abandoned the film. Dom gently eased Caroline and I aside and jumped up and out of the room, returning with a near-full bottle of whiskey and three mugs. A few drinks in and Caroline told us about her childhood, the bumblings of her dad and the loss of her sister. We talked about family, the loss of my dad and Dom's uncle Ron, who had apparently died last year. We indulged in that long, useless, beautiful drift of words about aspirations, let-downs, fears. And so we just talked until late. Above that clank of glass we talked.

DOM

The three of us spent the evening together, talking and drinking like it had always been that way, cosy and warm and intimate— all of that, with Caroline leant on my shoulder and Richard against my knee. I could feel his hair in my hand, her breath on my cheek, and all of us yammering away about everything, the hours dropping by and lulling me into security, a security which was broken when Richard went to bed and Caroline told me that,

"We need to talk," a phrase which is never good, a phrase used to bring about an ending. But why? I wondered, when we had been getting on so well. Was the evening some sort of goodbye? And so I worried, I worried whilst we brushed our teeth and Caroline went to my bed and I picked fluff from my belly button. I worried as I climbed in next to her, placing my arm around her shoulders, thin and clad in an oversized t-shirt which smelled of fusty cupboards. I didn't want to talk, I didn't want to break up, but at the same side I couldn't be silent, I had to say something. Finally I asked,

"So what do we need to talk about?"

She sighed, a long drawn out sigh, a sigh which was also not good at all.

"Look," Caroline explained. "I like Richard. I do. And to be honest, I didn't think I would be, but I'm perfectly fine with you guys being together. The problem is that it's not equal—"

I started to say something but she continued, squeezing my arm as she did so.

"It's not. Maybe it would be if Richard and I were in love— but we aren't. I like him, but I still don't know him, not fully. So at present that puts you in a position of power. You're with two

164

people you love. Do you see what I mean?"

I nodded slowly, feeling a lurch deep down, right in the pit of my stomach. So this was it, this was the real break-up conversation, this was the moment I'd lose her. I still didn't know what to say, so I just looked at her, not wanting her to leave.

"I want to see other people—"

This was it.

"—as well as you," she quickly added. "I love you and I want to be with you. With you and Richard. But I need to be able to date other people as well, or at least to try it. I love you and I'm still yours, but if I'm going to share you then you're going to have to share me too."

I nodded again, knowing that it did make sense, but at the same time not knowing how I felt about it—it was fair, sure it was, but it felt like losing her, like she was slipping away from me. She squeezed my arm again, this time leaning forward to kiss me at the same time. She knelt on the bed in front of me. Other men with Caroline.

"I've been talking about it with Steph, and she doesn't agree, but I think it's best to keep each other informed of everything. Every detail. None of this 'don't ask don't tell' rubbish. This is something we need to share."

"Sure," I replied. When had she been so assertive? Not that I minded, I didn't, but it was different. She placed her arm around me and I nuzzled into her armpit, then her breast, through the soft musty shirt, feeling the warmth of her through it, breathing in every time she breathed out, the scent of her breath on my tongue. I kissed her, the slow, light-tongued kiss of the soon to sleep.

Slowly and more than a little drunkenly I did fall asleep, all the while wondering whether a break up had actually taken place or not.

I lay back on the grass of the old quarry up the hill. The city centre was spread out before us, a haze of yellow lights swarming around a neon glow, with the occasional siren or drunken bellows from the closer streets. I pulled my blanket around myself as a sharp breeze buffeted our backs.

"Soup?" The thermos was held under my nose and the stench made my eyes water. High Hopes sloshed it into my mug. Steph held theirs up too. It was too dark to see. I was enjoying it, this night-time picnic—it felt like being teenage, just with less despair.

"So what's your real name, Hopes?" Steph asked, blowing into their cup.

"I just use Hopes," they answered.

Hopes had arrived at our house wearing eyeliner. I never knew how to feel about make up—on men it can range anywhere from interesting to tired, on women it just seems oppressive and faintly ridiculous. Aside from that they'd just been clad in jeans and a simple short-sleeved shirt. Their voice held a high-pitched ring and I imagined it didn't change much for their act. Their blond fringe hung in a fierce swoop over their face.

"I thought drag queens didn't use their drag name when dressed, well, not in drag?" Steph asked.

"I don't know," Hopes responded. "I've not been at it all that long. Besides, I'm not using the full name, exactly."

We heard a roar of male voices floating down the path to the other side of the blackened trees. The three of us remained silent, staring down at the city until they were gone.

"So where are you from, Hopes?" Steph asked, their voice low for yet another of the endless line of questions they always threw at new people.

"The valleys," Hopes replied, their voice also hushed low.

"And you survived?"

"Just about," Hopes answered. "I was probably less effeminate then though I suppose. Besides, is it really much worse than here?"

The chorus of heavy shouting now came from the streets below.

"So it's my turn to ask a question," Hopes announced, now raising their voice a little against the wind. "How do you children know one another?"

"An evil curse," I answered. Hopes laughed, a laugh which was deeper than their usual voice.

"I like you," they told me.

"Don't," Steph warned, "he's full of himself as it is."

"Well Steph, I want your number. Never mind why. Here, write it in—there, on my phone. Unfortunately I have to leave you wonderful people. There's something I want from you both though. I won't tell you now, next week perhaps. I'm not sure which of you will find it more difficult." With that, Hopes kissed each of our cheeks goodbye and bounded down the hill.

"Are you sure you want to go alone?" Steph called after them, but there was no answer back. For a moment the two of us sat side-by-side, gently fighting over the blanket.

"He seemed nice. Better than the last person you brought along."

"Absolutely," I replied. "They brought us food."

Steph held the thermos aloft like an award in response.

We sipped at the last dregs of the soup, listening to the singing spilling from one of the nearby houses.

I saw Hopes again the following night, after a long shift at the perfume palace—seeing Hopes was getting to be a regular thing, and I was starting to wonder if I'd actually managed to perform the impossible and dig up a decent friend from Swansea's gay scene. In fact, the city's scene was expanding—we were at a new bar which had opened up on the High Street, amongst a fanfare for the increasingly visible gays. This bar was closer to the centre of the city, away from the dark and homophobe-clogged alleyways of the marina. This bar wasn't to be hidden away. Somehow I'd missed all the news about the opening—I suspected Paul had kept it from me, though I wasn't sure why. Hopes, of course, had known all about it.

The new bar looked similar to the older one, but the walls were a bright blue and the drinks a little more expensive. I was fairly certain that the bar staff were the same ones who served in the old place, though that was hardly surprising—the scene recycled bar staff endlessly. They were kept on their feet darting back and forth making sure the cuter men got their drinks.

We hadn't been there long but already it was a busy night. Drunk twinks slathered their hands over each other while surly bears watched from the background. Hopes watched them with me under a heavy dose of eye make up, adding their own long commentary. They nodded toward the group of bears.

"God bears suck. Look at them, judging the bodies they think are too skinny. It's hypocrisy is what it is. I once heard that the bear movement was set up, like, way back in the seventies because the heavier, hairier, and older men didn't like feeling judged, but the sad fact is that most bears are far more image-conscious than even the twinks. They're certainly not afraid to let you know if you fail to live up to their big manly expectations. No, I'm being unfair, they're not all like that, but the ones around *here* certainly are. Here they just want to be safe and look normal—who can blame them for that? So those of us who dress in drag, we make them look bad by association. Even just being skinny makes them look bad in the same way, because skinny means weak and weak means faggy. Being big and hairy, even if you're camp as a Tory minister, it makes you a man. At least in their eyes."

Hopes took a deep breath. "The whole thing is sort of fucked up anyway. It's not like they're the only ones judging people—I mean, any one of those twinks over there would judge someone wearing the wrong clothes, who didn't look like a waify mannequin from some bland chain store. Even some of *them* hate the drag queens—to be honest I did, back in the day—and I suppose it's the same thing, the wanting to look normal and

168

not look bad by association. You can see the same little clubs and judgements among the lesbians, but maybe it's less extreme or something, I don't know."

I nodded along, doing my best to not smile. I didn't want to seem too enthusiastic toward Hopes, in case it turned out they weren't real. They were about to introduce me to a handsome but tired-looking bartender when I felt a hand on my back. It was Paul.

"Hello stranger." Paul gave me a hug.

"Hello Paul." I hugged them back.

I wanted to introduce Paul to Hopes but when I turned around Hopes had gone.

"You here all by your lonely self, then?" Paul asked, barely masking a look of delight.

"I guess so."

Without saying another word I left to look for Hopes.

CHAPTER TWELVE

LIPSTICK AND DUNGAREES

RUTTI

I found Hopes at the other end of the establishment, chatting to another member of the bar staff. It was dark in that corner, lit by a single overhead lamp above the bar.

"I thought you'd gone," I admonished, doing my best to maintain a casual voice. The bartender went to serve a small gaggle of twinks and their companions.

"I saw a friend of mine. Besides—" Hopes began, interrupted by the arrival of Paul, who looked Hopes—standing directly beneath the single light—up and down, a small sneer forming at the sight of their make up. Hopes introduced themself, undeterred.

Paul politely but coldly regarded Hopes. Paul told Hopes that they'd seen their drag act, then turned their attention to back to me.

"So where've you been?" Paul asked, continuing before I had a chance to reply. "It doesn't matter anyway. We're back together. Me and Tim. We worked it out." They were expecting congratulations.

I didn't say anything.

It annoyed them. Paul had never had to hide their emotions, and they never did. Their eyes narrowed and jawline tightened, and a part of me—a large fucking part of me—was pleased by the reaction. To not say the right thing at the right moment was worse than an insult, to Paul at least. I wondered what they would say, my limbs tense.

"Well, not that you'll care," Paul sneered. "You'll still be too hung up over that straight ex-roommate of yours, I understand. Well, that and..." they stalled. There was a mean glint in their eyes.

"And what?" Hopes asked, clearly already frustrated with Paul, their dress shining beneath their own private spotlight. Hopes was poised in a manner I envied—like a glamorous waxwork, as though it took no effort at all, hand on hip, head askew, lashes long.

"Well," Paul continued, dwarfed by Hopes and only half-visible. "You must be working on your whole pretence-at-isolation thing. You think I haven't seen you, sitting alone? You don't even want friends, much less deserve them. The amount of time I've spent on you, Rutti. Who else would have, aside from that lesbian dog of yours. But fuck it, whatever. You clearly had more important *things*—" they looked at Hopes, "—to do."

There was a moment of silence before Hopes smiled, red lips spread wide around a tooth-crowded mouth.

"Pay attention, you vertically-challenged mouthpiece of insecurity. I'm sure Rutti here is plenty ashamed to have made the mistake of letting you into his personal life, but frankly I'm more ashamed that you have so little in your own existence that you even gave it a second thought. You just said you got back with whoever it was who is equally insecure enough to have a relationship with you, and it surely can't be working out out too well if you're having to distract yourself with nonsense like this. You and your little boyfriend will break up again soon, I'm sure, but that's certainly not Rutti's problem. You have the emotional development of a suburban teenager. Fuck off."

There was another quiet moment before Paul swore and stormed away. I wasn't sure what to think: I felt vaguely pleased at Hopes's outburst but worried at what Paul would say later.

"That's exactly what I'm talking about," Hopes said. "Too many arrogant little fucks like that on the scene." They noticed my concern. "Oh, please, don't worry, I'm not that mean or anything. But I had to be harsh or you'd never be rid of him. And believe me, you want to be rid of him."

I watched Paul leave the bar, their face a furious shade of red. I made my excuses to Hopes and headed to the toilets. I stood in a cubicle and pulled out my phone, searching for Paul's name. I'd scrolled down 'A' through to 'M' before I put it back in my pocket and went back out into the noisy room.

It was the following week before Hopes revealed their surprise. I'd received a message simply stating:

Come over. We're dressing up.

I honestly hadn't felt too keen, but I didn't want to offend Hopes. I was fast running out of friends.

It's not that I thought dressing up in women's clothes was wrong—I've always felt that gender is an illusion, a construction after all. At least that was what I believed. But to do it myself made me uneasy. It was no longer pure theory, it was no longer just words. Then there was the fact that I had trouble enough meeting guys—did I really want to add transvestism to my list of off-putting quirks?

I had arrived at Hopes's house, palms sweating, the streetlight outside broken and flickering. I'd slowly felt my way up the path in between the bright-orange flashes. I couldn't see lights on inside. I'd pressed the bell.

"Rutti," Hopes had answered, planting their lips on my cheek. They were clad in a kimono and clutched a cocktail in their right hand as they pulled me inside with their left. They'd led me down a dark hallway which was decorated in a myriad of traditional watercolours overlaid in felt-tip, stuck over peeling

172

wallpaper. The hallway opened up into a main room.

"Take this," Hopes had demanded, thrusting a drink between my fingers.

It was about three parts gin to one part bitter lemon. I'd downed it. Hopes quickly replaced it and directed me to their dressing-up box.

It was working: the warmth spread through me. I was on my third drink. I felt half-naked and self-consciously vulnerable, a bra above my jeans, standing in Hopes's kitchen-cum-lounge. I kept envisaging Paul in the corner, watching with malicious joy. Hopes was trying on a bright-blue wig and a Japanese dress.

"So do you dress up outside?" I asked, feeling awkward in the bra and jeans. "I mean, out in the street?"

"Sometimes." Hopes replied, reapplying lipstick.

"Don't you get trouble?"

"Of course." Hopes took the blue wig off their own head, placed it on mine and followed it with a pink cowboy hat. "Perfect. Look." They turned me toward the cracked and grimy full-length mirror propped against the kitchen cabinets. I hoped they couldn't hear the nervousness in my laughter.

"You're going to have to dress up properly though," they informed me. "Let's find you something more glamorous." They started rummaging through the dressing-up box, muttering and throwing clothes about the room. I went to pour myself another gin, sugar, and tonic.

"Here," Hopes said, holding up a garish floral-print dress, black with pink and red flowers. They placed it into my hands. The static shot my arm hair on end.

"Try it on," they instructed. I slowly took off my jeans, hoping they didn't notice my fingers trembling, followed by the cowgirl hat. I pulled on the dress, wrestling it down, smothering my arms and body. It clung to my skin. Hopes burst out laughing again.

"Oh, that's just lovely!"

I looked at myself. The dress followed my shape as I pulled it straight. Hopes placed a garish handbag over my shoulder. I was just about to comment on it when the doorbell rang.

I could see something suspect on Hopes's face. I asked them who it was.

"A surprise," they giggled, jogging to the front door.

No, I thought. No, don't let it be—

"Hi, Rutti," Steph greeted, a large grin over their face. I felt an uneasy queasy sensation at Steph's being there, as though they'd walked in on me on the toilet, but it wasn't going to ruin the evening—besides, dressing in women's clothing was drag for Steph as well.

"Take whatever you find," Hopes instructed Steph, "except something red, I want my next colour to be red. Go on, Rutti, you too."

I carefully picked out some silver leggings and a faux-fur jacket, placed my trousers over the back of the battered stained couch—the likes of which were an omnipresent feature amongst our poverty-straddling generation—followed by my jumper and t-shirt. I felt too thin, naked. I squeezed on the leggings and clad myself in the ersatz corpse coat.

"Delightful," Hopes declared. They were busy dressing Steph, who looked at me and laughed.   Hopes made one or two adjustments before presenting Steph in an evening dress. It suited their body but looked unnatural on them, like animals dressed as tasteless humans. The two of us applauded.

A few more outfits and we found ourselves—Hopes and I— mixing cocktails in the kitchen. They were sternly concentrating on the jug and wooden spoon.

"So, Hopes," I began, "surely performing at the dingy bars round here doesn't pay the bills. Do you have a day job?" Dole. I had them down as being on the dole, like most of the city.

"I have more of a night job," they said, sipping their creation and adding lemon juice.

"Whereabouts?"

"St. Helen's Road."

I knew the place. Perched above the late-night kebab houses and Islamic book stores. Pink neon and a corporate rabbit's head. There were three more of those places within a five minute walk. But Hopes wasn't the first sex worker I knew in Swansea so I let it drop without any irritating questions. As they gave the cocktails a final stir, I noticed the small faded slash-scars on their forearms and wrists—another generational feature. They covered themself with a tasteful blood-coloured muppet-fur jumper.

We changed outfits until we reached the bottom of the clothes chest. I felt more and more comfortable as the chest emptied, and less and less exposed. It actually started to feel good. Finally Steph announced that they had to go to work in the morning. We searched for the clothes we had arrived in, and changed back piece by piece.

When we reached the door Hopes told us they'd had a lovely evening.

"Me too," I told them, genuinely meaning it. Steph was already heading down the front path.

"Oh, I have something much bigger planned for you, Mr. Rutti. No, no, I won't tell you now, it would ruin everything. You'll have to wait. What else is there to do around here?"

CAROLINE

I felt better for having asserted myself—for asserting my right to date outside of the three-way relationship. When it came, it came—I wasn't specifically looking for anyone right then, but that wasn't the point. What mattered was that I wasn't a part of some harem, that I was as free to fall in love as Dom was. So I'd proclaimed my space, but there was still the problem of physical space—of our shared living situation. And I did my best, I tried to leave my mark on the flat. Firstly, I told Dom I was taking down the posters of half-naked women from his wall. They were crude and unless he made a habit of standing by his bedroom wall and masturbating, I couldn't see the point in them being there. He grumbled a little, but relented. Richard and I

175

had taken the pictures down one by one as Dom stood around and sulked. Richard had gathered the scattered pictures up from the floor and sorted them into a neat pile for Dom. Dom took them and put them into the bin in the kitchen. He had an old wall hanging which we put up instead. It was frayed but quite charming, and had just been bundled up and shoved under his bed. The room looked much better. I had cleared a space for my clothes in his wardrobe, having almost bought an entire new set of second-hand outfits from Oxfam.

But I missed my own home. I missed living with the girls.

"You have to take action," Steph told me, the noise of the tavern blaring from inside.

I was about to ask her what exactly she expected me to do when she added, "Alright," setting her glass down on the wooden bench. "Well none of your old friends will come see you at Dom's place, that's obvious. It's walking straight into your territory and it's admitting they were wrong. But you know that leaving for Dom's makes it look like you're in the wrong and like you're running away, right? You know that, right? Say you give them a chance to come talk to you. Say we went and spent the rest of the evening in your old room. We could pick up some wine and drink it there, and if one of your friends comes to talk to us then that's great, if not then you've shown you're not afraid of them and we've had a nice evening drinking wine. What do you think? Is that a plan?"

It made sense. I still thought that as we wandered round the convenience store actually looking for wine. It did make sense. Even so, my stomach lurched as we reached the front door.

The lights were off in the hall but I could hear people moving around in the bedrooms upstairs. They were definitely home. The hallway was littered with mess: papers, an ashtray, a teddy bear with a giant novelty cock. We fetched two glasses from the deserted kitchen. As we walked up to my room I just kept hoping we wouldn't bump into them, but Steph's footsteps were especially heavy and loud, as though she were trying to tell me that this was the whole point: they should hear us.

My room. It felt familiar but I realised that I had left. I was still paying the rent, but the tenant here was invisible, the ghost of the woman who would never have gone to stay with her lover and his lover. I expected to feel uncomfortable in there but I didn't. It didn't feel like my room, but it did feel like the room of an old friend.

"Right," Steph said as we entered. "Let's stick some music on." Before I had chance to react she'd already switched on my radio and let it blast out Radio Six through the highest volume the tiny speakers could manage. She opened the wine and poured it into the two glasses.

"Now we have to wait. So what shall we talk about?"

I shook my head as I picked up my glass.

We had finished one of the two bottles and Steph was just telling me about the women she had dated in Swansea when there was a small knock at the door. For a second I wondered if I'd heard it, but then it happened again. They were more taps than knocks, three quiet taps.

"Come in," Steph called. I held my breath. I expected to see Nomi with the same angry expression I'd last seen her with, standing furious in my doorway.

It was Christina. She stopped for a second as I stood up in front of her. Then she stepped forward and kissed me on the cheek.

"Where have you been all this time?" She pretended to look angry but broke out into a smile. "It's good to see you, why didn't you call me?"

Steph put her coat back on and crept toward the door. She softly said that she would see us both later, and then left.

"Tell me," Christina said, "Tell me what you've been doing."

So I did.

"And that's all?" she cried. "I wish you had come to me, I am not Nomi. Do what makes you happy, don't worry about the other things."

"And Nomi?" I asked.

Christina pulled a face.

CHAPTER THIRTEEN

ABDUCTING RUTTI

CAROLINE

I was moving back into my room. Even so, Nomi made it clear she wasn't speaking to me—my time away was a betrayal, and so when I saw her in the corridor she offered a curt 'hello' before disappearing behind her door. I could hear her on the phone to Zebedee.

Christina and Steph helped repaint the walls of my room. Steph had insisted, because, given the circumstances, I had to 're-mark my territory'. So the walls were, section by section, going from white to green. I had already thanked Steph for her help in getting me back in the house, but she dismissed it—she said that all she had done was go drinking at a friend's place. She was actually still drinking, having brought beer round for us to down whilst painting.

The cracks and crevices in the wall were slowly being obscured, but made the task of getting the paint nice and even that much more difficult. Steph had taken my heavy curtains down, and the room was flooded with low early-autumn light. We were dressed in bin liners to protect our clothes, which were already dappled in green specks. We rustled with every movement, and the liners were hot, so I had only my underwear on underneath. The plastic rubbed against my skin, and the newspapers we'd draped over the floor kept sticking to my bare and painty feet. Even so, we were making quick and noisy progress.

"You are lesbian, Steph?" Christina asked, doubled over to dip her roller in the dripping paint tray.

"Certainly," Steph replied. "Why do you ask?"

"I was with a woman once," Christina casually revealed, slopping paint onto the wall. I was shocked into a moment's silence. Christina never really said anything about herself. I wanted to know more, but I really wasn't sure how I could ask. Thankfully she needed no further prompting.

It turned out that back in Barcelona she'd had this boyfriend. They'd fallen for one another in school, after some sleazy bloke at a party had tried feeling her up—against her will—and she'd thrown said sleazy guy down some stairs, right on top of the unfortunate soon-to-be boyfriend who'd happened to be standing at the bottom.

Christina took a moment to dip her roller in the paint tray again, then restarted, her voice straining as she stretched for the higher sections of wall.

She had been seeing her boyfriend for some years, but eventually they just stopped getting on and mostly even stopped speaking—somewhere along the way their words had 'just vanished' and there was nothing left to say to one another. Christina had, though, gotten to know his cousin, who was staying with him for the summer, and she and Christina started to spend more and more time together. When her boyfriend had passed out stoned, the two of them would drink wine and giggle and laugh at his bad music collection—"Made up of so much angry skater boy music." Christina said she felt a spark between them (her actual words were *a fire*), and one evening, the boyfriend had fallen asleep in front of one of the action films he loved but which bored her to tears, she had simply walked into his cousin's room, and then,

"And *then*," Christina finished, a wide smile and her eyes sparkling. "It was the only time so far, but I liked it." She returned her attention to the paint tray.

"Wow," I said, not sure what to say to her in return. I'd been attracted to women a few times but had never acted on it.

"You should stick with it," Steph said, "I was never into men. Not like poor Caroline here, with *two* of them."

So I had my room back. I hadn't been sure at first—I had practically moved in with Richard and Dom—to move back out again seemed as though, well, it might look like I was leaving them. It wasn't the case, not at all, I mean, I loved Dom and I was happy. But I knew how it would appear.

And if they'd had three bedrooms in the flat then maybe I would have fit, but sharing a room with Dom was too cramped. Perhaps it was because I'd spent so long with my own, but I needed somewhere to run to when I wanted space. There was nowhere I could go and read a book without being interrupted. And some nights—just some—it's nice to have your very own bed and to stretch your arms and legs as far as you can into the corners. After a week I told Dom I was keeping my old room. I told him I loved him, but it was something I had to do.

Christina had been delighted when I'd told her I was coming back, and had given a high-pitch squeal. Once I'd convinced him that we weren't breaking up, Dom said he was happy with whatever made me happy. I knew he was being honest: Dom's feelings are on the outside, like his clothes, where they can be seen. It was actually more difficult with Richard; he told me he'd rather I stay, though he did concede that he wouldn't want to share a room with Dom on a full-time basis either.

"I've enjoyed living with you both. I mean that," I told him, setting my bag down and leaning over to hug him.

"You're only going to be ten minutes away," he joked. "You have to leave?"

"I have my own territory. Besides, I miss the girls."

"You'll still be coming over? I mean, you and Dom—"

"Dom and I are still together," I told him. "You'd be the first to hear about it if not."

Richard looked subdued.

"Richard," I continued, "I'm not ready to move in with you

both. I'm not. That doesn't mean I'm not happy with us three. I mean, what the two of us have together beyond Dom, I don't know, but I'd like to see. You're a sweet guy, Richard." I leaned in again and kissed him on the cheek, for a moment welcoming the warmth of his skin.

"I may well be back in the future. Who knows?" I added.

"Who knows," he repeated.

RUTTI

Hopes staunchly refused to tell me where we were going—a worrying fact considering it was dark and we were getting on an intercity bus. They had a large camping-style rucksack on their back, marking them as some strange make up clad turtle. They insisted we weren't going camping.

"So where are we going?"

"Rutti, for the millionth fucking time, you're going to have to wait and see."

"The tickets say Bristol."

"Then we're going to Bristol."

Hopes had simply and mysteriously told me to gather a bag of overnight things, as 'For some reason the fucking buses stop at midnight.' I had a small bag with me containing my toothbrush, toothpaste, deodorant, phone, spare underwear, spare t-shirt, spare socks, and some gum. The bus station had been quiet, the bus even more so. Now Hopes was trying to fit their oversized bag into the overhead storage. We were wet from the rain, water sliding down their arms and dripping from their elbows.

The bus was almost totally empty, with the exception of a sour-looking middle-aged couple poring over the rantings of a rabid tabloid newspaper, and a young mother attempting to pacify two red-faced children, their hands a blur as they slapped at one another. The driver mumbled news of our departure through the fuzzy microphone.

"What's in the bag, Hopes?"

"If I'm not telling you where we're going I'm hardly going to tell you what's in the bag, am I?"

Hopes birthed a smaller, dryer bag from the larger one, taking care not to reveal any more contents. They sat down, pulling out an assortment of cheese and crackers.

"I thought it might be good to have a snack, keep our strength up," they explained.

Hopes then informed me that they had friends in Bristol, 'the type of friends you don't usually meet in Swansea or Cardiff', and that they had gone some way to 'discovering themself' there. They laughed at the melodrama of their own statement. 'Well, something nearer to myself.' I had never even heard Hopes mention Bristol before. I listened carefully, hoping for some sort of clue as to where we were going.

"The thing is, Rutti, you're getting to know yourself a little better." I felt patronised, but didn't say anything. I had a sneaking suspicion Hopes had rehearsed this.

"Sure, you could convince yourself that you're alone in the city, and I'm certain—I'm certain," they repeated, "that you could see your whole life ahead. It might be depressing, but it will also have made you feel comfortable. You feel as though you don't have to try with anything, because it's not worth it anyway. Well, discomfort is a very good way to reposition yourself, and—like I say—the very best way to get to know yourself better. Stick with things as they are and you'll spend your whole life with very little idea about yourself. I should actually say 'yourselves' because, as this little cross-dressing hobby of yours has proven, there is more than one you. This other you, the you that has been coming to my house every night for—what—the past week? This other you would never have seen the light of day if you'd given up.

"Before you think I'm being insensitive, I'm not. I thought I had my life mapped out. I've been engaged, you know. And he was something, or at least I thought so at the time. He was strong, physically, not as tall as me but with thick arms and a big chest. He felt like he was bolted down to the ground, whereas I felt so flimsy I might blow away. I thought of our upcoming marriage as being like him, strong and bolted down."

I didn't respond—I could tell Hopes wasn't finished. They stopped talking and stared out the train window at the dim sky and rain. It was about three minutes before they spoke again. Their tone was the same as before.

"But you know, he came home one day and saw me dressed as Hopes—though Hopes didn't have a name then. Or a wig of any kind. He was very calm. Extremely calm. He walked up to me, he put his lips near mine like he was about to kiss me, then he spat in my face." Hopes recounted this as though they were talking about the weather. "He said, again very calmly, that he wasn't going to marry a faggot. Can you believe he was serious? We were two men about to get married and he called me a faggot. He said he was leaving but it was me who left in the end. I had less to take.

"The funny thing is I got an email from him a few months later. He wanted me back. He was re-proposing by email. I printed the email and then I burned it. I had to go to the shop to buy a lighter. Then I moved the email into my junk folder. I'd found the name High Hopes by then, and a wig. I was miserable that the engagement was off, of course, but I had the space I needed to get to know myselves better. Fine, our situations aren't exactly the same, but trust me, things will be more interesting now than they would have been."

"So where are we going tonight?"

"I'm still not going to tell you."

They didn't tell me until we'd come over the river and were in England, standing together at the door of a tall Bristol town house. The houses were grander than you would usually find in Swansea, and coated in brightly-coloured graffiti.

"You've probably guessed," Hopes whispered, "that we're at my friends' place."

I nodded. Hopes pressed one of the brass buttons on a panel

183

by the door. A crackling voice asked who it was.

"It's me you fuck, you know that." They sighed. "High Hopes."

The door buzzed and clicked open.

The stairwell matched the outside—elegant and shabby, dusty, roughly painted. Two men in stockings were violently kissing on the stairs. They stopped when they saw us both and pecked us hello. Hopes introduced us—they each had names I managed to forget. Hopes offered to leave the two men to it and led me up to the third floor, lugging the huge bag behind them.

The apartment was smothered in white Christmas lights and Moroccan-style cushions. There were people—mostly men—splayed about them. The nearest stood when they saw us and lined up in greeting. Hopes introduced me to each in turn, and each in turn they kissed me on the mouth. The room was warm and three entered the room from a door opposite, wearing nothing but tiny pants—one pink, one blue, one white.

"Where are we?" I asked Hopes when the last of them had greeted us. I kept my voice low.

"With my friends," Hopes said.

"Who are your friends?"

"The Faeries." Hopes said no more, as though that were explanation enough. "Now come on, we're going to get changed."

We went into a small bedroom, also lit with Christmas lights, these ones multicoloured. I say it was a bedroom, though there was no bed, not unless you count a mass of mattresses which stretched wall-to-wall. We stepped bouncily across the room. Hopes finally opened the rucksack. It contained a series of outfits, nicer ones than those we had been trying on back in Wales.

"Hopes," I said, as firmly as I could, "I want to know what we're doing here."

"You know what we're doing here, Rutti."

"An orgy?"

Hopes laughed. "No, not if you don't want." They pressed a smooth red dress into my hands. "We're here so you can dress as you like and be around people who won't care. People who will see it as just another you."

I told Hopes I wanted them to meet me in my regular clothes first.

"Of course, if you like," Hopes replied. "I didn't bring you here to scare you—I only didn't tell you where we were going because I'd have made a mess if I'd tried to explain it. They can't even explain their gatherings themselves, it's why the little posters they make are so terrible. It's just something you have to experience."

I returned to the room with Hopes following. The space didn't appear to be someone's regular apartment—there was none of the normal living-space furniture—no coffee tables, or sofas, just a single armchair and a warehouse worth of cushions. The walls were bare but for the lights, and the kitchen, which took up one dark corner of the main room, displayed none of the usual day-to-day appliances. The ceiling had been painted in a swirl of colours, all mixed together at the light fixture at the centre, separating further out toward the walls. As a result, each corner had a single, vibrant colour, visible even in the dim glow of the Christmas lights: orange, turquoise, lime green, and lilac. The Faeries and their cushions were lounging above an equally-colourful and clashing array of rugs, the most vibrant occupant clad only in a fuzz of feather boas.

I spoke to three Faeries—the three in the tricoloured pants. The three were all in the early thirties, each with a different body shape: stocky, slender, and somewhere-between; hairy, smooth, and fuzzy; tall, mid-height, and smaller. Hopes had already told them about me. One of them was distracted. That one was rewording and reciting a poem they were going to read later. The remaining two asked me about my new hobby, until another was coaxed away, this time by an older man in a boa. The remaining Faerie leaned in and told me I must look sexy in a dress, until they too were finally called away to give directions over the phone. They were apparently good with directions, and someone was lost.

185

"They're nice aren't they?" Hopes said.

"Of course. Can we—"

"Are you ready to?"

"I think so."

And so we returned to the little room with mattresses and multicoloured lights. Hopes's rucksack was still there, filled with clothes. Hopes passed me the sleek red dress and helped apply make up. My hands shook, so most of the work was undertaken by Hopes. When we were done Hopes told me they had a surprise. They rummaged in their rucksack and brought out a box, wrapped in wedding paper.

"Sorry about that," they apologised, pointing to the wrapping paper. "It was all I had lying around."

I tore off the paper, scattering it in clumps about the mattresses. The box was corrugated card with a separate lid, which I slowly removed.

"It's a wig," Hopes exclaimed. "And it's the same colour as your hair. It's not the best quality, but it's what I could afford. I hope you like it."

It *was* the same colour as my hair. Almost exactly. It wasn't quite a style I'd have chosen but it was simple and inoffensive. Hopes offered to put it on me. I closed my eyes and took a deep breath. They guided me to the bedside mirror.

"Wow."

It was the right hair. It reached my shoulders and matched both my skin tone and the dress I was wearing.

"I need shoes," I told Hopes. I could feel my heart, heavy and fast, against the dress.

When we came out the room—Hopes in a blue dress, the same material and shape as mine, with blue hair—the three Faeries cheered. They were now naked: their cocks were three different sizes too. A few other nearby Faeries took notice of us and called out compliments.

"See," Hopes whispered, "You *do* look fantastic."

"I get the feeling they'd say that even if I looked awful," I whispered back.

One of the three naked ones announced they were about to read their poem.

"Come sit with me," another offered. They led me by the hand to the only armchair, collapsed into it, and pulled me down with them.

DOM

Perhaps, just perhaps, you would imagine that juggling two partners, two people you love, is hard, an effort, too time-consuming. It's probably not even that unreasonable an assumption, not when you think about some people, with their girlfriends or boyfriends or lovers or partners or wives or husbands, those people who obsess and pick at every detail of their loved one's life, those people who spend hour upon hour analysing and over-analysing those small words and actions, making their relationship into a PhD. For those people having more than one lover would be some sort of exhausting, endless, untenable endeavour, a double doctorate of love, love which for them means control. She loved me and it was different. She was leaving, but she loved me. I knew that much.

Perhaps the same person who might also suppose that it would be impossible to balance everything, that the same apparently-innate jealousy I was meant to feel would course through each of Caroline and Richard's veins too, so each would demand more attention, more time than the other, and each of them would resent each other as a result, that resultant resentment congealing until nothing could flow and that love had coagulated into hate. It's a common idea, one of the many assumptions against the sin of loving more than one person at a time, a toxic mixture of practicality and human nature somehow getting in the way, all to the sound of told-you-so tutting. It was real, that assumption that, ultimately, human beings only loved one-at-once.

Here's the weirdest thing—when you live it, it's not that

interesting. Everything we ever do, beyond the first moments, is mundane, it's ordinary. That's the most surprising thing, that's what people don't get, what they could only really get from doing it themselves. The fact that being in a trio can be boring. It's going to the supermarket, it's doing laundry, it's being glad of instant coffee when you have a hangover. I don't want to give the wrong impression, something can be mundane and precious, it can even be mundane and rare—but it's still the ordinary, it's still the everyday. What else could it be? People can be mundane, people can be loved, all at the same time.

When she said she was moving back to her old place I worried, I worried about losing her again, with visions of her announcing it was *enough*, that she *couldn't handle it any more*, or any one of the millions of clichés which were so often the only way of expressing ourselves. But she didn't. I had been waiting for her to leave, I expected her to leave, and so I'd counted every time we'd kissed or made love or cuddled on the sofa as the possible last time, when the next day I'd wake up to find her bags packed, the anguished look on her face announcing how 'it was over'. It didn't happen. Instead her and Richard had got along, and maybe it had been because she'd lost her old friend, the one who wrote her with messages such as *with you forever* but who, when Caroline did something she didn't like, abandoned her and ignored her. I don't know, maybe, somehow, it had actually helped.

The same had happened to me, Zebedee was gone and not returning texts—aside from the occasional one to say how they'd talk to me when I was 'honest'. We had to adjust against everything we'd lost, to our old connections, and even our old routines, we had to build something new, to find new habits.

That's how things had been, that was the start of the bond the three of us shared, finding a three-way space, that was how I'd lived with two people I loved. Perhaps those supposed questions, those assumptions, the ones I just mentioned, perhaps those came from me, the first night when the three of us talked together, or when we had dinner together in the first week, or even when we went for a walk in the wilds of Gower later that month. Perhaps I worried, whether I would wind up burdened and exhausted, or that they would grow angry and resentful, or that any one of a hundred things could go wrong, like no other relationships could fall victim to a hundred different problems. But I never felt burdened, because, really, a strong bond gives you energy, and two even more so.

"You're leaving me?" I'd asked her.

"I'm leaving the flat, not you. And not Richard."

I held her close and I said nothing more—I believed her. I mostly believed her. She'd left to go paint her place, refusing offers of help. This was something for her and the girls, and so I'd told her fair enough, but my hands were trembling a little by the time I'd texted Richard.

I peered over the edge of the stone jetty, trying to see the blur of the water through the darkness, trying to see what I could only hear. The air was wet and salty. In the distance the chimneys of Port Talbot belched fire, a proto-*Blade Runner* landscape. The seagulls were gone, the entire place utterly deserted. I was alone, and I was nervous—but that was why I came, that was why we were meeting here, here of all places. Somehow it had seemed important.

I paced the jetty, trying to figure out where it was that we'd been attacked, where it was Richard had been attacked. This was his idea: we couldn't be afraid of it, he'd said, and he was right. We had to be able to go where we wanted, be who we wanted, or what was the point? We were living alone together again, Richard had explained, and we had to face whatever made either of us afraid, and it made a sort-of sense, I suppose it did.

Was that where he'd been hit, where I had held him as he'd lain senseless in my arms? There was broken glass on the ground, but broken glass was scattered at regular intervals, gently glowing every time the clouds parted and exposed them to the light of the moon. Despite the clarity of that night in my mind, I would never be able to tell where it had been. The whole place looked alike.

There was someone there, there, over at the far end of the jetty, and I could feel my throat tighten, I could feel every muscle in my body contract, teeth grinding, head pounding. There was nothing I had to defend myself, nothing I could use as a weapon in case it was one of them—what the fuck was I going to do if it was? What the fuck was I doing? The figure lumbered forward through the darkness, toward me, something in his right hand, a blurry shape, anything. I gripped onto the stone wall as hard as I could, knuckles clenching cold rock. Glass tinkled beneath my shoes.

Richard.

It was Richard, carrying beer. He set the bottles down and hugged me, holding me close to him, the air cold and him warm.

"We can go somewhere else if you'd like," he offered.

"No."

Y STRYD FAWR, ABERTAWE
37 YEARS ON

"Mmmmm, good morning, beautiful."

Caroline shifted, turning over and feeling the bulk of Dom's younger body against them. They could feel the breath on their face, the same as every morning. This was how Caroline liked to wake up. Caroline smiled.

Richard sat up and looked at Beth. Neither would say anyway. They were each used to it.

Caroline circled their finger in Dom's chest hair.

Richard examined Dom's body—Dom had looked good for their early fifties. Despite always having had a build which fell on the chunkier side, Dom had avoided the middle-aged spread which Richard struggled so hard against. These days it looked a little strange: Richard, Caroline, and Beth had all seen the past ten years bring them grey hair, a few extra wrinkles, and one or two moles.

Not Dom. Dom was locked in time. This was it—a pre-recorded sensory apparition, played every day for a decade. Every morning— even as Caroline and Richard had started dating Beth, even as their relationship with Beth had grown serious, even as Beth and their daughter had moved in. Dom's apparition was there—Caroline had insisted.

Dom smiled. "Good morning, Richard."

Sunshine poured in through the window, the noises of traffic approaching the increasingly-busy Abertawe docks clackered and racketed outside.

"It's raining," Dom incorrectly exclaimed, the same slight disappointment shadowing their face: the same slight disappointment which had shadowed Dom's face every day for the past ten years. Richard had wanted to remove that line, but Caroline insisted: it was a part of Dom. They shouldn't lose it.

"Good morning, Dom," Beth greeted, knowing Dom would give them no response. Dom had never known Beth, but Beth was used to Dom by now. Beth had only ever known this morning ghost. Yes, it was strange, dating two people who woke up to an apparition every

morning, but then life was strange, and it was only a few minutes every morning—Richard and Caroline hadn't gone as far as most. Beth would probably do the same if they were them.

Caroline rolled over and kissed Beth. Dom's projection kissed the back of Caroline's neck—their lips were soft and moist. Dom's lips tingled Caroline's skin, every tiny hair of their body standing on end. All these years and Dom's lips had the same effect.

Dom.

There was nothing that could have been done. It had spread throughout their whole body before anyone had even realised. It had been in their bones. Dom had taken it so well. It never seemed to even bother them, they were more concerned with how Caroline was. And Richard. They'd recorded that morning on purpose, the three of them. A rainy day, Richard, Dom, and Caroline. They'd recorded it before it was too late.

Richard looked at the projection. You could see it, there in Dom's eyes. They were smiling, but there was always something behind the eyes. Dom knew that they were dying. Richard hadn't noticed that look at the time. Now they saw it every morning. Richard wanted to comfort Dom all over again, holding them and telling them that they loved them. That they'd never stop loving them.

But the morning ghost wouldn't notice. The morning ghost turned to Richard.

"I love you, Richard. I'll always love you."

The morning ghost turned toward Caroline.

"I love you, Caroline. I've always loved you."

"I love you too, Dom," Caroline replied. Beth held onto them.

"I love you," Richard mumbled under their breath. It never got easier.

The other two went downstairs to make breakfast for Beth's sulky teenage offspring. Richard rolled closer to Dom, holding them in their arms, feeling their chest rise and fall, feeling Dom's pulse. They could smell their sweat.

Dom fell asleep. The projection vanished.

CHAPTER FOURTEEN

AN UGLY, LOVELY TOWN

RUTTI

Caroline was having a house re-warming, a re-warming to which we had all been invited. I took my place between Hopes and Richard; on the other side of Richard, Caroline; on the other side of Caroline, their housemate. Hopes, Richard, Caroline, Christina, Steph, and I waited, whilst Dom clattered about Caroline's kitchen, spilling water and wine over the wipe-clean lino. When Dom finally got the drinks precariously balanced onto a tray they joined us too.

Caroline's place was decked out in mismatched Ikea furniture, with the heavy fire doors, over-active smoke alarm and scratchy-cheap carpets of government-regulated rental accommodation. Despite the surroundings Caroline had gone to some effort to warm the place up—evidently they had fished out some old tinsel, and it was draped over the walls and the backs of most of the chairs. There were two tables, each covered in a mass of candles, and I couldn't help but continually watch them for fear of fire.

I was wearing the wig Hopes had bought me, above a black-and-green evening dress I had bought for myself. Hopes was wearing their usual blue wig, above a garish maroon halter top and black mini skirt. I had waited for a comment from Richard—

or anyone—though so far no one had said anything.

"So how am I heterosexual, but not straight?" Dom asked me. "What do you mean?"

"Because," I told them, "gay is a culture formed around homosexuality, and straight is a culture formed around heterosexuality."

Dom gave an uncertain nod and glanced back toward the kitchen. Caroline's other roommate flickered briefly in the doorway, a sour look on their face, before vanishing.

"Think of it this way: you could be homosexual, or have a penis, or you might have an impairment—say you're deaf. You have these states, and then you have the social shit we pile on top of those—in these cases being 'gay', or a 'man', or 'disabled'. So if you're homosexual people wind up assuming you're gay, but all *homosexual* actually means is that you're a man who wants to fuck other men. Being *gay* means a whole lot more than that: that you want to build your life with a man and not women, that you fall in love with men and not women, and a whole load of other crap."

"Don't forget the lesbians," Steph said.

"Yes, right, thanks Steph, helpful." I pulled a face at Steph, so Steph leant over and punched me on the arm. "Anyway," I continued, "so your sex drive is towards women, not men, which makes you hetero—" Dom looked uncomfortable at the mention of their sex drive, whilst Richard leant forward, "—but your romantic drive, that obviously lies with both men and women. If you were straight then both would be purely toward females— women would be the ones you fucked *and* the ones you love. That's what I mean, that a homosexual doesn't have to be gay, a heterosexual isn't necessarily straight. That's how you can wind up hetero, but not straight."

"Right," Dom shook their head. "Would anyone like a drink?"

"Salut," Christina called, holding up a chipped Superman mug.

"Cheers."

"Iechyd da."

"Prost."

I was celebrating too, though I hadn't told anyone. At least I had wanted to celebrate, I wanted to be in the mood. I had lost my job. It wasn't how I'd imagined. I had always planned on quitting the perfume store; to smugly thrust a resignation in my manager's face, relishing the chance to sneer, as they had with me on so many occasions. But I was robbed of that chance. The pretentious shop was collapsed by the recession's aftershocks: the manager had entered the store, their face blotched with black tears, our redundancies given through quivering lips. The store was closing. All the stores were closing, up and down the island. No one was in the mood to purchase chemical stenches.

The manager had stood before us in the usual manner—but instead of a local empress engaging their illiterate subjects, there was just a tired middle-aged woman who had lost their job, surrounded by a group of students and local teenagers who had just lost theirs as well. There had been no big sale, no everything-must-goes—just last days of usual prices and hollow offers to stay in touch. I emptied my mug.

The consensus had been in favour of lounging. Steph, Caroline, and I had arranged the furniture in a circle. We found our spaces on the sofa, chairs, and cushions. We held up our glasses so Dom poured wine—only one of the glasses had been made for wine, the rest a variety of squat and tall tumblers, mugs, and one teacup.

Now I can't recall what we talked about. It doesn't matter. It didn't then. I barely caught a half-hour of idle chatter. Instead I watched the others, a feeling of unease curdling in my stomach. Steph was leaning forward a little, leaning over Caroline's knee, saying something very important, very emphatically. Caroline wasn't listening—they and Christina were having their own animated discussion. Caroline had lost the dizzy nervousness they had wrapped themself in when we had first met. As Dom passed, Caroline reached out and stroked their leg, running a hand up to Dom's arse, causing Dom to chuckle. Dom took

Caroline's hand and gripped it in their own. Caroline pulled Dom down toward them and pressed their lips together. Dom snickered. Caroline released them and Dom loped cautiously, gently asking each person in turn if they wanted more wine, wine? Would you like some wine? A gentle voice so not to override Steph's, whatever they were saying. Dom stopped when they reached Richard and sat by them, their knees touching but neither noticing. My guts clenched. Dom put their arm over their friend-lover's shoulder. Richard glanced over at me.

I wanted some fresh air filtered through nicotine. I went outside. The ground was dotted with rain and a chill breeze whistled about my ears. I decided I needed to stop smoking. It's the great ethical blind spot of the left. Even die-hard vegans burn up their bodies with tobacco. I had to hold my hand up to protect the flame as I lit my cigarette.

As I watched the twinkling lights of the terraced houses perched high on the hills above I found myself thinking of Craig. The Christian. I saw them huddled up beneath a doorway or overpass somewhere, sheltering themself. Perhaps they found someone else to crash with, in the hope of converting them to Christ. Perhaps they were never homeless, perhaps it was all planned, perhaps it worked sometimes. It seemed unlikely. I thought about Bristol, of the Faeries. I was unemployed. I was free. I could finally escape the city—there was somewhere else. Things could actually be better. The thought didn't help—the thought coursed down from my head, tightening at my throat.

"What're you thinking about there, Mr. Rutti?" Dom's voice was right behind my ear.

"I don't think."

"Well whatever you are thinking about, it looks important," Dom said, trying to read my face.

"It's not, really."

Dom lit a hand-rolled cigarette. I smelled pure store-bought tobacco, without a hint of weed.

I told Dom I didn't know they smoked cigarettes.

Dom told me that everyone our age smoked. Isn't that what

I'd decided?

I told Dom I supposed so.

So here it is, they said, holding the cigarette aloft.

Are you happy, Dom?

I suppose I am, and I say that even though I know I am. I am happy. Whatever winds up happening I know that, right now, right now I'm happy—I can't really ask for more, you know?

I nodded.

You shouldn't smoke, you know.

I know.

I went back inside, steering past the lounge and making my way to the kitchen, where I found a chipped mug and poured myself some more wine from a half-empty bottle. I peered around the corner of the doorway. Dom had returned to the living room, and they, Richard, and Caroline were seated together in animated discussion; Steph and Christina the same.

"What're you doing, Rutti?" Hopes asked, placing a hand on my arm.

"Just taking a breather," I informed them, keeping my voice as casual as I could manage. Richard took a sip of wine and giggled at something Caroline said.

"*Just* a breather?" Hopes asked me, their voice edged with suspicion. I decided to tell them.

"I could leave. I could. I thought that things would be the same everywhere—that it was me. But I don't think it is. I might actually be happy somewhere else."

Hopes paused, taking the cup from my hand and sipping the wine, before taking a deep breath.

"Rutti, a place is what you make of it. Sure, it might be filled to the brim with ignorant, conservative fucks, but that doesn't have to affect how you live your life. I mean, come on, I survive here. Your friends there, they have a fucking polyamorous trio thing going on, right in chapel country. Do you know where the largest Faerie sanctuary in the world is? Tennessee. Tennessee of all places. You don't need to move a thousand miles to fit in. Make the place fit you."

Hopes followed my gaze, handed the cup back to me and momentarily placing a hand on my shoulder.

"He looks happy," Hopes commented.

"They deserve to be."

I told Hopes about the time that Richard and I had tried to get to Ireland but only reached Carmarthen, how we had stayed in an out-of-time bed and breakfast run by an elderly Nazi—we had snuck in alcohol to defy them and pushed our beds together before we left, so they would be horrified at the implied sodomy and have to burn the sheets.

I told Hopes about the time Richard and I snuck into the pond by the university and drank Cava in celebration of their new call centre job. I had drunkenly tripped and splashed about in a metre of murky muddy water. Richard, in a perfect display of pointless and dramatic heroism, had jumped in after me.

Hopes listened to my ill-timed anecdotes with patience. When I had finished they spoke, as carefully and cautiously as before.

"Rutti, you have to get over Richard. Don't tell me you're not into him, because you are, and anyone who can't see that is a fucking idiot. He's hetero, Rutti. Do you hear me? Yes, he's in love with a man, but that doesn't mean he'll fall in love with you—if he hasn't done by now, he's not going to. He wouldn't have sex with you, anyway. He might not get many of them, but he obviously likes girls. Stop looking for what you can't attain."

And before I even processed what Hopes said, before I had chance to deny it, Hopes kissed me, their tongue reaching mine for just a moment before they pulled away, an uncertain look riding their face.

"I thought you weren't into me," I said, feeling faintly ridiculous.

"You've grown on me," Hopes stated.

So I kissed Hopes in return. We made our way to Caroline's

room. It was too warm, and Hopes creaked open the window. We sat together whilst Hopes rolled a spliff, each other's kiss still imprinted on our lips and with me lain against them. I could feel their stomach against my spine. We were still wearing our clothes. We took our time.

The tense odour of our sweat melded together and was slowly covered by the scent of the smoke. There was no music—no sound at all barring the random growl of passing motorists below. We were soaked in the cosy warmth of one another, that slow wallow of soft friendship.

We kissed in pieces. Part-after-part. We shed clothes, piece by piece. A face nuzzled in an armpit. The press of a cock on a thigh. Hands clenched together. Deep drawn breaths morphing into short shallow gasps, then into two long satisfied groans. A sleepy head on a stomach then another lick, a kiss as the darkness spread over the curtainless window, heavy thrusting through the dull lamplight.

The night fuzzed between slow sex and sleep. We had nothing to prove and all the time we wanted. Somehow no one disturbed us.

Then the room was bright with sunlight, and it was all too much. My head pounded. There was no air. Hopes was asleep. I checked myself in the mirror, then again. I picked up my phone then put it down. I walked out of the room and to the kitchen, filled a glass with water then went back. The water was bitter.

I lay back down, feeling the clammy warmth of the bed. The room was hot. I opened the window to find it too cold. It was too cold. I was sweating. Things were tangled. Hopes was wonderful, and I knew that given enough time I would love them. I would love them, and that would be it—I would be stuck in the city forever.

My phone bleeped from my desk. The screen glared at me. I had a text.

Caroline stayed at ours—we didn't want to disturb you. You looked wonderful. Richard.

I cried.

There was no one around when I got back to Steph's. I made a phone call. I took my suitcase from Steph's wardrobe and emptied it of all the junk I'd put in there. I filled it with clothes, important documents like bank statements and my passport, then toiletries. I piled my remaining clothes into bin bags, magazines into stacks, books into piles.

I wrote Richard a text message. *Thank you.*

I wrote Steph and Hopes a letter each, then stuck both to the fridge.

I showered, brushed my teeth and put my remaining toiletries into the case. I took one last look at Steph's living room—at the wilting plants, the gaudy décor, at the sofa bed. I ached. I made my way to the bus station.

It was early, so the beachfront was deserted. At some point the sea had sunk from bright blue to a churning metal grey, along with the sky. The seafront's summer lure had decayed, leaving nothing but the peeling-painted and vacant guest houses. They watched me with nicotine-net curtains for eyes. Now and then a car sped by, heading toward the giant supermarket further down the front.

I passed by the stone steps of the old bridge. When I first arrived here, a fresh eighteen-year-old idiot, the bridge was topped with elegant and crude Victorian ironwork. I had walked across it to the beach. Since then the council had decapitated it, removing the actual iron bridge part, leaving two sets of stone stairs leading nowhere. The newspaper had announced the grim news with a cheery headline.

NO FUNDS TO REPAIR BRIDGE

In place of people there was litter. It flowed from bins and crevasses and car windows. It whirled in circles. A used tissue hit me in the face.

As I passed the long stone jetty I felt drab, as though I was perfectly camouflaged amongst the shabby decline which surrounded us. But I was going. I was finally going.

HARVEY-MILK-PLATZ, BERLIN
55 YEARS ON

"Homosexuals and bisexuals were once attacked for making issue of their orientation, for marking themselves as 'different'. This was, of course, a total and utter perversion of truth. It was the heterosexual who first set themself as distinct; as distinct and apart from the homosexual and bisexual. This was true on both historical and personal terms. It was heterosexuals who invented these categories as a means of isolating and differentiating homosexuals—in response the homosexuals sought refuge amongst themselves as outcasts; watching, monitoring and criticising the heterosexual culture, whilst at the same time forming their own. Sexual minorities found themselves simultaneously imprisoned and freed. From the heterosexuals came 'straight' culture (an aggressive word in itself as the opposite of 'bent'), whilst from the homosexuals came 'gay' culture ('gay' having previously been used to mean 'deviant', as well as joyful).

"It was true also on a personal level. Homosexuals and bisexuals were criticised for their parades, closed meetings, and sealed-off nightclubs—for making an issue of their orientation. But there was no instance rivalling the promotion of orientation than the heterosexual saying 'I am not gay'. Back then this was the standard response of most heterosexual individuals when same-sex affection was directed toward them, and the phrase carried a certain degree of violence; it said, we are not the same. *Unlike now, It was far rarer for the response to be 'I'm just not into (men/women/others) that way'—an answer that does not rely on division and closed identities but places the emphasis on preference. It was true that homosexuals may have replied to opposite-sex affection with the phrase 'I'm gay/ lesbian,' but the response was never 'I am not straight'. On the level of personal interaction heterosexuals would defend their orientation with more rigour.*

"The key to ending this violent division was to allow all access to an identity based on the rejection of such categorisation. A term which was accessible to all who saw fit to question the state of things, who did not wish to be limited to an oppressive 'gay' or 'straight' culture.

We had that term. It was queer.

"I came to Berlin nearly sixty years ago. Do you want to know why I won't leave it? I'm going to tell you anyway. I won't leave because I came to this city for love. I don't mean that in the tack-tacky, clichéd sense that many do. Really, you know me better than that. But I do mean it. I came to this city with no job, no home and no German—just a ferry pass, a suitcase of my things, and equal amounts of optimism and pessimism. In the end I did it for love, open and endless.

"Of course it was possible to find that kind of love before. Some people can find it anywhere. After all, it's all chance, and I had to improve my chances. It worked. I found love in this city. Over and over and over. I regret nothing. I have loved and I have been loved, in constellations I couldn't even grasp, in deranged chains I could never see the ends to. That is love. That is love.

"These streets map it all. It was there, in fact—just over there—that I kissed in this city for the first time. It all looked different then, but I feel it every time I pass by. I found my first relationship on the U1 subway line. It isn't called that now, but it was there, it was there. I am sentimental. My life has been played through the city.

"And what would I have found had I stayed in Wales? I would have found a very different kind of love. Perhaps with someone wonderful. We may have stayed awake for nights on end, chatting and smirking and debating the fall of republics. But we would have been walled. We would have been two lights in an empty sky, two links and no chain. I'm old enough to see the value in what others do, and a walled love is still love. But it was never for me.

"Perhaps there will be new lovers, perhaps not. I am old. I am old, I am old, I am old. But there are those who will love the old.

"And I am not alone. Even after so many break-ups, even with days by myself. I have love. I will die in this city, the city where I found it, the city where I am surrounded by it, on streets and subway trains and parks and skyscrapers and lakes and kitchens and carpets, chairs and beds and once, a hammock. There is no such thing as a broken constellation, links still bear the scars of their chains, I still feel the touch of all I loved, I can still taste it. Even now, I can taste it."

CHAPTER FIFTEEN

ONE WAY

DOM

Zebedee's room was clean—this was now the permanent state of things, his space was now ordered and tidy, and smelled faintly of cleaning fluids, of sterility and old folk's homes and airport toilets and hospitals. The men's magazines were stacked neatly on his desk, the carpet was spotless, his mirror was leaning against the wall behind his non-overflowing hamper, rather than face-up on the floor and coated in hair trimmings. His bedroom door had been locked when we'd arrived, locked rather than ajar with last week's laundry hanging over it, and I couldn't see any ashtrays anywhere—perhaps he was no longer getting stoned, or perhaps he did so in the small, shabby back garden. There was a small potted plant on the windowsill, and I wanted to touch it to see if it was real, but I didn't dare.

On his coffee table was a single, tall candle with two used mugs to each side—the only hint of disorder, the only token to chaos.

Zebedee opened his mouth and started to pick up one of the cups, then seemed to think better of it. He left it where it was, and I got the message—he wasn't going to offer me a drink as I wasn't to be staying long, and in response I felt both dismay and relief. This was the end, there would be no pretence of it being any other way, and it saddened me, the sinking feeling plunging into my gut, but at the same time I hadn't wanted to stay, we were both awkward and uncomfortable around each other, you could see it in his perfect-postured body language, and I'm certain, I'm sure, that it was in mine also.

We were sat opposite one another, each in a high-backed dining chair, chairs which hadn't been there before, when we used to sit together on the bed, or on the floor. Seated opposite each other felt like an interview, though to be totally frank I had no idea who was interviewing whom, and it added to the feeling of unease, the awkward, sad, grey feeling that I wanted to leave and that he wanted me to leave.

The reality was that he was the one that would be leaving, leaving with his girlfriend Nomi, the friendly-looking girl who had made it clear she'd never liked me, but who'd always done so in a mostly-polite and easy way, which meant I hadn't minded at least, that was the way it had been up until Richard had come along. We didn't mention his name. Nor did we mention Caroline.

Zebedee scratched at his ear as he told me that he was moving out to one of the city's austere, pebble-dash-fronted suburbs, where the city's young but never-leaving couples moved and gained mortgages, where they could wallow in affordable space and not bother with the drunks and heroin-addicted folks of the city centre, where they wouldn't have to deal with corner shops and bars, and roommates.

I found that I was rubbing my chin. I was extremely conscious of the gesture as I asked him how he would manage, seeing as he'd never learned to drive. He told me that there was a bus stop fifteen minutes' walk away, and he'd checked, there were three buses to the city centre every hour. Besides, what did he need those for? Nomi could drive him to the supermarket and drop him off at work, where he'd landed a job in one of the gigantic hardware stores in one of the boxy warehouses in one of the sprawling out-of-town shopping centres. I noticed he was sweating as he told me that Swansea had one of the highest ratios of such windowless shopping Meccas in all of Europe, its new claim to fame now it was no longer the copper-smelting capital of the world. He gave no clue as to whether he found this fact impressive, or was giving a subtle dig at the suburbs, the old Zebedee poking fun at his upcoming life. I rubbed my chin.

He told me about the new house in a halting, reluctant, confessional kind of way, as though I were a priest, or a policeman. I'd be lying if I said I was comfortable, I really didn't fucking like it. I wanted to tell him to talk openly, that I wasn't judging him, he could move away and we'd still be friends, but it wouldn't have been true and he wouldn't have believed me. I leant against the stiff back of the chair. Zebedee and I had once been able to be open with one another before because there'd been boundaries, invisible lines of conduct in which we could be free with each other—but I'd pissed all over those boundaries with Richard, and that had fucked things between me and Zebedee. Because deep down, we knew they could be broken with us, too. These things can't be fixed with words, and to be honest I was different, the boundaries with Zebedee were also gone, something we both knew, and without that container our friendship had somehow evaporated.

Or maybe it was something else for him, who the fuck knew? I couldn't see inside his head.

He pushed back his chair and stood up, not taking his eyes off me as I myself stared at the candle, at the cups, and with that the awkward, stunted talk or confession or declaration was over. He picked up the stack of men's magazines and handed them to me, a young large-busted woman on the cover licking at a red lollipop, the red matching her shoes and the text next to her, text which promised a translation from girlfriend-speak into boyfriend-language. I shook my head and refused the parting gift, I didn't want them and, as he said, he was going to throw them out anyway.

But there, in his eyes, there was a dull hurt, a dim betrayal, so I changed my mind and offered to take them, but it was too late—they were already in his new wastepaper basket.

I stood outside and looked back at the closed front door. So he was leaving, off to start a new life with his girlfriend— romantic anniversary dates in chain restaurants, getting a cat, or more likely a dog, and then a child, then drives to school, lack of sleep, birthday trips to theme parks, exhausted evenings in front of the television, all of it. I might have done it myself, before everything, before all of this. I wouldn't have even thought about it, it would have happened, just like that. Maybe I'd have been happy, I certainly hoped Zebedee would be.

It would be a lie if I said I never saw him again, because I did, now and then, in town or a little way away on the beach, and once in a bar. It would be a lie if I said I never spoke to him again, because I did once, in a supermarket. But we never made plans again, we never had a beer or a smoke or a laugh again, and standing there outside his house I knew that, I knew that enough that I rounded the corner into a quiet alleyway, and with my hand covering my eyes I cried, until I wiped my face with my sleeve and made my way back to the street.

When I got home preparations for the counter-demo were in full swing and, I am ashamed to admit, I was glad that no one noticed I'd been crying. Our fold-out table was covered in tubes of paint, and the signs they'd been making were carefully lain over old newspaper. Richard came over and placed his arm around me, directing me toward his poster. Caroline was on the phone but turned momentarily to smile at me, before returning her attention to her long-distance conversation.

"You can try, I'm not saying don't. I can't tell you how I think it'll go—"

Surprisingly Richard's sign was predominantly in a purplish colour, pale though, quite pale, almost lilac. To compensate for the less-than-visible colour, he had edged the lettering in dark oranges and reds, giving the whole thing a very visible, gaudy look, and I must have been looking at it strangely because

Richard added,

"I'm not great with colours."

But somehow it worked—the thing was hard to look at for long, sure, it had a sickening appeal, it assaulted the eyes and the gut, it was a sort of weapon on its own, the colours serving to strengthen the wording, a simple 'NO TO RACISM'. Somehow it worked.

Caroline had already finished painting, and without breaking her telephone conversation she whisked her sign from the table and propped it face-away by the door to the kitchen, before picking up a blank A3 slab of card and laying it on the table for me. Richard returned to his own, carefully finishing the edging around the final word, his face stern with concentration, the movements of his hand small, careful, neat.

We left the flat together, the three of us, each holding our placards, each unsure what to expect—there had been demonstrations in other poverty-saddled cities, there had been violence, blood and uniforms. I stopped just before we reached the end of our street, our house and the tatty old betting shop still in view, and I placed my hand on Richard's shoulder, memories of skinheads and broken glass and the dark sea, and I asked him,

"Are you sure you want to do this?"

And he didn't say anything, but he nodded. Caroline turned to us, beckoning us along. She and Richard strode on ahead but I stood still, watching them, the two people I loved, and as they linked hands there was a swell through my body as though I would burst, and whatever happened, whatever I'd lost, I had found something—something fucking wonderful, something extraordinary and mundane, and at that very moment I froze in fear, today and the future sprawling on ahead, a path we could never have chosen, everything decided. Blood thudding through veins, nerves screaming, but those two seemed so sure, and as the two of them turned back toward me I moved on, their certainty pulling me, drawing me as I stumbled, and then ran toward them, to those two. Oh, those two…

The train was heaving with passengers, a heady jumble of bodies clambering past one another on various missions: toilet, buffet car, vending machines. Parents shouting at children, children wailing at parents, a young group of Italians sharing cans of lager. Dom had considered plugging his ears, but fuck it, they wouldn't drown out the experience.

Dom had slept with no one on the train—it was too crowded, and they had never enjoyed having sex in toilets. The private bunks of the trans-Atlantic ferry had been a different story, but the boat was docked back in Brittany, its Quebecois colours glaring. That one had been larger than the Passage ship, and on neither had Dom wanted for company. They looked good for their age, or so they were told. Dom didn't care—Dom wanted to age, to look old, to watch the lines slowly etch over their face. It was natural. And they would age, they had aged, it was just too slowly. After all, ageing was beautiful, and Dom was impatient. A young man bounced their two children, one on each knee, as the kids screeched with delight.

Richard, for example, had already gone grey. Dom had teased them about it, though they envied it. Even Caroline had a few good wisps of white, white which had not been there when they'd last seen each other in the flesh. Dom searched tirelessly for greys, but their own hair remained resolutely brown. Perhaps they would look distinguished when they were older.

Dom was late—there had been a storm, and the boat had remained in St. John's harbour, its solar sails dull against the grey sky as they watched it from the dockside hotel. Dom may have still been on time if they hadn't missed the last train. They'd tried messaging the others, but usage on the train had been too high, and the signal too weak. Had their messages got through? Were Caroline and Richard waiting for them at the registry office? Fuck. They tried to think of something else—if they worried then they would sweat, and their spare shirts were locked in the luggage compartment.

Instead Dom thought of Caroline's white hairs, how they longed

209

to run them through their fingers, to experience this new development, to bury their nose in it. It had been too long, they'd all been too far away. Not any more. Dom wouldn't leave again. They wanted to feel Caroline's breasts against their chest, the light fuzz of Caroline's arms, the soft hairs on their legs which Dom and Richard had convinced them to grow out—well, Dom suspected it had more to do with their friend Steph, but Dom had been pleased, regardless. They thought of running their lips over Caroline's legs. They were sweating.

Dom longed to hold Richard too, in that very different way they had—that soft and sensual way, not the hard thrust of sex. Richard's breath on Dom's collarbone, the jerk of their leg as they fell to sleep, the tight clutch of their fingers on Dom's arm, as though it was Dom which kept them from falling.

The lights overhead grew slowly brighter, the last flicker of the green French countryside plunging into dark. It would be dark for a while, as the train burrowed deep beneath the Pyrenees. It wouldn't be so much longer before they got to Barcelona. Dom pictured them waiting there, clad in strange formal attire; waiting for Dom in dismay. Worrying about them. The last thing Dom wanted in all the world was to disappoint those two—Dom wanted to be there for them. Would they be too late? Once more Dom willed their attention to something else. The Italians were singing—no—they weren't all Italians, one or two sounded French. Dom couldn't hear any Welsh people, or English for that matter. They closed their eyes and thought of the others whispering into their ears, Richard remarking on how hairy they were.

They could feel the wet circles around their armpits. They wanted a shower. They hoped that the hotel bed would be large enough. Marital bed, wedding night, it all seemed ludicrous, though the three had shared many beds before. Dom had once wondered if their shared sexual antics might make them bisexual, that some latent sexual urge for Richard would reveal itself and they would delve into mad lust for each other. It hadn't, though as they'd aged they'd experimented a little, stroking and sucking. It was pleasurable enough, though not frequent, and not what either of them felt for Caroline. It was different. Dom longed for both their bodies, sweating beneath the hemp t-shirt which was too thick and heavy.

Dom didn't care. They felt giddy, like a teen anticipating fucking for the first time. Their bodies, Richard and Caroline. How Dom longed to feel them again.

RICHARD

Caroline wrapped her arms around me, holding her paintbrush in her teeth. I held my arm at a distance, anxious not to get paint on her clothes.

"What was that for?"

She resumed painting, long and quick strokes of placid turquoise-blue. Her placard was already almost finished, whereas I'd barely started mine.

"Does there have to be a reason?" she answered. I presumed that was the end of it, she was so focused on the painting, until she glanced up at me. I recognised the look. Her phone rang as soon as she'd finished, and she was still in conversation when Dom came in through the front door. It was obvious he'd been crying, but I didn't say anything. If he wanted to talk about it, he would talk about it. I glanced over at Caroline, but she was still busy with whoever was at the other end of the line.

He put his arm around me as he examined my half-finished poster. I knew Dom enough to know that he'd be worried about me going to this demonstration, after what had happened that night on the jetty. I actually felt fine about it—the scab on my forehead had healed, and I wasn't going to let them bother me. As there was no way of convincing Dom of that—his worrying would trump anything I could say—I diverted attention to a different subject (namely my lack of painting skills and poor choice of colours).

Once we'd finished, phones in pockets and placards in black bin bags, we made our way into the street. Caroline took my hand (I wasn't certain what to make of it—if she was being friendly or conveying something else, but I didn't want to press the matter). Dom caught up with us and the three of us turned onto St. Helen's Road with its Islamic book store, mosque, and the kebab shops. There were one or two small groups of other people headed in the same direction we were. One group of dreadlock-haired students were carrying a 'People and Planet' banner.

It was only as we got nearer that I realised the possibility of there being more of them than there were of us—that we might be outnumbered and the situation could turn dangerous. I had a feeling that I should have been afraid by that point, and I wanted to be afraid: I did my best to will an appropriate sense of danger, but it wouldn't come. Dom looked the more anxious of the three of us. Caroline looked somewhere between his quiet panic and my ill-fitted serenity.

There was someone familiar standing near the mosque. A young man with slicked-down hair and a white shirt was handing out leaflets, eyed warily by a small group of old men in kufi caps. I waved to the man and in return he handed me a leaflet advertising the Baptist Church.

"How's Rutti doing?" the young man asked. I recognised him as the stranger in Steph's apartment, and felt a slight sense of embarrassment. I'd run out the door as he'd been making us a cup of tea. I didn't answer. He turned his attention to Caroline.

"Hello again. This must be your boyfriend." He extended his hand to Dom, who shook it over-enthusiastically. Caroline told him we had to leave. I followed.

"God bless you!"

Part of me wondered if I should have stayed behind and asked him where Rutti had gone—had he broken down and joined a mission in some developing country? Or was he holed up in the basement of the church, folding up leaflets and putting them into sacks? Of course these were ridiculous conclusions, but Rutti hadn't told anyone where he was going. He'd made no mention of his destination in the letter he'd written to Steph. At first Steph had been quite blasé about his leaving, insisting that it was only a gesture and that he'd be back after a week. It was only once three weeks had passed that she'd started to grow concerned, evidenced by her calling me once a day to see if I'd heard from him yet.

It was over a cup of tea in Rutti's favourite battered coffee shop during that third week that she'd grudgingly shown me the letter, as though it might have some clue about where he was going, written in a code only a geek like me could understand. But the letter was short and simple, telling Steph that he'd had to finally escape, and that he'd contact her once he had things sorted out.

"Leaving me here to worry," Steph had complained, "when he could contact me any time and just let me know he's doing all right. It's selfish, is what it is."

She was right, it was selfish, though I understood. If Rutti spoke to a friend back home before he was secure in his new place (wherever it was) there was a chance he'd come running back. I'd have been the same.

Deep down I was disappointed that he hadn't written to me.

"If that Hopes did anything to drive him away—" Steph'd threatened, leaving the end of her statement hanging. She'd been repeating the same threat ever since she'd begun worrying, and we all knew that Rutti and Hopes had spent the night together, right before he left. I couldn't be sure, but I doubted Hopes had done anything to upset him. It wouldn't be like Rutti (or anyone with half a gramme of sanity) to leave because of one night's cruelty, or thoughtlessness, or whatever it was Steph had imagined. We would hear from him eventually. I felt calm about his leaving; there was nothing we could do. Steph said that I was being too fatalistic. But what could she do about it?

It didn't mean anything that I'd seen the Christian. There was a point when I would have taken it as some sort of omen, my drive toward fantasy envisaging Rutti's return, or his death, or something equally implausible. Seeing the stranger hadn't meant anything other than he'd chosen to leaflet outside the mosque, and that was the way into town.

We left St. Helen's Road and reached the Kingsway. The noise hit me suddenly, a chaos of people with banners and flags, a police line beyond, the remains of the club looming grey over everyone. I couldn't see the fascists anywhere. Perhaps they weren't coming. Dom squeezed my arm, telling me it wasn't too late to leave. I wasn't leaving.

I saw one of the members of the group who had organised

this solidarity protest, standing atop a red van with an old megaphone in his hands. Though the megaphone only caught the odd word, he repeated himself over and over, making his message clear. Do not leave the area. They were coming.

The chaotic jumble was comforting. There were nervous murmurs about the crowd, and questioning glances at the faceless line of police officers. Slowly three police vans rolled into place, forming a barricade behind the officers. Caroline was at my side, standing on tip-toes, trying to find someone she knew.

The concrete was baked hot by the strange glare of unexpected October sun, the hard ground pounded by the endless stamp of furious feet. Here we were: students, hippies, Muslims, teachers, professors, socialists, anarchists, liberals, mealy-mouthed politicians, gays, and dragged-in onlookers, all for now allied. Flags, banners, and signs all littered the sky, a flurry of colours declaring unity from this group or that. The air was thick with chanting.

Nazi Scum... Off Our Streets
Nazi Scum... Off Our Streets
Nazi Scum... Off Our Streets

And there they were, this mob, this clan of skin-headed drunken white anger, people every lecturer and homo and hippy would usually cross the street to avoid, here we were facing them. Shouting at them. And they shouted back, beneath their sub-literate-scrawled signs which were marked 'CYMRU TALIBAN HUNTERS' and 'PATRIOTISM ISNT RACISM', the 'defence league' shouted,

EEE—EEE—EEE—DEE—ELL
EEE—EEE—EEE—DEE—ELL
EEE—EEE—EEE—DEE—ELL

Clearly forgetting they were supposed to be the Welsh—and not the English—Defence League. Between our multicoloured sea and their band of blue-white tracksuits was the luminous-green of riot police, a uniform wall dividing the flow, forcing back the surge of the two crowds, their horses threatening behind. They issued their decrees, printed on white paper, ordering our side to leave or face arrest, but their orders were lost in the chaotic noise of the chants and their papers littered the ground.

Years of anger had flowed from the tabloids to the streets. Now they burned in the heavy daylight. Dom looked as though he was going to be sick.

"Do you need to leave, Dom?" I asked.

He shook his head. Caroline and I made eye contact. She no longer looked concerned at all—she looked as I felt. Resolute. We would be all right, her expression said. We would be all right, we were strong enough, us two. We could look after Dom.

I couldn't help myself. I leant over, and I kissed her on the ear.

THE PYRENEES
23 YEARS ON

The man opposite Richard was sleeping in their seat, head slung back and mouth gaping, gasping in the cold air from the blower above their head. The attractive woman the young man had spent the past few hours fucking rested their head on the man's bare shoulder, swayed to and fro by the rocking of the bus, their gentle snores accompanied by the whirr of the bus's electric motors.

Good show

Richard wrote, finger poised in the air above their reader, unsure as to whether they should flick the message to over. Richard hadn't watched, not really, but the couple had been hard to avoid. Did Richard mean the message sincerely, or was it the sarcastic prudery of an older man? They weren't sure. They flicked their finger and sent the message anyway—it would almost certainly be taken as a compliment. The easy-going young.

A half-hour later and the bus slowed—the road through the Pyrenees was ricketed with potholes, each scar in the tarmac a tiny inverse mimicry of the sweeping mountains around them. The route was a mere two lanes wide, and with the way in such poor condition, Richard reasoned, the driver did right to take caution. Even the birds in the back of the vehicle were quiet.

Where are you?

Rutti's messages had grown more and more frantic the later Richard was. How was Rutti, of all people, on time?

Trekking through the mountains

Richard replied. They knew what Rutti's response would be— why the bus? And Richard wouldn't be able to answer, because in truth they weren't really sure. The bus had meant going through the border checks with England—something few others bothered with, what with the mess it was in—then through crossing to France, changing in Paris, another bus to Catalunya. Why not a boat, or the train, like the others? Richard preferred the bus, it was that simple.

Late for their own wedding. Richard wasn't the anxious young man they had once been, but this should trouble even the sturdiest of people. Even so, they didn't mind. They felt calm, they felt relaxed. The situation was beyond their control, so there was no point in worrying. There was some comfort in that—so much of Richard's life had seemed beyond their control, it seemed only fitting that this was too.

Dom and Caroline aren't fucking here, either.

Richard replied:

So why worry?

Dom and Caroline were late too, then. All three. All three of them were late to the wedding. Richard giggled, covering their mouth as they did so. Richard wasn't one for baring all to everyone, unlike the beautiful young couple opposite, whose bodies were now glowing in the golden sunlight, the clouds parting to reveal the autumn sun. A sunny day in the mountains. They found themself wishing the windows opened. They turned off the air conditioner, followed by the reader. The last thing they wanted was another call from Rutti. Richard was going to enjoy the journey.

The bus rounded a particularly tight and treacherous corner, then the road evened out. The driver picked up speed, a bird squawked, the couple awoke with a jolt. The near-fully-naked man checked their own reader and gave Richard an impish grin. Richard used to envy this pansexuality, now it no longer bothered them. They closed their eyes and felt the afternoon sun on their face.

CAROLINE

I had waited in the laundrette for two hours. Actually, I felt pretty guilty I couldn't stay much longer—the previous day I'd waited for four, the day before that four and a half. If I hadn't had work I'd have stayed even longer. I watched the cream-coloured wall-mounted clock as the black hands worked their way over the tobacco-stained face. I didn't read the book I held in my hands, instead listening to the rumble of the machines and watching the door. Nomi had to arrive sooner or later, there was no washing machine in Zebedee's house, and this was the only laundrette for miles around.

I watched the swirl of the machines, paying particular attention to the customers stumbling in under big bags of hefty laundry. No one had a problem with me waiting here, everyone just presumed that one of the machines was being used by me— so far nobody had actually counted them, working out that there was one fewer running than there should be. I hadn't been inside a laundrette in years, we'd made do with the battered old machine at home. It had only ever chewed through a few of my clothes so far.

Where was Nomi? Why hadn't she come in? I knew she hadn't taken so many of her clothes to Zebedee's, her wardrobe was still mostly full. I remembered my trips to Oxfam when I'd stayed with Dom and Richard, but that wasn't Nomi's style— she would never have browsed the same shelves as kindly old women and tired single mothers. I looked around the laundrette again—two men, three women, none of them Nomi.

"Come on, Caroline, we need to go."

I hadn't seen Steph enter. She put her hand on my shoulder, but I couldn't go. I told her what Christina had told me, how she'd had a phone call the night before from Nomi. How it had been very prim and proper, how she had formally told Christina that she was moving out. She was going to go and live with Zebedee.

How could I let her go without even talking to her? Yes,

Nomi had been a pain, she had overstepped the mark on more than one occasion, but she had always been there for me, she'd protected me. Before I'd heard she was leaving I hadn't been too bothered—we lived together, we'd have to make up sooner or later. Now there was a chance we never would, and I was flooded with guilt—after all, hadn't I left her first? We had needed each to stick together and I'd fucked it all up. I wanted to say sorry.

"She's moving to Port Tennant, not outer space," Steph told me. "I know what you're thinking, Caroline, and you have to stop. She was going to leave sooner or later, that's what hetero couples do. Ones that don't acquire an extra boyfriend, that is."

She sat down next to me on the cushioned bench, resting her head on my arm, being too small to reach my shoulder.

"Do you need to talk about it?"

I was going to, but there was no point. Not really. If Nomi wanted to contact me she'd still be able to, and really I'd been deluding myself if I'd thought the mere fact of living together would be enough to patch things up. If Nomi was anything, she was stubborn. And Steph was right, she would have left, sooner or later.

"Don't we have some little protest to get to, or something?" Steph informed me. We left the laundrette. I asked if she wanted to come make signs with us, but she told me she'd agreed to go meet Christina, and that they'd meet us there.

"Wish me luck," Steph called back. I had no idea what she was talking about.

When I got to the flat Richard was already there, carefully painting. He'd set newspaper around the table and arranged the paints. He didn't even notice me enter at first. I stood in the doorway and watched—I watched his careful, curious look of concentration, a considered intensity. It was cute, if I'm blunt. Cute. When he saw me he looked startled, and that was cute too.

I painted quickly—I was never really any good at it and

I wanted to get it over and done with. It was a sign, it didn't exactly have to be a work of art. I suppose I didn't have Richard's diligence. Would Nomi come to the protest? I couldn't work out if she'd consider it worthy or a waste of time. It would merely depend on her mood that day.

The second I put my brush down, my phone rang.

"Is everything all right, Steph?" I looked over at Richard, but he was still wearing his concentration face.

"I'm chickening out, that's what." She sounded panicked.

"What're you chickening out of?"

"Christina! I wanted to ask her out," Steph revealed, in a voice which told me I should already have known.

"Oh," I replied. I hadn't really considered Steph being attracted to Christina.

"Oh? Do you know something?" Steph's voice grew louder.

"I don't know anything. Honestly. I'm just sort-of surprised." I saw Dom come through the door. He looked upset, and I wanted to say something, but Steph was clearly having her own mini-crisis, and Richard already had his arm around him.

"So you think I shouldn't try?" she asked.

"You can try, I'm not saying don't. It's just that I don't know how it'll go, it could go either way, to be honest."

"That's not very helpful," Steph replied, sounding a little rejected. I wished her luck and told her that I'd see her in half-an-hour or so. When the others were finished I put the posters into bin bags—Dom had done his in a vivid green, 'swansea diversity league' in lower case. Once we were outside I began to feel nervous, so I took Richard's hand as we made our way into town.

It was funny, but I felt better when I saw the husk of the club. All those people. Somehow I'd pictured us alone, against men with stones and bottles, but there were so many of us, how could I not feel relieved? Things were going to be fine. Dom nuzzled his face against mine, his other arm around Richard.

There was music in the street, music from our side—the beats of drums, someone playing a violin. A few people were stood in the middle dancing. It was nice—it wasn't Swansea, it was like a festival. The city looked hopeful with all the people. Black people, white people, Asian people. With all of us, I told myself again, what could go wrong?

There were police vans. On the other side, outside one of the chain pubs ('McDrunks', Dom called them), there were the skinheads. Not just skinheads, but angry-looking women and men gathered in clumps and giving frustrated gestures. They'd been drinking.

It was then that I saw the others—Steph, Christina, and by them the entirety of the Women's Circle. They looked aggressive and defiant, and their signs were angrier than the ones we'd painted, 'fascists fuck off', 'eat shit, thugs', that sort of thing. I was glad they were with us. Steph and Christina joined me, each kissing my cheek in greeting. For a moment I found myself wondering if Steph had propositioned her after all. I clutched at one end of my sign, Christina the other. We would be fine, we told each other, we just need to stick together. Don't get separated. As soon as we'd said it, I realised Steph was gone.

The square jostled with people who streamed in from the streets all around us. I saw that Steph was dancing. The rest of us huddled close. Christina held onto my arm. Dom leaned in toward me and pressed his face against mine.

"There are more of us." He pulled away and said something else, but whatever he said it was lost in the music and chants of the crowd.

Christina pointed to the other side of the police vans. One of the skinheads was trying to climb the outside of the ruined club, clutching an England flag. A new line of police officers marched in from the High Street, holding small shields like ones from ancient Greece. Their shields were catching the sunlight and kept blinding me. The man climbing the outside of the club made it half-way up, before losing his footing—he managed to catch himself, sliding most of the way down, falling the final few feet. The flag fluttered down after him, and some paramedics hurried over. The Women's Circle jeered.

A senior-looking officer and a senior-looking anti-fascist were having an argument. They both kept gesturing at the growing number of increasingly angry skinheads on the other side of the police vans. They had grouped around the one who had fallen from the building, chasing the paramedics away. They were shouting at us, but what, I couldn't hear. Steph stopped dancing and joined the rest of us.

Then the chanting and loud chattering turned into a roar. People started moving. The drumbeat stopped. Christina hung onto me. I thought of Nomi. Dom moved to follow the crowd. I could see horses.

"Over there," he shouted, "They're over there."

The fascists had moved too. They were marching down in front of the club, slipping past the police vans, I could see flashes of them in between bodies. They had their tracksuits and their badly written cardboard signs. They had glass bottles. I felt Christina's grip tighten on my arm.

A row of luminous police officers started pushing bodies back, but the skinheads burst through the line toward us. The police grabbed at them and caught some but missed others, others who surged toward us. We prepared ourselves, we prepared ourselves to fight. I was ready. I was ready for them.

People collided, face-to-face or legs kicking out. I saw a woman pushed to the ground, pushed down right near me so I reached out my left arm, trying to grab her hand and help her up, but I was pushed away as the crowd surged backwards.

Stones flew through the air above us, in all directions, stones and bits of brick, and I put up my arm to shield my face, I couldn't hear anything above the roar of all those voices, the scuffle of arms and legs and someone's face being kicked, a spurt of noseblood spattering over the concrete.

Then the guys in front were on the ground, a skinhead on top of a student, an Asian guy hitting the skinhead with his bag, and I saw that the skinhead had a bottle in his hand so I tore it from his fingers and threw it to the floor. This was our city, it was ours, however broken it was it was ours and they weren't going to wrench it from us. Richard was shouting something, but I couldn't hear what he was saying, and then the police piled in, dragging bodies in different directions. Richard pulled us away from them, back into the crowd.

There was the chanting, from all directions, all different words.

"I love you," Dom shouted in my ear. I twisted around to see him. He was saying something to Richard.

Christina let go of my arm. She looked fierce, waving her fist over at the enraged group opposite. Some were giving fascist salutes. Glass smashed against a lamppost. Steph had my sign and held it as high as she could, but she was short, too short. I saw paper and placards scattered to the ground, I could see a series of scuffles, a woman pulling a tracksuited man off another woman, a student struggling with a police officer. Some were running away and I could hear whistles ringing from somewhere, whistles and more shouting, loudest of all though was my own blood in my ears until...

The roar of voices stopped. The poor, stupid fascists were gone. So were the police, with their bright vests, bright shields, their vans and their horses. So were the students, the Muslims and the bystanders. It was just us.

We were stood in the middle of the city on a bright autumn day. We were huddled together in a little group, we were clinging onto one another. We were shouting. Whatever happened, if things got too much, if things broke down, if everything fell apart... for that moment, it was just us...

THE EUROPEAN ATLANTIC
23 YEARS ON

"I've managed to get through to Rutti," Steph announced, holding the rail of the boat to steady themself. "Everyone knows we're late. In fact, no one's shown up. You're jilted and you're not even there."

"I'm hardly jilted if I'm not there," Caroline responded. "And Richard? Dom?"

"On their way too."

Caroline was relieved. They were also unsurprisingly excited— though they'd seen Richard at home just the previous week, it had been months since they'd seen Dom, really seen them.

"Hola chicas!"

Christina arrived on deck with a small tray of smaller drinks.

"I said to them I wanted adult size, not the children's cocktail. They pretended not to understand me," Christina explained, handing a glass to Caroline; a glass to Steph.

Christina had met them at Brest and boarded with them—it was such a long way, and it had been such a long time, but they'd insisted. Christina's husband and son were nowhere to be seen. Christina had said the loner type suited them—it gave them more freedom. Steph had told them the same could be accomplished with sex toys.

"So anyway," Christina announced, raising a glass and motioning to the others to do the same. "To the wedding, if we ever get there. To Caroline, and Richard, and Dom. The strangest relationship I know."

The three glasses clinked in the salty air, the yellow liquid golden in the warm October sun. The deck was almost empty, save for someone being sea sick over the edge of the boat. The boat, of course, had been delayed—some unspecified mechanical problem at the Abertawe port. Steph and Christina had kept Caroline's spirits up, and Steph had only begun teasing once they knew that Caroline had stopped worrying.

"To the three-way jilting," Steph declared, their half-full glass raised once more. Christina rolled their eyes. They and Caroline humoured their friend, bringing their glasses lightly together.

In truth, Caroline hadn't allowed themself to think about it, and they didn't begin thinking about it until they were all safely in their bunks and lying under scratchy sheets, the snores of the other two rolling with the creak of the boat. In the darkness Caroline stared at the slats of the bunk above, all dark lines and swimming colours. They'd had too much to drink, but then they were celebrating. Hopefully. Perhaps the ceremony could take place the day after, instead? But the venue was fully booked. There were a lot of poly marriages going on.

Caroline knew that Richard was taking the bus, and Dom the train. They pictured Richard rocking in the semi-darkness, the glare of street lights passing by. Was Richard asleep? No, they were awake too, they would be thinking about the wedding, about the fact that they were late. Richard would be alone, Caroline had no doubt about that—Richard always took their time to meet people, to get to know them. It was a slow process, Caroline had learned that from experience. It felt so long ago. Richard would be alone, on the seat next to them an ordered pile of food, travel-sickness swabs, and a reader. Caroline knew Richard well. Richard wouldn't be worrying. They would be calm, especially if they knew that Caroline and Dom were late too. These days it was difficult to shake Richard.

Steph mumbled in their sleep, and Caroline thought they heard Christina respond. Caroline realised that they were slipping into sleep themself, but they didn't want to, not yet. They eyed the dark underside of the mattress above.

Dom would be on the train by now, at least Caroline hoped so. Would Dom be alone? Dom'd had their dalliances on the boat, they'd told Caroline and Richard about that. Steph—whose snoring was reading cavernous levels—had always insisted that a 'don't-ask-don't-tell' policy was better, but the truth was that Caroline liked hearing about it. They gained a vicarious pleasure from hearing about the curve of a hip, or the pitch of a moan. It wasn't as good as seeing it in person, of course, but they liked it all the same (Caroline liked hearing about Richard's encounters, too, though of course these were less frequent).

That last one, for instance. The boat woman. Caroline had listened intently as Dom had described the crooked curve of their mouth. Caroline had liked that—they'd have liked to have met the crooked-mouthed woman.

It was Caroline who had started it, these shared details, the gift of these small moments. It had been a long time ago, and they could no longer remember the man they had told Dom and Richard about—it had at least been a man, it was before Caroline had started seeing women. They were less old-fashioned than the other two. Less. They sank into sleep.

"*Happy wedding night. At least the bed is big enough—is that your leg, Richard? Sorry, I think I'm squashing you, I hope I'm not hurting you, wait, is that comfortable? Can I put my arm there?*"

"*It's all right, Dom, don't move it. Don't move it. You know, it's dark in here with the lights off. Are the windows shuttered? The room seems bigger, like it stretches off forever in all directions. Like everything stretches off in all directions.*"

"*How much did you have to drink?*"

"*Someone had to drink the champagne. I had as much as you. How much did you have to drink, anyway?*"

"*I forget. I mean, I remember drinking from a few of the bottles, That is, I'm sure they were different bottles, but then I handed back to you, back to you and Caroline.*"

"*Is Caroline still awake?*"

"*Caroline, are you awake?*"

"*Grrnnnggh.*"

"*Caroline, I just travelled here from North America, all that way over the sea, we haven't all three been together in over a year, you can't fall asleep on us just because it's—wait—five in the morning. Five-thirty in the morning.*"

"*I'm not asleep. I'm awake. I think I was asleep. Where's Richard?*"

"*I'm here, Caroline. I've been thinking, about something Dom just said. It's funny to think of this as our wedding night. A wedding night without a wedding.*"

"*Are you bothered by that, Richard? If you want we can reschedule this, if this matters to you, we can set a new date, no problem—I mean, I'm happy to if you want to, you or Caroline. Is that something you'd want, Caroline?*"

"*I don't know. I don't think so, though I'm happy to if Richard wants it. The ceremony is nice, so're the politics. I don't think I need it, though. And we've already spent the money getting to this one.*"

"*Richard? What do you need?*"

"I used to think I needed this. I mean, I used to think about it, even after I fell in love with Caroline. Especially then, actually. I came after you two were already together. Of course there was that doubt, that you two would want to be just you two again. I thought, if we had some sort of ceremony, then that would bind things together. It's why I mentioned it in the first place."

"I'd no idea. But Richard, I love you as well as Dom. You know that."

"I do know that."

"Come on Richard, we've been together—what? Over twenty years now."

"Glad you had to think about that, Dom."

"What I mean is, that's a fucking long time, for anyone, and I'm happy, I'm happy with the two of you, still. If the marriage thing makes you more comfortable then we'll do it, but I want you to already feel comfortable."

"We love you, Richard."

"I know. I know that. Honestly, I don't think I need it any more. I'm not just saying that, I really mean it—I feel secure with you guys. Dom, why did you agree to it?"

"To marrying you both?"

"Yeah."

"Yes, that."

"Because you asked. I was far away, and I thought that you two needed that, like Richard says, to bind things together, and I wanted you both to know I was coming back—I mean, I know I said that, I just wanted it to be official, that I'd done travelling and was going to live with you both again. I guess in that way I wanted it myself, like a sign, something to mark me returning, or something along those lines."

"And you don't need that, now?"

"Richard, I have you in one arm and Caroline in the other. If I needed anything to prove that I was back, it's that, feeling the two of you, knowing nothing's changed."

"Wait, I want some time next to Richard—wait, I'll move— there we are."

"Happy?"

"Sure. So that's definitely the decision? Dom? Richard? We're definitely not trying this again?"

"Never say never, but no, I don't see a way I'd need it, not if I'm home with you two. Not if I'm home."

"Richard?"

"No."

"Then this is it, my gentlemen. This is our wedding night, the only one we'll ever have. Sure, it's not after an actual wedding but if none of us need it then who gives a fuck? The girls'll say I'm nuts, but the girls always say that, and I might as well give them something else to talk about. This feels nice, I can hear you two, and feel you both—"

"Hey—"

"And it feels perfect. Even with Dom tugging at my hair."

"Sorry."

"I love you guys."

"We love you too."

EPILOGUE
BERLIN

"Hello, is that Dominic?"

"[coughs] Yes, yes, that's me."

"Oh, I'm sorry, did I wake you?"

"Don't worry about it, it's fine, but who is this?"

"Oh, right, I'm Hopes, I'm a friend of Rutti's—I don't believe we've met."

"Right, is that, well, can I help you with anything?"

"No, no, this is just a social call. Hello! You know, you have a really sexy voice, all gravelly and sleepy. Are you naked there in bed? Do you sleep naked, Dominic?"

"What? [coughs] Yes, usually, I just—what?"

"No, Dominic, this is not a social call."

"Then, Hopes, would it be too rude of me to ask you why exactly it is you're calling? Not that I don't enjoy getting calls from sexually aggressive strangers at [pause] six-thirty in the morning—Jesus Christ—I only ask because—"

"Stephanie gave me your number in case I heard from Rutti and couldn't get through to anyone else. Well, I've heard from Rutti."

"Oh right."

"Oh right, indeed. He is in Berlin, of all places, though I don't know where he got that idea. He's staying with one of the Faeries."

"He's staying with one of the what?"

"That doesn't matter. Just make sure to tell Richard. He's been sounding terribly worried. I told him, 'Rutti can look after himself, he's a big boy,' but it didn't help anything."

"Right, then I'll make sure to tell him, don't worry about it, he'll get the message."

"Good boy."

"So I'm the second person you called, after Richard?"

"No, first there was—let's see [pause] Steph, then Richard,

then a 'Caroline', and a 'Christina'. They all turn their phones off at night, apparently."

"Christina—Christina was before me? Rutti barely even knows Christina."

"Don't shoot the messenger. Personally I quite enjoy talking to handsome deep-voiced young guys while they lie around their bed with a hard-on, I find it quite—"

[DIAL TONE]

RICHARD

I'd booked a flight the second I heard that Rutti was in Berlin. His friend Hopes came over and together we booked one for him too—he had been to Berlin before and knew where to go. I called Steph to ask if she wanted to come, but she said she didn't have the money for a last-minute flight and besides, she had something else on her mind. She made me promise to let her know how Rutti was doing, and to 'smack him in the jaw' for leaving so suddenly.

That evening Hopes and I threw our bags into a big black taxi. I'd wanted to walk to the station but Hopes pointed out that Rutti needed a few things, and with them we had too much to carry. Dom and Caroline were stood silhouetted in the doorway. I kissed them goodbye and told them I'd be back in a week. I could see the taxi driver eyeing us through the driver's window, but I didn't care. Hopes had already climbed into the back of the cab and was saying something he clearly found hilarious, but which made the driver scowl. Hopes threw his head back as he guffawed.

It was a short taxi ride, one which took us by the burned-out club. The city had done a decent job of cleaning up the mess after the conflict—by the next day the street'd been spotlessly clean. Now a month has passed you would never have known anything had taken place. Slowly the two crowds had been drawn apart, the stragglers herded into police vans, others fleeing into nearby alleyways. The skinheads were marched to the train station. The rest of the protesters slowly vanished. The square had been a mess of banners, of broken glass and paving slabs, but we were all fine. Steph had a scratch on her face from an arm that had flailed toward her, but that had been the worst of it. We'd sat by the shell of the old club and watched the police slowly drive away.

The sky was November grey and the cleared pavements were spotted with rain. A young couple were walking by the club, the man waving his arms about as they engaged in some sort of argument (she, in turn, was red-faced with anger, but saving her response for later). We reached the train station a few minutes later.

The journey went quickly, more quickly than I'd expected. I'd always felt that Berlin was far away (like Moscow, or Istanbul), even though I'd studied enough maps to know it wasn't. We didn't talk about Rutti—instead, Hopes spent much of the hour-and-a-half-long plane journey telling me about his new drag act, a retro-futuristic character who had come from a future where everyone was androgynous. He insisted I come see it, so I told him I would. It sounded interesting (I'd never seen a drag performance), but I'd always avoided bars like the plague. Too many people, too many drunks. It had never been my thing.

By the time we'd landed in Berlin, navigated the airport, made our way into the city's train network and found some seats on a battered sixties-looking carriage, he'd finished talking about his new act. Seated opposite me, he cocked his head and asked how I'd wound up in a three-way relationship.

"I mean, Rutti mentioned it, but never gave me the full story. I want to hear it from you."

I told him I'd tell him later, and in response Hopes shrugged and started fiddling with his phone. I suddenly felt extremely tired. I watched the blur of allotment houses from the train window, high-rises scattered beyond. We didn't even have anywhere to sleep for the night, we were hoping we could stay at Rutti's. Apparently he was working at a queer bar in Kreuzberg, though if Hopes was telling the truth that was all we had to go on.

At the next stop a man stumbled onto the train, skin blush-red and blackened feet in old sandals. He pulled along a mangy dog by a string. He slumped down across two seats and began to snore. The dog licked at his toes.

We changed at the next station, then another, struggling with the bags between each one, up and down steps and dashing behind trams, before boarding a bright yellow train which crossed the river Spree. Through the window I could see the tall TV tower. We were in the centre of the city and entering Kreuzberg, or so Hopes told me. I was working to hold myself awake, the sequence of trains, punky-looking people, and buildings were whirling by like a dream. Hopes nudged me. We got off the yellow train.

"Kottbusser Tor," Hopes said, gesturing at the tall, ratty-looking buildings, which were covered in gigantic old satellite dishes. "We're almost there."

It was true—we rounded the corner and entered the bar. It was dark and the furniture was old and mismatched. Hopes told me that was common in Berlin, though to be honest it just reminded me of Wales. My legs ached and my head pounded. I slumped into a dusty armchair, as Hopes made his way to the bar to ask about Rutti.

I was poked on the arm again. Hopes. There were two cocktails on the table in front.

"He'll be here, soon," Hopes said, grinning and taking a seat next to me. We waited in silence.

Every time the door swung open my breath caught in my lungs. There was a young gay couple, then two lesbians, there was an angry-looking hairy man, then off went the bartender investigating some commotion on the street. A group of young guys entered, their clothes tight and glasses too big for their faces.

Would would he say? At first I had an image of him storming in angrily, furious at us for following, not wanting to see us. Then

234

I had a worse vision—of a shy Rutti, who couldn't talk to us and meet our gaze, who was nothing like his old self. Loud music suddenly pounded through the room. What if he breezed in with devastating apathy, aloft and uninterested, only to float away again with barely a word? I scratched at my neck, nails scraping red-raw skin. What would I say? Could I tell him I missed him, that I missed him more than I would have expected? Would I tinge the air with humour, joking and teasing, making our scene too light for depth, avoiding discomfort or confrontation? There was always the chance I would throw up my feelings, vomiting them over the table, over him.

I couldn't give Rutti what he wanted, but perhaps the two of us would find affection again. We could greet with pleasure, full of relief, like no time at all had passed, nothing blocking the way to each other, no spiteful words or shyness. Words that actually meant something.

Hopes excused himself and made his way to the toilet. I realised he looked as tired as I was. He was nervous too. I stared into my drink and watched the swirl of bubbles clinging to the glass. It was a tongue-curling kind of sweet with a lemon slice perched on top for authenticity. It looked sort of like—

"Did you do this for me, Richard?"

And there Rutti was. The long wig and tight dress were flawless.

Rutti regarded me with a warm smile and took me by the arm.

They were stunning.

TWILIGHT MEMORIAL BLOCK, ABERTAWE
55 YEARS ON

Richard and Caroline held hands as they made their way through the quiet corridors, strewn with flowers. They no longer needed to say anything: they didn't need to tell one another they loved one another. They were old enough to know it. Affirmations are for the young and insecure, so Caroline said. That always made Richard laugh.

The pair made their way to the elevator, past a young man who was watching an image of a lost girlfriend, holding the projection's hand, tears running down their cheeks. Caroline patted the young man's shoulder as they passed. The young man spun round, as though seeing a ghost. Richard apologised on Caroline's behalf. Caroline shook their head at Richard.

Dom and Beth's graves had been set together, plaques side-by-side on the huge expanse of wall—the fifth level, Taurus Row. Richard and Caroline stood together, watching scenes of their old loved ones.

"Do you think those two get along?" Richard asked.

"They're dead," Caroline replied.

"That's not what I asked."

"It's the right answer," Caroline replied.

Dom and Beth side-by-side. Every photograph and recording entombed—hundreds of thousands of walks, birthday gatherings, orgasms—even petty fights played out message by message. Their faux-wedding anniversary, the morning ghost. Everything. Dom with Richard and Caroline. Then, all those years later, Beth with Caroline and Richard. They knew that it was the two of them which tied Dom and Beth together. Dom and Beth had never even met, but this is what Beth had wanted.

Richard and Caroline would join them, eventually. Caroline placed a hand to their lips, then placed their fingers against each plaque in turn.

"You'll go first," Richard said.

"I'll be taking you with me. I could slip something in your tea."

"I don't want to be placed next to you for all eternity if you've murdered me," said Richard.

236

Caroline laughed. Richard gripped their hand ever more tightly.
"Goodbye, guys. I love you."

END

AFTERWORD
BY MEG-JOHN BARKER

I'm so pleased to be able to contribute an afterword to this new edition of Redfern Barrett's book, *The Giddy Death of the Gays and the Strange Demise of Straights*, and to see it back on the shelves after the success of their more recent novel, *Proud Pink Sky*.

First a note: I'm going to use the word 'normativity' a lot in this afterword! For any readers who aren't familiar with the term, it means the ways in which societies view some kinds of people and behaviour as good, normal, and acceptable, and others as bad, abnormal, and unacceptable, valuing the former over the latter. Cisnormativity is the social assumption that it's better to be cis than trans; heteronormativity that it's better to be straight than gay or bi; mononormativity that it's better to be monogamous than non-monogamous; amatonormativity that romantic relationships are the most valuable kind of relationships; and sex normativity that such relationships should be sexual—to summarise some of the main normativities that Redfern weaves into their novel. Other than that I'll try to avoid the big words here, I promise!

On reading this novel, I was struck that Redfern succeeds in doing something in their fiction which I have always endeavoured to do in my non-fiction books. That is to demonstrate how such normativities hurt all of us, not just those who are obviously oppressed by them. Also, how this happens at all levels from the deeply personal level of our intimate relationships with ourselves and others to the global level of the workings of nationalist violence and structural oppression.

By exploring these themes through the eyes of multiple fictional characters, Redfern brings home both the diversity of ways in which normativities can damage us, and the emotional impact of this damage on individuals, on relationships of all kinds, on communities, and on whole cities and nations. Perhaps this is something that fiction offers which non-fiction can't. It enables us to fully feel this impact because it's happening to characters we've come to care about.

For me, the mark of a good novel is that I feel a sense of loss on finishing it. I miss the characters who had become like friends during my short time in their company. This is how many of us feel about classic queer series like Armistead Maupin's *Tales of the City* or Alison Bechdel's *Dykes to Watch Out For*. While people will rightly praise Redfern's fiction for its impressive world-building and speculative elements, for me it is the warmth and tenderness of their beautifully-drawn characters, and the dynamics between them, that lingers the most. We can really feel the struggles these characters experience internally, and between them, because of the—often violent—normativity of their upbringings and of the world around them.

This becomes all the more powerful when we realise that we're hearing directly from the inner experience of such a diversity of positions in relation to (cis/hetero/mono) normativity. Characters in *The Giddy Death* run the whole spectrum from those who have always experienced a sense of difference and not-fitting, and who now build their identities and communities around this, all the way through to those who fit absolutely within normativity and who struggle with others who don't. In between these poles are those who resist their sense of difference, those who find it later on in life, those who are normative in some ways but not in others, and those who are comfortable with their normativity and with others who don't fit it as they do.

This diversity of representation is deeply refreshing in a world where so few mainstream books include queer characters at all, and those that do often only include them in exoticising or tokenistic ways, while few queer books include characters who are not explicitly queer but who are also grappling with their gender, sexuality, and relationship style. As with masculinity/feminity, gay/straight, cis/trans, and dystopia/utopia, this is yet another binary that Redfern gently but firmly challenges in their novels.

While most people—both outside and inside of queer community—accept the common sense notion that we live in a world that is majority straight and minority queer, I have always found this understanding troubling. From all my studies—and still more from my lived experience—I feel that it is equally true to say that no-one is queer, that everyone is queer, and pretty much everything in between! We could say that nobody reaches the full potential of queerness because nobody can entirely step outside the (cis/hetero/mono) normative dominant culture. However much we may resist it, we remain in relation to it. Being truly queer could be seen as akin to being spiritually enlightened: not a state available to many, if anyone, while perhaps possible for anybody to glimpse in a given moment. At the same time we could say that everybody is (eventually) queer, because nobody manages to fit the rigid normative standards gender/sexual/relationship normativity throughout their life: embodying the ideal of femininity/masculinity and expressing this through a lifelong monogamous procreative relationship, wherein the only sexual desires and practices are a consistent, fulfilling, form of penis-in-vagina sex! Between these extremes we could posit queerness as a minority position (people who identify as gay/bi, trans, or polyamorous, perhaps), or as a majority position (the third to two thirds of people who report experiencing themselves as neither/both/the other gender, and/or as attracted to the same—or more than one—gender, and/or as having ongoing—or periods of—asexual/aromantic and or kinky/non-monogamous experience).

Through *The Giddy Death* we get the sense of this complexity. We meet gay characters who are—in some ways—straighter than many of the heterosexual ones, and heterosexual characters who are—in some ways—queerer than many of the gay ones. We are gently cautioned to be careful of our own assumptions, for example that someone who appears normative is actually, or that the position someone currently occupies in relation to gender, sexuality, and relationships, will remain the same over time.

We also encounter both the normativities of mainstream culture which are challenged in many queer communities, and also those that are not, as well as the new normativities that sadly spring up within queer communities themselves (around which is deemed queer enough, for example). Redfern particularly highlights normativities that exist across mainstream and alternative communities about how relationships should be conducted, about what is deemed attractive, and about how gender should be expressed. Rutti's often hilarious observations, in particular, shine a light on the ways in which people's talk, lives, and relationships are shot through with normative assumptions, while, at the same time, we see the ways in which Rutti's own position in relation to normativity can become a kind of aggression against themselves and others.

I love the way in which each chapter of this book is told through multiple perspectives (Rutti, Richard, Caroline, and Dom) so that we get to experience the same situations unfolding through their four very different viewpoints. The *aha* moments when something previously baffling is explained are particularly satisfying. I love how the surrounding characters are drawn just as warmly and tenderly as the central four, so that we get a sense of how things appear through their eyes also, from the diverse positions they occupy in relation to normativity.

As we gradually come to know each person, the relationships between them, the group as a whole, and the city around them, we feel the ways in which the same kinds of expansions and contractions, struggles and possibilities, are flowing through them all. Individuals, relationships, group, and city are all both warm and cold, flawed and full of possibility, traumatised and capable of traumatising. There are moments when characters open up towards greater freedoms and intimacies, and moments when they refuse, resist, or rage against such potentials. Relationships and alignments flicker, form, and deepen, and they also rupture, wither, and end. We get the sense of how the wider culture around the characters—and the specific city they occupy—is both opening up and closing down in similarly complex, fraught, and dramatic means, and how these changes continue to enable and constrain our characters in all kinds of unpredictable and important ways.

Overall, it is a rigid adherence to normativities—of all kinds—that causes the most hurt through this novel: whether that is when it prevents characters from being kind with themselves or others, when it becomes an impassable block to a relationship deepening or a friendship continuing, or when it erupts into violence on the streets or operates in a deadening way across workplaces and nightlife venues. This makes it all the more moving that the characters are able to find tender intimacies with themselves, with each other, and with the world around them: through and around the edges of these rigid normativities. Hopefully this is something that will inspire readers to find their own flickers of freedom, genderqueer intimacies, and unexpected kinships and communities, where possible.

— Meg-John Barker, author of *Life Isn't Binary, Rewriting the Rules,* and *Queer: A Graphic History*

ABOUT THE AUTHOR

Redfern Jon Barrett is author of novels including *Proud Pink Sky*, a speculative story set in the world's first LGBTQ+ country (Amble Press, 2023) and *The Giddy Death of the Gays & the Strange Demise of Straights* —which was a finalist for the Bisexual Book Awards and featured in *Paste Magazine's* "10 Audiobooks to Listen to During Pride Month (and Beyond)."

Redfern's essays and short stories have appeared in publications including *The Sun, Guernica, Strange Horizons, Passages North, PinkNews, Booth, FFO, ParSec, Orca,* and *Nature Futures*. Their writing has been shortlisted for Scotland's HISSAC prize, was a semifinalist for the Journal Non/Fiction Collection and Big Moose prizes, received an honourable mention for the Leapfrog Prize, and has exhibited at the National Museum of Denmark.

Born in Sheffield in 1984, Redfern grew up in market towns, seaside resorts, and postindustrial cities before moving to Wales and gaining a Ph.D. in Literature from Swansea University (Prifysgol Abertawe) in 2010. Redfern is nonbinary queer, and has campaigned for LGBTQ+ and polyamory rights since they were a teenager. They currently live in Berlin.

AMBLE
PRESS
ANN ARBOR

Amble Press, an imprint of Bywater Books, publishes
fiction and narrative nonfiction by LGBTQ writers, with
a primary, though not exclusive, focus on LGBTQ writers
of color. For more information on our titles, authors, and
mission, please visit our website.

www.amblepressbooks.com